After
Ever After

After Ever After

HANNAH LUCKETT

Bedford Square
Publishers

First published in the UK in 2026 by Bedford Square Publishers Ltd,
London, UK

bedfordsquarepublishers.co.uk
@bedfordsq.publishers

ISBN
978-1-83501-443-1 (Paperback)
978-1-83501-444-8 (eBook)

2 4 6 8 10 9 7 5 3 1

Typeset in 11 on 13pt Adobe Caslon Pro
by Avocet Typeset, Bideford, Devon, EX39 2BP
Printed and bound in Great Britain by
CPI Group (UK) Ltd, Croydon CR0 4YY

The manufacturer's authorised representative in the EU for
product safety is Easy Access System Europe, Mustamäe tee 50,
10621 Tallinn, Estonia
gpsr.requests@easproject.com

For my parents who gave me fifteen perfect French summers.

And Wyn, because it's all for you.

Chapter 1

'I've been thinking about the book,' Sam says to me, as she runs her finger down the wine list. It's the one thing I respect the most about Sam, she doesn't mince her words.

Her colleagues call it a 'Sam special', the kind of needs/must communication that has helped secure her Editor of the Year three years in a row. Even her email inviting me for dinner this evening was brisk. It contained all the information necessary in the subject line: 'La Brasserie. Seven PM tonight'. Signed off with a warm and courteous EOM.

I think with anybody else she may have flowered it up a little, given them more notice perhaps, but Sam knows me; she has been my editor and almost-friend for just over a year and she knows that I very rarely have any evening plans.

Sam briefly shows me the menu, pointing to some forty-five-pound-bottle of red halfway down the page. 'This do?' she says briefly. It's all in French, italicised to make it look fancy, and I feel the tug of familiarity. Three years ago, I would have understood almost every word, enjoyed the cadence and flow, loved how I could fit into two worlds. The words are gone now, locked up in a place in my brain that can only be accessed by a key that I have hurled off a bridge.

'Yeah,' I nod, swallowing down the tightness in my throat.

'Great. We'll take this one.' She manages a tight-lipped smile in the waiter's direction, hands over the menu and then crosses her forearms on the table.

'So, the book...' she tries again, bringing us back to the reason we're here. To talk about *The Book*. The book about grief that we've been working on for a year and a half. My book.

'It's missing an ending.' Her face tries its hardest to stay neutral but I notice how she stops blinking.

'An ending?' I repeat.

'Yeah, like a destination. Right now it's brilliant and modern and totally heart wrenching of course… but we need some sort of resolution, a post-script kind of thing.'

'A resolution…' I try the word on my lips, 'to grief?' I can't help but smile into my wine. 'I hate to break it to you but you haven't read it properly if you think he's coming back.' I bring my face in line with hers. She winks at me. We have had many conversations about grief over the past year and a half; she has seen me at my rawest and my best, she can't be put off by my bad idea of a joke.

'Save the gallows humour for the page, eh?' The smile that radiates off her face disappears as quickly as it arrived and instead, she returns to professional Sam. 'It needs something more, otherwise why read it? People can just scroll through your blog for free, we need something to signify that there has been progress, that others in your situation might find it too.'

'Right…' I draw it out, the universal sign to let her know that I am not sure she is indeed right.

'I have an idea.' She proffers an olive on a cocktail stick in my direction. 'Don't worry, I think it can all be easily resolved.'

I feel a prickle of frustration, that her 'easily resolved' will probably mean many more nights staring hopelessly at yet another Word document. 'I'm all ears.'

'Go back.' She waves her hands a little as she says it, leans her body over the table, eyes wide.

'Back where?'

'To France!' I feel a heat that comes with such intensity it makes me choke. 'To where it all began, to the village…' The waiter interrupts, delivering the wine and pouring out two glasses.

'Monpazier?' I say the name of that village, the place that I had spent seven of the most important years of my life, a place that was, at one time, my home. Sam picks up her glass and starts swinging it around enthusiastically.

'Ava, you've come so far I think it would be the thing that makes this book fly, that *homecoming.*'

I pull at my sleeve. I feel entirely at her mercy again, the way it felt when I was on submission, thinking I would sell my soul if someone wanted me. 'What does everyone else think?'

'In all honesty?'

I don't respond, instead I nod apprehensively. I have never been one to take criticism on the chin.

'I just get the feeling they want more. The premise is great, and you have the readership in all those followers, but right now it's just a lot of stand-alone blog posts. I spun the team a line about you coming up with this idea and they're on board.'

'And if I don't go, I don't have a book?'

Her silence answers the question. It's strange, how bereft I feel at the thought of it. If anyone had asked me when I was a little girl what I wanted to be, a writer would never have been top of my list. Instead, 'the bug' got me slowly: a good grade in secondary English, a great teacher at Sixth Form, a very persuasive sales pitch at a university open day and suddenly it mattered, words and experiences, and cadence and vocabulary, they all mattered. The thought of the last three years resulting in nothing seems too cruel to comprehend.

'We'd pay of course. Treat it like a holiday...' Sam cuts across my glazed silence.

'A holiday?' I scoff.

'A break then, away from your parents? I'll make sure we spare no expense! What do you want? Luxury hotel, B&B, villa...'

'An apartment,' I counter. 'Somewhere of my own.'

Her brow puckers slightly. I feel like Sam would never willingly turn down a hotel in favour of self-catering. But Sam hasn't had to move back in with her parents after her life exploded so Sam doesn't truly understand how appealing the promise of solitude really is.

'How long do you want?'

'A month.' It's a joke at first. A challenge of sorts, to see how serious she really is about all of this but Sam doesn't even blink.

'Fine. I'll even pay for extra legroom on the plane.'

I feel the clammy panic set in. 'You spoil me,' I manage, my voice devoid of any emotion.

Sam notices. Her job is to read between the lines. She softens a little. 'This book means a lot to me too, Ava, as do you. I care about this.'

I soften. 'I know. I… I just never thought I'd go there again, that's all.'

'You know I'm the last one to want to make you uncomfortable. I appreciated that when I took on this project, that it is so personal, and losing him – the rawness of it all – is what made me fall in love with you as a writer, but something good can come out of it all. You can be a writer. You can have a book that people read. This can be something special, it's just going to have to take that little bit more to get it there.' Her phone buzzes. Our conversation has been punctuated with sporadic pings from emails and texts and missed calls. She turns it over and winces. 'I've got to take this. Why don't you take five to think it over?' she offers. I nod as she gets up from her seat, phone already on her ear as she leaves.

When the door closes behind her, I reach into my bag for my own phone for some sort of distraction, hoping on its cracked screen there would be a reason not to take her up on her offer. But the only reason that would fly would probably be resurrection, and I think that may be off the cards. Instead of my phone, my fingers find fabric. My diary peeks out at me, green and covered with pink and blue paisley prints, half-filled and slightly beaten up.

I take it out, brush my fingers over the cover and then turn to the inside page. It's an exquisite torture, seeing my name in his handwriting in the top right-hand corner. The words *just write something* capitalised and underlined below. It was supposed to be an incentive to start doing the thing I had been saying I would for the first five years of our relationship. It hadn't worked in the way he intended; those pages had remained completely empty until the ninth of May, three years ago.

The day Etienne Grenaud, my husband, died.

The door to the restaurant opens and I can see Sam cutting through the tables towards me. I close the page, go to slip my diary back into my bag, but it's too late.

'What's this?' She gestures to the book I am now hiding under the table.

'It's nothing.' I try to play it off but the look on her face tells me that she doesn't believe me. I shrug. 'Just a diary.' It's not a lie. Inside this cover is every single thought, idea and revelation I have had about losing Ettie since the day his heart stopped. It isn't the blog I started a few months after he died that has racked up enough followers to lead Sam to signing me; it isn't even coherent in places, it is just a companion. I put it back in my bag gently and then when I note Sam's raised eyebrow I smile softly at her. 'When you upload every single one of your weaknesses to an ever-growing following you have to have a place for everything else to go.'

She leans forward, eyes sparkling. 'Now that's something I'd like to read.'

'And I'd like it noted that it is to be burnt before that ever happens.' I place it safely back into my bag.

'Fair enough.' She raises her glass to mine and we clink them together before taking large sips and I know she's waiting for my answer.

I try to think of an excuse – that if she could just give me a month, I could bring about an epiphany right here in London; I could find God, go on a retreat, start meditating. But it's useless because I know she's right. As much as it pains me to admit it, she has managed to find the glaringly obvious plot-hole in my life. That despite the blog and the book detailing every part of my grief process, I'm not even close to getting over Ettie.

I swig back the rest of my wine, take one last fleeting look at my diary and nod. 'Okay, I'll do it.'

Chapter 2

'ONE DAY YOU'RE GOING to stay for breakfast,' Archie says as I slip out from under his arm and the quilt.

'Cornflakes and a carton of old orange juice? I'll take my chances on the street, thanks.' I start to hunt out my clothes that are scattered over various corners of his bedroom. I had arrived without warning, knocking on his door, slightly tipsy. I knew he'd be home; knew he would let me in, knew he would want me, and that was exactly what I needed to try to process Sam's meeting.

The first time I slept with Archie, I was blind drunk. I had to be, otherwise I wouldn't have gone through with it. He was a friend's younger brother, a friend who can no longer look me in the eye. I had just signed my book contract; we spoke about Ettie and I cried and then took him a little by surprise when I launched myself at him in the taxi on the way home. I was awful, emotionally and physically, lay there not doing much and vomited into his pot plant when we were finished.

Things have improved in recent months.

He yawns. It's seven o'clock; I have no need to be up this early apart from the fact that if I linger it means this is something more.

He props himself up on the pillows, rubs his eyes. 'I'm actually a very good cook. Not that you'll ever let me show you.'

I start to wrestle my jeans back into submission. 'It's nothing personal.'

'It's hard to not take it personally when I'm naked in my bed and you can't get your clothes on fast enough.' He passes it off as a quick joke, but I know there's truth there. 'I mean you were the one who turned up at my door last night.'

I go over to him in the bed, press a kiss into his cheek and run a hand through his hair. 'I love it when you get all paranoid and sensitive.'

'Fuck off.' He pushes me away, splutters off my affection with a shake of his head and a boyish smirk.

I find my phone on the side, look at the missed calls from my mum, the late-night email that Sam had sent to 'put our conversation in writing' and everything seizes up. I feel the weight come back to me.

'Coffee.'

Archie raises his eyebrows. 'Is that a question?'

'Sorry. Yes. Can I have a coffee?' I remember my manners.

'Yes, Ava, I will make us a coffee.' He gets up, making no immediate attempt to cover up his body. He doesn't need to. Archie and I have seen each other naked enough times to know what we're hiding. I watch him, tall, solid, dark, and wonder if it's appropriate to start this all over again, whether morning sex was a 'casual' affair or whether it turned this into something more.

He pulls on some pyjama bottoms and a hoody and opens the door onto the rest of the flat.

I take a moment to make his bed, and then perch on the edge of it, turning my phone around and around in my palm until I summon the courage to reply to my mother who is threatening to call the police if I don't respond by nine.

I tell her I'm alive.

Archie's flat is a novelty; it is his, and only his. He doesn't have a roommate (or a parent) who can pop in and out at any moment and ruin the mood with a poorly timed question about the recycling. He feels like a proper adult, which is pretty humbling considering that he's younger than me, a whole two years younger, but he's the kind of person I would trust to do their taxes in time and has credit cards for the benefits not just for the overdraft facilities.

'Sugar?' He holds up a little glass container.

'Two, please.'

'Heathen.' He scowls but dutifully scoops it in and then hands it to me with a little grin. We stand there, resting up against his kitchen cabinets, unsure of how to proceed.

'Hey,' he says after a moment. In its attempt to sound casual it sounds strange. 'Some guys at work have been talking about this new Japanese restaurant, said it was amazing but really hard to get into so I put my name on the list and they've called me back… think you might want to go?'

I gulp down some scalding coffee and try not to wince. 'When?'

'Next Thursday.' I feel my chest constrict with the weight of the thing I now need to tell him. The flight that Sam had promptly booked for Wednesday before I could change my mind, my month-long absence, the realisation that this fucked up little *holiday* is, and will be, happening.

'Ah.' I look at my bare feet, the chipped nail varnish that has almost worked itself off of my toenails. 'I'd love to but I'm actually going away for a bit,' I counter and I see his expression change. It clearly wasn't the response he had been expecting, not a yes but not an outright no either. 'It's a work thing.'

His brow furrows. 'You don't do "work things", you're freelance and barely that.'

I hesitate. We have managed to keep the fine prints of our lives almost entirely separate. It's like we have the summaries – a synopsis of major events, jobs, bereavements, any outstanding STDs – but we don't really talk about specific nuances. 'It's a book thing.'

'Oh…' His eyes shoot up a little and I can see him chew over the details. 'Like a publicity tour?' he guesses. I appreciate his optimism.

'Not exactly. It's my editor. We went for dinner last night… before I came here.' I watch as something passes over his face, a hardening of his jaw, the acceptance that yet again he was an afterthought.

'What's the deal?'

'She wants me to go back to Monpazier, to go back to where it all happened... you know, Ettie and that.' It's like his name's taboo here, I lower my voice a little, like when anyone says the word 'sex' in public. I don't like Ettie and Archie to co-exist, it feels wrong.

'Oh shit, yeah.' I can see the awkwardness fall back on his face.

'Sorry, this is probably far too deep for a post-shag chat, huh? Rule of thumb, men don't like it when you bring up your dead ex-husband.'

'I'm not that bad, Ava.' He looks genuinely hurt; I reach out and grab his arm.

'No, I know, I'm joking, I do that when I don't know what to say.' He looks down at the connection, the entirely platonic show of support that we rarely show each other.

'You don't want to go?'

'Of course I don't want to but it sounds like I don't have a choice. They say I need to find some sort of "*conclusion to my grief*".' I put on a voice and screw my face up in a poor imitation of Sam.

'Bullshit.'

'I know right!'

'When do you go?'

'Wednesday. Decided it was better to just go and figure things out when I'm there.'

'How long?'

I pause, pull my shoulders up. 'A month.'

He nods, returns one hand into his pocket and the other cups around his coffee protectively. 'Maybe it will be nice?' His affinity for positivity never fails to shock me. 'You know, see some old friends, does he still have family out there? Sure they'll be happy to see you.'

My singular arched eyebrow and scoff say everything I need them to.

'Not good, huh?' he pushes.

'His mother could never quite get over the fact that her son's main ambition in life was to run a café in the village he was born in. And of course, as all totally non-toxic mother of boys will attest to, that was entirely my fault.'

'She's one of those?'

'Yes. That, and in her eyes, I am also the worst thing a woman can possibly be.'

I watch Archie's brow furrow a little, an almost imperceptible panic in his eyes, wondering what could be quite so terrible. 'What's that?'

'English.' I try to emulate her accent, screwing up my face in disgust. Archie laughs, partly in relief. I enjoy it.

'And that's it, all the people you had?'

'Kind of.' I shrug. 'It was all quite seasonal. There's a brother too. Florian. I can count on one hand the number of times we ever saw him. They weren't exactly close.'

He looks at me pityingly. I'm sure Archie isn't the kind of man that has ever found himself short of company. 'You can call me you know.'

'Sorry?'

'When you're there. I mean if it gets a little lonely, you can call me.'

I nod and raise my mug in his direction.

We drink the dregs in silence until the cups are drained and there is no need to prolong my departure any more. I dump it on the sideboard, pat myself down for my phone, keys, cards. When everything's in order I stand awkwardly in front of him, aware of his sad face scanning my body. I close the distance between us, my hand reaches for his cheek, and he stares at it as if it is some alien appendage.

'Sorry about next Thursday,' I offer.

'There'll be other restaurants, when you get back?'

I nod, stand on my tiptoes and kiss him quickly on the lips. I think it might be the most intimate thing we have ever done.

Chapter 3

Dad checks the departure board for the fourth time since we arrived three hours early for my flight. We are sitting in a Wetherspoons on the wrong side of arrivals, Mum cupping her tea, Dad pretending to read the paper.

'And you've got the documents for the car rental?' he quizzes, his eyes appearing over the masthead.

'Yes.'

'And you're sure you'll be okay with a manual?'

'I'll manage.'

'It's been a while since you drove and everything's the wrong way round over there, remember.'

I do remember, I remember the faded red Citroën that rarely made it to a destination without at least one breakdown. It was my first car, the first one I had bought for two-hundred-and-fifty euros from an old man who had moved into a care home. That car belongs to Etienne's brother now, along with anything else that couldn't be dragged back on a Ryanair flight.

Dad lowers the glasses back onto his nose and surveys the itinerary he had insisted on printing out, including the address of the place that Sam had booked on my behalf: an old Grenier apartment a few roads away from the square. It's not on a street I'm familiar with, and I'm grateful for that. I figure that the stranger things feel, the easier it will all be.

He puts the papers back into a plastic wallet that he had found in his study. 'I can run this all by Steve?'

I scrunch up my nose. 'Who's Steve?'

'He's one of your father's friends from golf, used to work in property law,' Mum fills in. 'You met him last month at the Round Table lunch.' I think about that awful lunchtime outing where I was sandwiched between my parents like a ten-year-old amongst a sea of pensioners. It was one of their many attempts over the past three years at getting me out of the house and talking to some people that I wasn't directly related to.

'Can Steve speak French?' I proposition, leaning over the table towards my father who I know is only trying to be helpful but has never quite adjusted to the fact that I am a certified adult. Perhaps, in his defence, I had used my first taste of independence to take a year abroad where I swiftly sacked off my university degree for a man ten years my senior that I had met at a café, so his trepidation might be valid.

Dad shrugs. 'He can probably use Google.'

I can't help but grin, take his arm in my hand and squeeze. 'You don't need to manage everything, Dad, I managed to survive perfectly fine for seven years before…'

Mum can hear the waver in my voice before I can control it. Her hand reaches out for mine and takes it. She is making that face she does when she's trying to appease me, when she's trying to avoid a scene. 'We know, love, but you weren't doing it all by yourself for long were you? You had him and now… well, we're just trying to help.' She doesn't want me to cry at an airport. She is very English when it comes to things like public emotions, she gave me a Valium at the funeral so I wouldn't have to feel things 'too hard.'

Finally, the plane pops up on the board and Dad pats down his thighs and coughs loudly.

'We'll leave you to it then, you should have enough time to get through security.'

'I've got two hours, Dad, it's Stansted, how big do you think this place is?'

'Well, better safe than sorry.' I can feel my eyes begin to roll again and I stop it before he sees. I don't want to leave like this. If Ettie's death taught me anything it's that you only get one goodbye, and it counts.

He kisses me on the cheek. His hand grips onto the top of my arm, pinches it a little too tightly.

'Now I know you won't accept anything now but if you need it, we can send you over some—'

'Thanks.' I stop him before he can finish the sentence. I have a few thousand euros in a bank account I haven't touched, Ettie's parting gift.

'Well anyway, give us a ring when you land, hope it's a good flight.' Mum calls Dad off the attack with a wave of her hands. She hugs me. She smells of patchouli oil and linen, smells I only notice on the first and last hugs.

They wait in their seats, watching me, whilst I steer the trolley towards the sign for check in.

I sit down at my departure gate. It is quiet, only a few ageing faces peering down at their newspapers. I open my passport. Take a glancing look at a younger me, early twenties, trying not to smile, excited about where it was going to take me. It turns out it wasn't the ticket to a host of exotic places, just multiple hops across a small stretch of channel to Ettie and back home again.

My phone lights up with another message from Mum asking how things are going. I shoot back an update that I am not currently being frisked in a back office behind security. There's a message from Archie too. I try to ignore the small warmth that spreads through me; it feels entirely treacherous.

'Thinking of you,' he says in a little blue bubble. 'Think I might even miss you.' My thumb hovers over the keyboard.

'Thank you,' I reply.

Chapter 4

I PULL THE SILVER rental Fiat up the curb to the red dot on Google Maps. 22D Rue Saint Jacques. It feels like the only street in Monpazier that I have never walked down. The more I think about the café with its faded red umbrellas, a mere kilometre up the road, I feel a sudden and immovable weight on my chest.

I step out of the car. The street is shadowed by tall stone buildings with shuttered windows and wonky balconies. As for signs of life? They prove to be minimal. Someone's washing is fluttering out of a window, there's a skinny ginger cat that slinks its way up a side street. The only proof that I haven't landed in some simulation of a tiny French market town is that there is the low hum of conversation coming from the square, the voices and words indistinguishable, but it's proof enough that I'm not entirely alone.

'Ava?' A voice cuts through my train of thought. An elderly woman emerges fully out of an imposing doorway. She is long and willowy and whilst she is sporting entirely white hair that she has pulled up into a bun, her bright red lipstick and black horn-rimmed glasses make her difficult to age. She could be both sixty and ninety. Her lips pull up into a large grin showcasing impressively perfect teeth as if she realises the riddle. It is only when I step towards her that I notice her outfit. She is draped entirely in a black satin kimono, with tassels on her sleeves which almost touch the ground. I get a sudden and powerful urge to curtsy. She feels like someone I should at least bob my head to.

'You're the… estate agent?' My voice is strangely hoarse. It is the first time I have spoken since I left my parents at Stansted.

She lets out a short, sharp puff of air through her lipstick and gestures to her outfit. 'Do I look like an estate agent?' The words slip out in American, a broad unidentifiable transatlantic accent that adds to the impression of misplaced grandeur.

'Well… no.'

'I'm the owner, honey.' She winks, and another year falls off her.

'I'm sorry I'm late, the plane—'

'In France, this is early.' She wafts away my apology with a hand. 'Shall we?' She gestures to the door, and I nod, stepping over the threshold.

Behind the bottle-green door, there is a communal hallway that hasn't been touched since the eighties. It is dank and large, with greying tiles on the floor and chipboard paper on the walls. It smells stale. The American appears to notice this too. I wonder if she'll ignore it but she looks at me and raises an eyebrow.

'Stick with me. I promise you it's nicer inside.' She leads me up a grandiose-looking staircase that has seen better days. The ascent is slow; she has to pause at every landing, pretending to inspect some socket or dado railing and I politely wait with her, grateful for the thirty seconds or so to get my bearings. By the fourth flight, the pretence disappears entirely.

'I don't do this very often,' she pants, 'I normally get one of the boys down at the immobilier to show the renters but it's a national holiday today – apparently the one last week wasn't enough. Honestly, it's a miracle the French ever get anything done. Still…' She smiles softly at me. 'Part of the charm.'

After three more treacherous flights of stairs, we reach a small landing with a singular skylight letting in a crack of the early afternoon light.

'Most of the people who enquire about this place can't make it past the second floor.' She fumbles for the key.

'Well,' I shrug my shoulders and try a smile myself. 'I wouldn't say no to a stairlift.'

She cackles. It is a loud and sudden noise that makes me jump. 'Well, that's just cheating.'

The door opens gently and light floods the landing. She steps in first, holding the door back as I follow her.

Nothing matches – even the windows appear to have been added in different centuries – but considering it is in the attic, it is surprisingly cool and airy. The ceiling is vaulted with white-washed beams that snake their way through the space. I notice the sofa first, large and white, covered partly by a crimson blanket and punctuated with scatter cushions. There is a low square coffee table, already laden with a few magazines and coasters, to the left of the sofa is an armchair pointing towards the bookshelf and between them, the only place where the roof is high enough to cater for it, is a floor lamp that has already been turned on, illuminating some of the books that litter the shelves.

'There's no TV.' It's not an apology. More of a statement.

'That's okay,' I shrug. 'Don't really watch much anyway.'

'The kitchen has everything you'll need though.' She gestures to her right, where a mismatch of wood and tile greets me where the roof is at its lowest. There is a breakfast bar with two stools and the cooking space consists of an oven, fridge and a counter for prepping. It is tiled almost entirely with perfect white squares illustrated with hand painted food items. I spot a courgette, a prawn, a pepper, a questionable peach.

'All my friend's doing, I'm afraid.' The American notices my inspection. I look at her; she is smiling wistfully at the splashback.

'It's beautiful, all of it, it's just lovely.'

'She was an artist. I tried to get her to move to something a bit more "age-appropriate" later on but she wouldn't hear of it. Said the stairs kept her young.'

'I like the sound of her.' The American glows at the comment until something passes over her face and she stiffens.

'Now don't get me wrong,' she starts, wagging a finger in my direction. 'It's not perfect, things creak and break and you'll need to run the taps for a few minutes before the water's clear, but it's cosy and clean and rather modern in comparison to some other places around here.' I look around at the wooden beams, the yellow shaker cabinets and tiled splashbacks. It is not modern, not in the slightest, but I know what she really means is that there's no gingham curtains, or an avocado bathroom suite.

On the other side of the apartment, where the roof pitches down more than the other, is a dining table set up for four, flanked by two more waist-high bookshelves.

'The bedroom and bathroom are through there.' She points to a door. 'I might stay here for a moment, prepare myself for the descent.' She thumps herself onto the sofa with a soft groan.

The bathroom is sparse but clean enough, with a diamond-shaped window letting in enough light that I can catch a look at myself in the mirror. I wish I couldn't. The day has clearly caught up with me.

The other door opens into a bedroom that is flooded with light. The bed, an entirely unnecessary double, sits in the middle of the room against the wall with a bureau to one side and a small side table to the right. There are two full-length windows flanking a set of doors veiled only with a thin gauze curtain. I try the door. It's stiff but a few pulls do the job and I am thrown out into a courtyard that has been built into the roof of the neighbouring building. It must only be a few metres wide and the same in length, but there is enough room to house a bistro table, an umbrella and a couple of pot plants that are bathing in the weak afternoon light.

'Everything up to standard?' The American asks as I close the door behind me. She is perched on the edge of the sofa, her ankles knitted together.

I nod.

'Perfect, I will leave you to it then.' She struggles to her feet. I resist the urge to help, it feels patronising, and she looks like a woman who wouldn't take too kindly to that. 'I hope you don't mind me asking,' she starts as she straightens out her sleeves, untangling her kimono tassels. 'What brings you to Monpazier?

The email was vague, something about work but that crowd normally go to Bordeaux. I'm sure there's more opportunities for a good time there?'

Normally I might have felt riled at the question, put her down as nothing more than a nosy landlord trying to figure out if I'm going to wreck the place, but she looks genuinely interested.

'It's complicated.' I shrug. It isn't a lie. It is bloody complicated. 'I'm not here for long, just need to… tie up some loose ends.' I end up performing some half-hearted jazz hands, as if the story had some punchline that wasn't my ex-husband dying.

'You have friends here?'

'No.' I shake my head quickly. 'Not really. Just me.'

She looks at me for a little too long. 'It's going to be a lonely month for you.'

I let out an ugly snort. 'I'm used to it.'

'The market is on tomorrow. Come for lunch afterwards. L'Auberge at one-thirty. I'm rather bored of my own company myself.'

'That's kind of you, but you really don't need…'

'One-thirty.' She closes down my objection and I nod slowly. 'Thank you.'

'I hope you'll be happy here.' She smiles. 'Tying up those loose ends.'

I start to unpack my suitcase in the apartment that suddenly feels all too quiet without another soul in here to make the floorboards creak. My things take up two drawers and three coat hangers.

There is an old cassette radio on the kitchen countertop; it jolts to life in a static crackle. I turn the dial until the music becomes clearer and then adjust the volume until it fills every corner of the apartment. The American had left a bottle of red wine, a baguette and some butter in the fridge. The addition of a cereal bar in my handbag makes it a meal.

I pour myself a glass and collapse onto the sofa and feel everything start to close in. So I do what I have learned to do when I feel like this; I reach into my bag and take out the diary.

I turn to a fresh page, bend the spine some more until it is flat and scrawl out the date. I write Monpazier in the centre and underline it three times. It looks strange now, that word, this place back on the page, like a word that loses its meaning when you say it too many times. I write a simple sentence.

I'm here. Now what the fuck do I do?

And I dry up. There's no burgeoning feelings that need to be explored, contained and cemented. Just a kind of numbness.

It's not something I'm used to – the block. When I first started to write about him, in those heady, Valium-laced days after he died, my mum used to have to come in and put me to bed. She would physically take the diary and put it downstairs, tuck me in and turn the lights off, because if she didn't, she knew that I wouldn't stop. I would write it down, every little detail from Ettie's shower routine, to our arguments, to the description of his body in the mortuary, because I felt like if I didn't, then I would lose it all, forget everything. As long as it was hurting, it bought me closer to him in some way.

The only thing that helped stop the writing addiction had been a comment from my dad, hovering in the doorway of my bedroom, with that wary and concerned look of a parent terrified of his child's emotions.

'You're almost halfway through,' he said, pointing at the spine. It was a simple thing to say, a half-hearted observation, but as I looked through the pages, the ones heavily lined with writing and the fresh ones yet to be touched, I realised what he was saying. If I kept on going, then in a couple of weeks, even my little coping mechanism would be gone. I cried some more and Dad stepped into the bedroom and hovered again, but this time over me, patting my shoulder. The next day we drove to a tech shop and he bought me a laptop, a proper expensive one, all the bells and whistles. I protested but he insisted – I think he would have bought me a car to try and make me feel just a little bit better at that point.

So it's hard not to feel the irony that now I'm here, the words stop. A kind of cruel joke that has been played on me before – let's give it all to Ava, lay it all out in front of her and then when it matters the most, take it all away.

I pull out my phone to try to distract myself from the pressure building in my chest.

I text Sam that the apartment is fine. I tell my parents that I'm alive, arrived and settled – even though the last bit is so far from the truth I'm sure that the lie is blaringly obvious – and then I do the unthinkable.

The phone rings twice before he picks up.

'Ava?' Archie's voice is full of concern.

'Hi.'

'Is everything okay?'

There's a long pause. It is weighted and heavy until I fill it with a whimpering 'No.'

'Give me two seconds, Ava.' Archie's voice is steady. I can hear him say something to someone on his end of the line. A chair moving. It's four o'clock on a Monday in London. He's at work.

'Shit, I'm sorry... I forgot, I'll go.'

'No! It's fine. It wasn't important, I'm just heading outside.'

'God,' I stammer. 'I'm such a shit.'

'Right, I'm here. What's going on?'

'Sorry, you just said I could call you and there is literally no one else... and I have no clue what I'm doing here and fuck...'

'Ava, just breathe.' He is calm, authoritative in a way I didn't know he could be. 'Just breathe.'

I do as he says, keep breathing until the shudder goes, until it feels like my throat isn't going to close up.

'Good,' he coaches. 'Now tell me.'

'I just freaked out.'

'I can tell.'

'I haven't really been on my own in a place like this in forever and...'

'So you're at the apartment?' he cuts through.

'Yes.'

'Is it okay?'

'It's lovely.'

'What are you doing?'

I look down at the very full glass of red in my hand. 'Drinking wine.'

'Maybe wine isn't the best?'

'Thanks for that assessment.'

'Have you got dinner sorted?'

'Yes.' I lie, my eyes darting towards the cereal bar. I choose not to be so honest about that. 'Can you just… tell me about your day?'

'There's nothing really to tell.'

'That's exactly what I want to hear about right now.'

'Sure.' I can hear him smile through the phone. 'I got up at seven, went to Gail's, got a coffee.'

'You basic bitch.'

'You love it. Got to the office for eight. Forgot my key card but Jerry on the door let me in. Checked my emails, did some admin… is this boring enough for you?' he checks in.

'Perfectly boring,' I nod, rooting around in my bag for the cool silver cigarette case that had once belonged to Ettie. I barely smoke any more, but sometimes on particularly hard days I allow myself the luxury.

'Had lunch in the canteen.'

'What did you have?'

I take the wine through the bedroom and onto the balcony. It's almost dark now.

'Ham and cheese panini.'

I light the cigarette and inhale deeply. 'You rockstar.'

'I'll hang up.'

'You wouldn't dare.'

His laugh subsides, 'Maybe I can come out and see you when you're more settled. I have some holiday. Could do a long weekend?' My silence on the other side seems to scare him. 'But no pressure or anything. I appreciate your head's probably all over the place and everything and you're there to do some work not to just entertain some random guy you hook up w—'

'Yeah sure,' I say to stop him saying anything else self-deprecating.

'Yes that's why it's a bad idea, or…'

'Just yeah, I mean maybe at some point. If we get some time.' It is the most pitiful invitation.

'Oh.' His voice softens. 'Cool,' he adds.

'Maybe I can call you again, like tomorrow? When you're not at work,' I offer, desperate to move off the topic of Archie flying all this way to stay in this attic with me and my ghosts.

'Of course.'

'Great.' I take another long drag.

'Ava, I have to go.' He sighs.

'I know, thanks Archie.'

'For what?'

'For answering. I— It means a lot.'

'Anytime.' And whilst it might be something that anyone says to finish a call, when he says it, I believe him.

Chapter 5

I SLEEP IN UNTIL nine. Enjoy the luxury of not living with retirees who seem to surface horrifically early and like to hoover.

The shower eventually starts to spit out warmish water after five minutes of running and I try to scrub yesterday off into the drain. When I feel slightly more human and the headache from the wine has been reduced to a dull fug, I reach for the towel and stand by the sink. I can hear my mother telling me to try to make an effort, that if I at least looked like I was coping, the rest would follow. I wasn't quite sure about the psychology behind the sentiment, but still dig around in my make-up bag, searching for a face that might show the world I'm better than I am.

I never turned the radio off last night, so I'm welcomed into the kitchen to what clearly is the French version of Best of the Seventies, but it is nice to not be in silence. I make a black coffee and launch my laptop into life at the breakfast bar.

I go through the motions of my usual morning routine. First, I log on to the blog. There are forty more comments on my last post and twelve messages. I had told them I was off on a short, book-related break but would be back in a couple of weeks. It managed people's expectations, stopped randomers messaging you asking if you had died.

I used to make sure I replied to everyone when it all started, but it was smaller then, a few dozen maybe here and there, and it took up a morning. About five months after the blog started, a post went viral. I had shared a picture of Ettie and me, the first time I had put our faces on the internet. It was a selfie, the first date, when phone cameras were still blurry and imperfect. We looked so young. I wrote something so unguarded I look back now and wonder where I got the confidence to ever publish it. It had travelled somehow into the feed of a TV presenter who had lost her husband a year before and she had shared it. The next day I had gained 17,000 followers, and my meandering passion project to stave off boredom had become something much more.

This morning though, I decide to read through the messages. They used to just be women but there's men now too. All explaining to me how my 'strength' inspires them, how I am the only one who 'gets it'. Now, as I sit in the empty apartment, terrified about the prospect of stepping outside, I know it's all one big lie.

My mission today is to buy food. It is almost eleven; I can get my shopping, walk around the market for an hour and then meet The American for lunch. The thought of eating with a stranger would normally bring me out in hives, but there's something about her that makes the prospect a little more appealing. I want to know her, to be invited into her confidence. I think if I was more like her then everything might be a little easier to handle.

I take a large canvas bag from the kitchen and make my way down the stairs onto the street. The road up to the square is as empty as it was yesterday. Familiarity seeps through me. This had been my town, the one I had discovered and built my identity around, the one that wasn't heavy with shared family stories and awkward teenage moments.

When I round the corner towards the square, I see a queue of people snaking out of the boulangerie door. Ettie had told me once that it was a legal requirement for every village in France to have somewhere you could buy bread. Like a lot of things Etienne told me, I never felt the need to follow it up with a Google search. I had a sort of immovable trust in him. Later I realised that this is a trait that lots of young women who fall for older men often have in common. There's nothing quite like finding out you're a cliché.

I skirt around the edge of the square, until I can't avoid it any longer. The stalls are huddled around a covered market built back when chainmail was a wardrobe staple. In the height of the summer the weekly Thursday market is the place to be, where hastily made shanty stalls sprawl down the side streets to the delight of the tourists, but now it's just for locals offering a meagre splattering of the basics: namely vegetables and jars of paté. It means there aren't enough distractions. It means that the moment I look up across the square I can see it.

The little red sign with the gold writing still reads 'L'Avenir,' the wicker tables, already laid out, the shutters and parasols sun-bleached and all a bit wonky. The café. Our café.

A waitress I don't know looks at me, notices me staring. She points to the sign with the opening times, 'Nous ouvrons en dix minutes, madame!' she shouts across the void of all of the ten metres between us.

I turn and walk towards what I hope is the supermarket. My bearings have left me now. When I see the Spar sign I feel as if I have made it to a bunker of sorts. It is safety with its fluorescent lights and refrigeration – it's hard to feel sentimental in a supermarket.

I take a basket and shuffle around the aisles, clutching at the torn-up little shopping list in my hand. I'm sure there are glaciers that would complete a shopping list faster, but I think I would stay all day in here if it meant I didn't have to look at the café again.

Chapter 6

THANKFULLY L'AUBERGE IS DOWN a side street, and I go the long way round to try to make up the time. Even when I try not to be, I have always been frustratingly punctual.

I didn't need to worry, The American is already here, sitting at a bistro table on the terrace, sunglasses shielding half of her face with her shoulders wrapped up in a grey scarf I fully expect to be cashmere.

'Ava, you made it!' She doesn't make the effort to get up which I am grateful for, instead she leans over the table for me to kiss her on the cheeks. She smells expensive.

'I thought I was going to be early but looks like you beat me to it.'

'I'm a bit of a cockroach. I turn up at nine for a coffee and they won't get rid of me until dinner.' The waiter, a middle-aged man who is smoking by the door, looks up.

'She brings in the customers.' He shrugs and then grins widely at her. He stubs out the cigarette and transports a cumbersome chalkboard menu to the table. We are the only ones here.

'What's good?' I ask, plastering on a smile.

'Depends what your position is on animal welfare.'

'Easily swayed depending on taste.' Her eyes sparkle at my response and then she gestures to a scribble under the entrées. 'Well then I'd go for the Normande.'

'What's in it?'

'I find the quickest way to lose your appetite here is to ask for the ingredients.'

I am satisfied that she's right and let her give my order to the waiter who has already managed to deliver a carafe of red with two glasses.

'Are you local?' I ask.

She smiles. 'Yes. I'm a long-term resident of Chateau Eleanor.' I rack my brain until the image of a rather grand hotel on the edge of the Bastide is bought into my vision.

'The hotel?'

'Yes. I came one summer a few years back to meet my friend – the one who owned the apartment – never left.' She lights a cigarette and then offers one to me. I take it, grateful to do something with my hands.

'I didn't know you could live there?'

She smirks. 'I don't think they did either. I'm sure it's an imposition in the summer but the manager and I came to some understanding. At least in the winter the bills get paid.'

I wonder how open she is to questioning, whether she will think I'm nosy or interested if I push further. I punt for the latter. 'Why there?'

She nods her head from side to side as if weighing up her response. 'I like getting waited on. Back in the States I'm sure I would have been lumped in some "assisted care facility", probably charge me more than they do, and at least they don't talk to me here as if I'm senile. Probably get fed better too.'

'I read about people doing that on cruise ships.'

She shrugs. 'I get seasick.'

She greets the waiter who has swapped his cigarette for a tray of steaming food. He places the plat du jour on the table with a flourish. I hadn't realised how hungry I was until I start to eat.

The American looks on proudly. 'I thought you might need feeding.' She elegantly takes a bite of her own and nods her approval at the waiter. 'Your best yet.' She raises her glass with her spare hand and I think I can see him blush.

'It's so good,' I mumble through another mouthful.

'You never came here before?' The American asks quizzically, I'm not sure if the glasses are magnifying her eyes or whether

they have always been this large. I know now that it is my turn
to swap some information.

'No.' I wipe some sauce off my chin. 'We didn't really venture
this far out of the square.'

'We?'

Shit. A slip of the tongue and now we're here. I weigh it up.
There isn't much point in lying; if she does live in the hotel there
will be people who eventually will recognise me, put two and
two together. 'My husband and I.'

'Oh.' She doesn't look taken aback. I realise that in the
same way I have been guessing what brought her here, she has
been doing the same about me. 'And your husband is back in
England?'

'No.' I take a swig of red from the carafe. 'He died, brain
aneurism, all very sudden.' I have learned that the best way to
deal with delivering the news is similar to ripping off a plaster.
That if I give all the information at the outset there's only space
for one sympathetic, kind-hearted response. If you give the bare
minimum, people get curious, and the whole thing gets dragged
out for weeks.

'I'm sorry.' She's taken aback now, but unlike a lot of people
who are met with that sharp statement, she doesn't shrink from
it.

'It's okay, I'm guessing it wasn't your fault.' I let out a little
snort. 'Sometimes I say I'm divorced. It's easier.'

She looks at me differently now, but not in a way I'm used to.
She looks strangely proud. 'Has it been long?'

'Three years, almost four.'

She looks up at me, chewing what's left in her mouth, her
fork balanced in a knotty hand. 'I bet it feels like no time at all.'
It isn't something I've heard before in the multitude of pointless
things people say. It is the comment of someone who knows
loss. Who has been told 'time heals all wounds' and has also
wanted to stab them with a fork in response.

'No. It feels like yesterday.'

'And you lived here? Together?'

'Yes. It's where we met. He ran L'Avenir.' I gesture in the general direction of the café. I used to love telling people that, back when Ettie was alive. It cemented the fact that I was more than just a tourist.

'The one in the square?'

'That's the one.'

'Life can be so bloody relentless, can't it.' She shakes her head. 'You miss him.'

'Lots.'

'And your loose ends?'

'A book, about him, well more about losing him really.'

'Ah, a writer.' She smiles widely. 'I thought there was something about you I liked.' I feel in that moment that I have been brought into her confidence and it is glorious.

The waiter brings out coffee and madeleines to finish and we smoke another cigarette whilst sitting in a comfortable silence, watching people come and go, the traders hauling their wares back to the vans on the outskirts of the walls.

And then I see him.

A figure walks past, quickly, his phone pressed to his ear so it's difficult to make him out entirely but just the way his body moves takes the air from my lungs. He's in the café's rust-red t-shirt showing the same lean, muscular arms, with the same long slender frame. Just as I think he'll turn his head, look me directly in the eye, he pivots and jogs down a side street away from me.

'Ava?' The American pulls me out of my trance.

'Did you see—' I can feel my breath come back, pulling at my lungs, thin and clawing. I feel like I'm drowning.

'Ava, you don't look well.'

'I need to go.' I pick up my things. A cup falls off the table and shatters by my feet. I don't even have time to apologise. It is like some force is in control of my body, moving it of its own free will. I break into a jog, down the same cut through, my eyes desperately trying to make out the ghost that had just appeared in the middle of the street.

I had of course imagined the possibility. What if it was all some ruse to dump me? An exit strategy. I think I could understand that eventually. It made more sense than all of that life suddenly being extinguished overnight.

The alley reaches a fork, and I see the flash of red at the end of a passage on the left and follow. My jog has turned into a clumsy run, my trainers occasionally catching on an uneven bit of stone, but I am determined to catch up with him.

The passage widens. There are voices now, a large cacophony of lunchtime chatter, as I am catapulted into the square and this time I don't care that I'm here, this time there is no creeping dread and fear of bursting into tears.

I start pirouetting, my head a lighthouse, searching the crowd for any sign of him. I think of the shirt he was wearing, the very basic uniform of the café that Ettie insisted we wore.

People move out of my way instinctively; I must look mad. I see the parasols, smell the cigars and the coffee, it hasn't changed at all. Of course he's still here, he never died. I must have hit my head, imagined the last three years. He's going to see me and wonder what on earth all the fuss is about.

I reach the terrace. There are a few occupied tables, mostly it's empty. Behind the archway of the stone cloister there is the familiar sight of the coffee machine obstructing the bar, the shelves of glasses, the TV blaring out some horse racing. I look for him behind the counter, but I can only make out a woman. And then there he is, I can feel him behind me, footsteps and then a hard, and very real, hand on my shoulder.

Chapter 7

I THROW MY ARMS around him. It seemed like the right thing to do at the time but almost immediately I realise my mistake.

It's the smell that I notice first; it isn't unpleasant, woodsmoke and coffee, so close to Ettie but not the same. Then I realise that the body isn't quite right, too tall, too lean. I can feel his bones beneath the crushing weight of my arms. The horror begins to dawn on me that the rigid body currently in my strangle-hold is not my Ettie.

'Ava?' the voice says again, so close but not his voice. He knows my name. The figure pats my back gently and for a moment I cling harder because I don't want to wake up from this momentary lapse of sanity. In the melee of delusion, I am the happiest I have been in years.

It's the stranger who peels me from him piece by piece, limb by limb, until we unstick and are staring at each other. I take him in, so much of the same – the shape of the face, the dark eyes, the frame, the café shirt – but he now looks like Ettie only in stature and uniform.

I know his face because I have seen it before, granted only a handful of times, but I have studied his features over dinners and birthdays and a funeral. I know the face because in front of me now, looking utterly panicked as he examines my face for any signs of recognition, is Etienne's brother.

'Florian?' My voice is strangled, wispy. I shake my head, step away from him. I realise that his hands have been securing my shoulders, stopping me from bolting, and now that he has released me there is a lightness, a sudden urge to run. I step back again, looking desperately around for an exit. I can see the faces now, the faces of the locals who have all stopped to watch.

I look back to him. His hands are held up in mock submission; his eyes wide and lips expressionless, he says my name again. It is like he's trying to get back some spooked dog. In fairness, that's how I feel, that there should be a poster about me with a warning that reads 'Do not approach, will bolt.'

'I'm sorry… I thought…' I gabble out a response, but I don't sound like me any more. I can't form the words, can't find the strength to even put on the pretence that I'm fine.

My eyes fix on the exit route, the street that will guide me back to the apartment, back to safety.

'No. Don't.' His voice is soft, raspy as if the emotion is contagious, sticking in both of our throats. He reaches out for my arm, in that moment entirely understanding what I am about to do, but I snatch it away. I do as the runaway dog does, and charge towards the exit. I have never been much of a runner, but I don't feel the effort of it, just the adrenaline that is flooding through me. I can feel it in every limb, in every muscle, deep in my lungs; my fingers tingle with it.

I round the corner, disappear down the maze of side streets. I can hear my name being called again. I don't like the way it sounds in his accent now. It sounds like an alarm bell. The drumming of his feet running after me becomes louder until he is closing in. His arm finds my shoulder, pulls me to a stop.

'Ava, stop please – just for a moment – you're upset,' he pants.

I turn to him. There's desperation there, a sort of pitiful sadness mixed with something else that a frantic mind can't quite translate.

'Just come back with me. We can sit down, get you a drink. I can explain.' His grip on my shoulder tightens as if he has learned from my last escape. He looks terrified of me. I think I am terrified of myself.

'Let me go.' I tug at my shoulder but he is a rock.

'Ava… Please, come on.'

'She told you to let her go.' Another voice thunders through the street. Florian and I both look at the willowy figure walking with some speed towards us, a stick being waved in her hand. The American.

Her expression is enough to make Florian release me.

I stagger back towards her. She is a few inches shorter than me but her arm still snakes its way around me protectively.

'It's not what it looks like. We know each other. We're family.' He attempts to neutralise the situation. I scoff at the mention of family. Feel my shock turn to jagged rage. We are not family. He is a stranger who has spoken more to me in the last five minutes than he ever had in the seven years I was married to his brother.

'Well then, I'm sure you can see that she isn't in a state to talk to you right now. I suggest you respect her wishes.'

'I—' he starts, his lips forming words that he can't actually get out. Excuses maybe. 'Fine!' He throws his hands up in defeat and storms back up the street leaving me and The American reeling, arm in arm.

The American forces us to sit down on a bench, she says it's for her knees, but I know it's so that I can catch my breath and gather the rest of myself together. I lurch forward, bury my head into my hands and let out a few strangled sobs. She rubs my back protectively.

'I'm sorry,' I manage after gulping back some of the tears.

'For what?' Her voice is gentle, it sounds like the sea.

'For making a tit out of myself. I'm so embarrassed.'

'There's nothing to be embarrassed about. We've all run away from a man at least once in our lives.'

I manage an exasperated little laugh. 'Why do I have a feeling you've done it more than once?'

'You already know me so well.' She squeezes me playfully and I feel the sanity returning. 'Now, do you think you can walk?'

I pull myself to my feet and dust off my jeans. My legs have an ache in them which lets me know my involuntary athleticism will now come back to haunt me.

'I can manage to get home.'

'Oh, we aren't going there.' She shakes her head and points down the street towards the silhouette of the imposing Chateau Eleanor standing sentinel over the town. 'You're coming to my place, for a cup of tea…' She tries to gauge my reaction; I clearly look less than enthused. 'Or something stronger?' she tries again.

I snigger. 'Both?'

'Great idea.' She gestures for me to help her up and when she is planted on both of her feet, we walk arm in arm towards the hotel.

Chateau Eleanor perches on the edge of the Bastide with two square turrets flanking the white stone front. It is one of the only buildings that looks like it has met an architect in the last three hundred years and has been restored into one of the only hotels in a five-mile radius. Normally buildings like this would be left to decompose until they were worth less than a modern little three-bed on the outskirts of town, but this place has managed to escape that fate.

She points to a quiet corner by the fire with two small sofas and I slump myself down in the closest one. Without having to ask, a waiter brings over a pot of tea.

'And two martinis please.' She points to the bar. 'Better make them strong,' she whispers to the young man with a wink. He nods approvingly and scurries off.

'So…' she starts, pouring some tea out of the pot and into the cup. 'Care to tell me who *that* was?' She puts the teapot back and without asking, adds two sugar cubes. 'I had thought some long-lost lover until he mentioned the family bit.'

I force out a sharp laugh and shake my head. 'God no. *That* was my brother-in-law. Or ex-brother-in-law. I'm not really sure what happens when your only connection together is dead.'

The American pours out some milk and then holds the cup up, looking me in the eye for the first time since we got here.

'When was the last time you spoke?'

I take the cup. 'The funeral.'

'I'm guessing they weren't close.'

'I always got the distinct impression that being related was nothing more than a major inconvenience for the both of them.'

'I think you've just explained a vast majority of sibling relationships.'

'Well they were something else. Whilst I guess you could call this place their hometown, they grew up all over the place. Their dad was a diplomat and their mum was happy to be anywhere other than stuck at home with her boys. Ettie always thought his mum had children because she felt like it was the right thing to do. She was young, she wanted travel and dinners and once she realised that children didn't exactly fit in with that lifestyle it was a little too late. To be honest, I think it's why Ettie and I never really imagined ourselves having kids; he didn't want to risk the same thing happening to them.'

The American takes a gulp of her tea.

'They spent their summers in the area but were sent off to boarding school to try to give them some consistency, but from what Ettie told me it was a rather torturous childhood.' Some people get seated next to us and my monologue is interrupted by the scraping of chairs on the stone floors. 'Sorry, this must be pretty boring, I should stop.' I blush but The American shakes her head so fervently that I think she might lose an earring.

'Honey, I love nothing more than a good old family saga. I'll tell you mine one day.' I try to gauge whether she's being serious but I don't think this woman is capable of being insincere.

'Well, their dad died when the boys were in their twenties and gave them some money. Florian used his to go to art school in Bordeaux, which he was actually quite good at until the money started evaporating; turns out he'd fallen into the role of tortured artist a little too well.'

The American leans over, clearly intrigued. 'Drugs?'

I nod. 'Yes, there were drugs.'

'Was it bad?'

I pull at my sleeves. Despite the hot fury that has been hibernating under my apathy for Ettie's family for the last three years, it's difficult to ignore the guilt about spilling someone else's secrets. I grimace, choose to stick to the facts. 'Yes, it got bad, really bad. It was this constant cycle of getting so bad that he had no choice but to try to do something about it, so he'd get clean for a while before the whole cycle would start again. Ettie and him fell out big time over it. The last Grenaud family meal we had together ended up in an actual fist fight.'

'And that was the last time your husband saw him?'

'Not quite. He turned up at the café three months before Ettie died, completely fucked—' I pause, waiting for a reprimand of my language, but it doesn't come. 'He had his face all bashed in, bloody nose, black eye, fractured cheekbone. He stayed with us for a night until Ettie drove him back. We were trying to buy the lease off the owner of the café, almost had the money together too, but the day Ettie took him to Bordeaux, the account was empty. Ettie played it off at first until I threatened to call the police and he told me in no uncertain terms that that wasn't going to happen. When we both calmed down, he said that one day he would tell me what happened, but... well... then three months later he was dead, so I guess I'm never going to find out.' It's cathartic to let it all tumble out. Cathartic and exhausting in equal measure. I look around for the waiter, hopeful that the drink will be making itself known in the near future.

The American reaches for my hand, squeezes it tightly. 'I'm sorry, Ava.'

'It's okay. It's Ettie's fault for being so stubborn,' I smirk. 'It would have never dawned on him that he would be the one in the body bag before his fortieth birthday.' The American lets out a sad little sigh and I feel everything slow down, my heart coming back into a manageable rhythm, my breath returning to me. 'I just never thought that Florian would come back here. Ettie said that he'd spent his entire life trying to run from it, why come back now?'

'You could always ask him?' she suggests.

'No.' I shake my head fervently. 'I don't want to hear anything he has to say.' The waiter delivers the martini to the table. I grab it off the tray before he has a chance to set it down on the coaster and finish it in three large gulps.

I watch as The American smiles and then leans over to the waiter, stroking his arm. 'Laurent, you better make up another.'

Chapter 8

FUELLED BY THE CONFIDENCE of two martinis I walk back to my apartment alone. The American had tried to wrangle one of the hotel porters into acting as a bodyguard. I think it was more for Florian's safety than my own – in case he was stupid enough to still be lingering by the door.

There *is* something waiting for me when I round the corner. Thankfully not a man but instead a bright blue cool bag perches in the doorway. I hesitate before opening it, wondering for a moment if something might explode, and then calm myself with a reminder that I am not some undercover spy; instead I am a woman hiding for much more mundane reasons.

I peel off the velcro lid to find my canvas bag full of the groceries I desperately needed but had abandoned at the café when the 'situation' arose. I hadn't even realised they were missing.

It feels slightly like a peace offering. He could have left the bag there, maybe even binned the lot. I would have probably understood, but there is a nagging feeling of gratitude that I can at least eat tonight.

I lug the shopping, cool bag and all, up the stairs and have to immediately strip off my jumper when I reach the safety of the apartment. There is a warm familiarity to the space now. I am grateful that I'm here, able to shut a door to a space that is my own, a space that can't be invaded by ghosts.

My phone rings. I see Archie's contact card, a professional yet approachable picture of his face that makes me automatically smile until I realise what my face is doing and try to straighten everything back out.

'Hi,' I pant.

'Are you running?' I can hear the shock in his voice, the lilt that suggests he is smiling at the thought.

'Less of the surprise!' I scold and take off my shoes. 'But no. I've just climbed some stairs.'

'Bloody hell, Ava.' He laughs, a genuine belly laugh. 'Maybe we should hit the gym when you get back.'

'Charming!'

'You sound better,' he says as I lug the bag into the kitchen and unload the contents on the counter. I let out a scoff. 'No?'

'I ran into Ettie's brother.' I fill in the blanks.

A pause. 'The weird one?'

'The only one.'

'Fuck!' Archie clearly remembers our rushed conversation on the subject. 'Was he alright?'

'Don't know.' I secure the phone with my shoulder as I start to look through the bag. 'I kind of legged it, but I dropped my shopping and it was waiting on my doorstep when I got back.'

'How does he know where you live?'

A cold shiver runs down my spine. I wish he hadn't asked that because paranoia begins to set in. 'Good question.' I notice a little postage tag attached to the handle of the bag. 'He's left a note.'

'Read it,' Archie orders.

I do as he instructs, reading it to him before I have time to digest it myself.

Ava,

You left this. Sorry if I scared you earlier, I was shocked to see you. I can tell that you were shocked to see me too. There is so much I need to explain and that you should hear. Meet me at Fromages et Vins tomorrow at seven and we can talk.
Yours,

Florian

'Seems legit,' Archie muses. 'Estranged brother who knows where you live wants to meet up tomorrow at a cheese shop.'

'Fuck off.' I start putting away the groceries until my hand passes over something papery on the bottle of wine.

It's a neon yellow Post-it note:

The wine's shit. Try this instead.

I pull out the bottle, realising that it is not the one that I had bought in the shop, but something else entirely with a cork and a dusty label. I can feel the heat crawling its way up my neck. It strikes me that Florian had not only retrieved my shopping but had also gone through it. An intense frustration starts to prickle through me. I imagine him trying to decode me, judging me. Then I think of the tampons also hastily bought and the prickling heat turns into an all-encompassing redness that sticks to my cheeks.

'The bastard!' I screech.

'What?' Archie sounds incredibly alarmed.

'He swapped it.'

'Swapped what?'

'The wine, the wine I bought. He said it's shit.'

'Is it more expensive?' Archie replies after a short pause, his voice soft and measured.

'It doesn't matter if it's more expensive. I wanted the wine I bought.'

'Well, maybe try it before throwing it out?' he tries to placate me.

'Yeah, well I don't have much of a choice.' I pour out the wine into a glass and start chopping some vegetables for dinner. Despite the large lunch I needed something more than just the martinis.

'Are you cooking?' Archie sounds perplexed.

I feel my body stiffen; I appreciate that Archie has only really seen the worst parts of me but I really do question how he thinks I functioned for thirty years without being able to feed myself. 'I *can* cook.'

'What are you making?'

'An omelette.'

'Alright Heston.'

'I'll hang up!' I throw the vegetables into the pan and start to whisk up the eggs. 'Do you think you could stop questioning my cooking skills and help me decide what to do about stalker brother-in-law, please?'

'I'd meet him,' he says quickly and entirely unexpectedly. I assumed he would err on the side of caution, tell me that I should lock my doors and be on the first flight home.

'You'd go?' I repeat, making sure I had heard him correctly.

'Yes.' He sounds level-headed, his voice clear. 'I'd hear him out.'

'Well, you're a man. You can meet other strange men in random bars and not end up buried in a ditch.'

'He's hardly a stranger, Ava.'

'He's strange to me.' I mumble and pour the eggs into the pan, watching with satisfaction as the mixture almost immediately begins to curl at the edges. It smells good.

'Look, whatever happened, things are different now. The drama was between the brothers, not you. This could be an opportunity for a fresh start.'

'I don't want a fresh start, I just want to go on pretending he doesn't exist.' I am aware I sound like a petulant teenager but if he is getting fed up with my whining he doesn't let it show. In fact I think he is enjoying listening to me rant and moan. There's an intimacy to this moody part of me he doesn't often see. He's right.

'But he does exist, Ava, and by all accounts, he's existing a few metres from your house in a place where you will have to go again during your month-long stay. You meet up, have a drink, get things out in the open and then you can go about your life, write your book – hell, this could at least be an interesting chapter.'

'You're missing the point.' I flip the omelette. 'I. Don't. Want. To.' Archie chuckles, it's low and deep and I can feel another, different heat in my cheeks that isn't from anger, embarrassment or cooking.

'Don't you want to know how he got your address?' Archie tries another angle. One that always had a better chance of succeeding.

'Yes.'

'Well then, you'd better meet him there tomorrow at seven.'

Chapter 9

Florian is an island; he is perched on a bar stool on the veranda of Fromages et Vins looking intently at his phone. He has changed out of his workwear, keeping the jeans but swapping the café's top for a thick flannel over-shirt in a burnt-orange plaid.

My resounding and limited memory of Florian was that he had always been slightly scruffy. No matter what the occasion, there would be holes in his jumpers, scuffs on his trousers and paint smears on most of the cuffs of his jackets. He's tidier now, like he has thought about what clothes he's thrown on. The most notable change, however, is his hair. It's shorter, loosely tousled with some wax that makes it darker than I remember. It had been shoulder length the last time I saw him. He had tied it into a scruffy bun for the funeral which he let down for the pathetic excuse of a wake that I was far too anesthetised by Valium and whisky to take much of a part in. He looks younger, his face only shadowed by a couple of creases here and there, the kind that make a man look distinguished, not haggard. The three years have been kinder to him than they have to me.

'Hello.' I approach carefully but he still jolts and then lets out an awkward laugh. 'Not expecting me or…' I trail off as he slips from the stool and greets me, quickly pressing his lips to my cheeks.

'I guess I just thought you wouldn't come.' He shrugs, his English word perfect, only the faint echo of an accent.

'I thought about it.' I pull myself up onto the bar stool facing him. 'But I figured that we were going to see each other again at some point.'

He assesses me and then nods. 'That's why I thought this would be good. And I also thought that somewhere new might be less...' He searches for the right word.

'Triggering?' He weighs it up, whether it truly does fit, and when he tries it on his lips he nods.

'Yes. Triggering.'

He calls over the waitress and a young woman comes over. She smiles at him, a hand on his shoulder, and she looks nervously at me with the same appraising look that Florian had given me moments before. I know they have been talking about me. Probably placing bets on whether I would turn up, giving her a one-sided version of our limited familial interactions.

'Would you like a drink?' she asks. It feels impolite to ask for a vodka so I gesture to the carafe of wine on another table. 'Red, please.'

'Two glasses.' Florian chips in.

'Sure.' She smiles sweetly and heads back into the bar.

The terrace is lit with festoon bulbs and patio heaters and I think I have been concentrating so hard on what I'm going to say, on trying to puzzle out what's happening, that I haven't really taken in the fact it's almost warm.

The waitress brings out the wine immediately, catching Florian's eye as she places the glasses on the table and sweeps back away.

'You two a thing?' I ask as I pour out a glass that is so large the carafe is now only half full. We both know why we're here, but it is a subject that I will need to be tipsy to broach and so a conversation about Florian's love life is a much more interesting appetiser.

He shrugs, taking the carafe off me and pouring himself a glass that is equally as big. 'Not really.'

We descend into an awkward silence, both gulping back our wine and refilling our glasses quickly.

'Thank you for bringing my shopping back,' I start. Archie had told me to make sure I wasn't starting the conversation on the attack. He said that he imagined I could be quite wounding when I went into things with an attitude. I felt strangely proud of that.

'You're welcome.' He doesn't look at me as he says it.

'You owe me a bottle of wine though.'

He looks up then, his neck whipping straight, his eyes bright and fixed on me. 'I gave you a better bottle.'

'I don't need my shopping delivered with suggestions.'

'You're telling me you didn't enjoy the replacement?' He already knows my answer. He knows it would be near impossible to not enjoy the bottle that did arrive in the bag.

'I—' I stumble for the right words but give up and just shrug. 'I want my bottle back.'

'Fine.' He drums his fingers on the table. 'I will get you another shit bottle.' There is an irritating smile at the corner of his mouth. I didn't come to entertain him. There is another awkward beat in the conversation and I watch as the attempt at a smile flattens, turns into a thin-lipped line.

'You thought I was him, didn't you?' He doesn't look me in the eye when he says it but his face is pained. He knows my answer before I say it. I think he has been thinking about it since I ran off.

I brush a hair from my eyes and tuck it behind my ear, thinking about yesterday, how in a moment I had managed to convince myself that I had run into my dead husband. The husband I watched being lowered into the ground. 'You know, it's funny. I never thought you two looked alike before. I don't even think you do now but… I don't know.'

'We're more alike than strangers.'

'I think perhaps I saw what I wanted to see.'

'I'm sorry,' he says sadly.

'For what? It's not your fault I thought you were him.'

'I don't know…' He pauses, shrugs and then he points briefly to my cheeks. 'Your face – when you realised – I just feel like I need to apologise for it.'

I can't help but soften, feel that heavy pang in my chest that makes me want to reach out, touch his shoulder, tell him that it's okay, he doesn't need to be sorry. It's instinctive; I don't like making people feel bad. But he isn't just anyone, this is the person who had made Ettie's life so much harder than it needed to be. The thought grounds me again, the memories pull me back into the anger. I take a breath, bring my eyes up to his, without the emotion this time.

'I didn't think you'd be back in Monpazier.'

'Why not? I grew up here?' he says sharply, matching me.

'Yeah,' I smirk. 'And left as soon as you could.'

He looks stung by the comment. I'm glad. 'It's complicated.' He shrugs. 'After he died, I just wanted to be back here.'

'Go on then. You said you wanted to explain, that there were things I needed to hear…'

'I thought maybe we could be a few more glasses deep before—' he starts but runs out of steam when he sees my clearly unimpressed face. He takes a breath, looks briefly towards the direction of the café and then when he looks back, his eyes lock on to mine. 'I'm clean, Ava. That's probably the first thing I should say, the reason I needed to see you.'

'Congratulations,' I say flatly.

'It's been three years… and a bit,' he adds. 'And when I got clean I realised that I needed a fresh start somewhere different. I tried Paris for a bit – that's where I was when Ettie died – but it was too busy, too many distractions. I came back for the funeral and something clicked. I liked it here, it reminded me of him.'

An involuntary scoff forces itself out of me. Florian ignores it. 'I know that you never exactly saw the best version of me, but we were close once, before you were on the scene, before I went to Bordeaux. I had always imagined we would be close again, that we could start afresh when I – well when I sorted myself out.'

'So, you were clean before he died?'

'Yes.'

'Then why didn't you see us? Why didn't you see him? He took you back to Bordeaux and you never phoned or called or came over. He never saw you again.'

Florian leans over the table towards me, his hands interlocked in front of him as if in prayer. 'He never told you?' he asks quietly, seriously.

'Told me what?'

He waits a second, reading me, trying to ascertain something that I don't quite understand. He shrugs and then relaxes, his hands releasing and floating into the air. 'It doesn't matter.'

I want to push him, because it clearly does matter. I have spent a lot of time trying to understand the meanings between the words that people say. I know that what people really want to say gets lost in silence.

'I stayed with Mum for two months and that was as torturous as you can probably imagine. I worked here for a bit, did the odd shift and ran into Thibot, you know, the owner of the café,' he fills in, in case I may have forgotten. 'He saw I was back, needed some help, offered me a job. Everything kind of fitted into place.'

I take a large swig of my wine. 'So you run it?'

'No, I just do a few shifts a week. It pays the bills when the commissions are slow.'

I can feel a sentimentality pull at me, memories of a few of the paintings we had scattered around the apartment, the ones in Madame Grenaud's house on the rare occasion we visited. I may not like the man, but there was no denying that he was talented. I think that's what made it all so much harder for Ettie, the fact that there Florian was, young and healthy and talented and willing to squander it away for the promise of a good time. 'You're still painting?'

He plays with a napkin on a table, folding the corners methodically. 'Sometimes, but I sculpt now.'

'Sculpt?'

'Yes, stone mostly, wood sometimes too.'

'I didn't realise people still did that.'

'Well, I mean it's not a lucrative career.' He smiles, it's a nice smile, one that you can't help but find slightly endearing.

'Why?'

'Why do I do it, or why is it not a lucrative career?'

'Why sculpting?'

'It's slower. I need things that take more time, I guess. Keeps me…' I can see him weigh up his words carefully, 'distracted.'

'Sure.' I try to sound as if I understand but I don't. I like the immediacy of finishing something in an hour. I like panicking about it, ruminating on writing a chapter all day and then the joy of sitting on the sofa with the laptop, seeing a project through to completion in an hour and feeling like I have at least accomplished something that day. The thought of working for months on something for little reward seems soul-destroying.

'So, you do that in the apartment?' I ask warily, scared to bring up the little slice of the world that belonged solely to Ettie and me. The flat with its large sash windows that never entirely shut, the red Formica kitchen that we barely used and the constant sounds of life from the café below.

'The apartment?' He cocks his head to the side; his lips silently mould to the word as if his perfect English has somehow failed him now. I gesture in the direction of the café and his face illuminates with recognition.

'Oh! No…' He shakes his head a little too fiercely. 'I couldn't do that. He rents it out to a family now, nice people.'

I try to not let the relief be all too obvious. Florian swills the wine around in his glass and grimaces. 'So that's it really, why I'm here, what's happened in the last three years of my life.'

There is an interval where we both gather ourselves together, re-fill our glasses and take a breath. I study his face further, see every month of sobriety on his face, the fullness of his cheeks, the shimmer back in his eyes.

'I wonder what Ettie would have thought of it, you back here.' I break our mutual silence.

He smirks into his glass. 'I like to think he would have warmed to the idea.'

My phone starts to buzz on the table. Archie's name pops up. I cancel the call quickly but not before Florian has registered the name, and I feel like I want to tell him it's nothing serious, list off excuses for why I have let another man into my life.

'It's late. I'm sure you have somewhere to be.' He starts to gather himself up before I have a chance to respond. 'I'll walk you back.'

'You don't need to do that.'

'It's on my way.' He shrugs, pulls some cash from his wallet and throws it onto the table. I go to object but he is already walking off the terrace with a quick wave of his hand to the waitress. I catch her eye; she is young, younger than me, pretty and curious. They are definitely a thing.

'And dare I ask how you know where I live?' I have to jog to catch up with him and when I do I can see an eyebrow raise. He must have thought he'd got away without me asking. He manages a small grin, understanding that it was pretty weird to have been able to figure out my address a mere few hours after realising my existence.

'One of my customers was there when we—' he searches for the words, 'ran into each other. He also happens to be your downstairs neighbour.'

The warmth of the early evening is fading and I pull my jacket around me. 'I haven't met any neighbours.'

'Ava.' He stops, stares at me with an exhausted look in his eye as if he is explaining something obvious for the third time. 'An English girl appearing out of season, people are going to hear about it.'

I can't pretend that he isn't right. I've forgotten what it's like to be in a place where strangers take an active interest in your life. London and its busy streets and endless noise brought with it a total anonymity. There was always someone prettier, cooler, smarter, sexier to fixate upon; us mere mortals, with bad dye jobs and last year's clothes, didn't really deserve a look in.

'Are you staying long?' he asks, not looking at me.

'A month.'

'Specific.'

'I…' I go to tell him about the book, about the blog and all that comes with it but something about it sounds cheap. I have often wondered where becoming successful from Ettie's death sits on the morality scale. In some comments that I was told not to read but did anyway, I had been referred to as an 'opportunist' or an 'unfunny bitch who was profiteering off of her husband's death' so, obviously, I had weighed up whether there was indeed some truth in the torture.

'I missed it.' I choose to lie instead.

'This place or him?'

I look around at the buildings, the flaking shutters, listen to the sounds of our feet on the cobbles that are starting to become cold and wet from the cool spring evening. 'I thought I might have missed the place, but it turns out it's slightly lost its magic without Ettie waiting for me.'

We round the corner onto my street. 'Well, I mean it was like you were blind to anything else when he was in the room.'

I feel my heckles rise from the comment. 'What do you mean by that?'

'I don't *mean* anything by it, just that you were young and in love and Etienne was – well Ettie. He was the kind of person that was the axis to which everything else spun around him, including you.'

I don't respond.

'Well…' He looks around, hands in his pocket. 'Thank you for coming. I just needed to tell you that things have changed for me. And… I'm sorry,' he adds, and I note the look of complete discomfort on his face.

'What for?'

'For how I was back then. I was selfish and I made life so much harder for you and Ettie than it ever needed to be. The person you met back then, it wasn't really me, not the person I am now, or at least trying to be. In therapy they made us write a list of all the people we've hurt that deserve an apology and on the top of that list were you two. I wrote out this letter and everything, planned on coming back in the summer and giving it to you both and then… well you know what happened. When you left, I thought that I was never going to get the chance to apologise and explain until I saw you yesterday and something kind of took over. I'm sorry if I scared you, it wasn't part of the plan. But I just needed to say my piece. It's different now.'

I kick some dust around by my feet. 'It's a shame that Ettie isn't around to hear it.'

'I know,' he says. 'That's something that I'm going to have to live with for the rest of my life.'

I feel bad. I know his sadness, understand that stabbing the knife into someone who is already prostrate on the ground is a pretty shit thing to do.

I look at him, how his jaw has tightened and his eyes are looking everywhere except at me. 'Hey,' I say, my voice losing its sharpness. 'He would be really happy to know that you've changed, Florian, I think he always knew you would one day.' I take my keys and start to move towards the door, hoping that this might be the end of the ordeal.

Florian hovers. 'You know where I am if you need me for anything,' he adds hopefully.

'That's kind.' I manage a straight-lipped smile. I have no intention of seeking him out for anything, there is nothing that he could offer that I would be remotely tempted by. 'But I'll be fine.'

'I don't doubt it but still, the offer's there.' He is standing metres away from the door, as if to show that he isn't a threat, that even though he has stalked me, sent messages via my shopping and stolen a perfectly good bottle of wine, he is a decent, upstanding member of society.

'Good night,' I nod at him and shut the door behind me.

Chapter 10

I STARE AT A blank screen for a whole hour and a half. Well not literally, of course, that would be maniacal. Instead, I sit at the breakfast bar and look at a blank Word document on my laptop, the cursor flickering to an invisible beat. I glance at my phone and then Instagram scrolling magically sucks up twenty minutes. I stare back at the Word document vaguely frustrated it hasn't miraculously become populated with something profound and worthwhile. I sigh, go back to Instagram and the cycle continues.

It's Sunday morning, a day I had usually reserved for writing. It was easy to do back home. It wasn't like I ever had any wild weekend plans that took precedence. Mum would wake me up at eight with a coffee and bowl of Fruit 'n Fibre. I would eat it in bed and brainstorm what I wanted to say and then I'd migrate to Dad's study where I'd start to write.

I hadn't told my parents about the blog in those early days when I was lucky if a post earned a few hundred likes, mainly because I had started it in the hour on a Thursday that I was meant to be in therapy. Mum had actually stumbled across it herself; there was a small article dedicated to grief in her *Women & Home* magazine and my account got a mention. She had cut out the segment and presented it to me over an Easter breakfast – she used to like sharing the latest 'griefluencers' with me. I came clean then, had the wonderfully strange experience of seeing my parents' utter excitement and pride that I had done something worth celebrating, that my half-finished English degree and their patience in waiting for their only child to be successful had finally paid off. Mum brought it up any time she could, to friends, neighbours, her doctor when we ran into him in the supermarket, and it felt wonderful in a way that I never truly expected. So, when the book idea came about, I let them in on it from the beginning. It was nice to have someone to celebrate with, to toast the deal too, to hold me accountable when suddenly it all became a little too real. They were counting on me too.

They aren't here to make me breakfast now, they aren't here to shoot me judging glances when my screen time overtakes my writing time and I realise just how much writing isn't a solitary existence; I need the accountability of someone watching.

I type out a title – *The return*. I bold it. I italicise it. I underline it. I change it to a different font. And then I close my laptop and replace it with the diary, the scrawling record of my deteriorating mental state.

I write the date, close my eyes and try to clear my head. The nib touches the paper and then it happens. The words start flowing verbatim from my brain, a stream of consciousness so removed from what I present to the world that it's like having a conversation with an entirely different person. I like her. She is angry. No. She is furious.

Florian's name is mentioned twelve times, which means that as much as I pretend that yesterday's meeting was a closure of sorts, it has done the opposite and that he has riled me more than I would ever care to consciously admit. Archie's there too, somewhere in the middle.

When I reach the end of the page, I slam the book shut.

At six, I leave the apartment in favour of the first night market of the year, which is pretty much Monpazier's equivalent of Glastonbury. The soiree is the one event of the week where the elderly ladies will take their hair out of their fresh set and silk scarves.

There is an unmistakeable buzz in the air of life returning. The sun sits low on the horizon, not quite day but not quite night either. The streetlights start to click on as I trace the short walk back to the centre. The steps are easier now; every memory doesn't sit quite as heavily as it had done a few days ago.

I hear the party long before I can see it. At first, it's the sound of an accordion, a rhythmic guitar and violin, and then the voices come in. The singing is entirely in French, slightly drowned out by the instruments desperately fighting to stay in tune. Then there's the conversations, the laughing, the passionate arguing, children squealing and chairs scraping on the cobblestones.

It is as if the place has expanded, unfolded. There are people in every corner, huddled around a hog roast, mingling under the market hall, drifting from stall to stall laden with plastic cartons of chips and mussels and paella. Scattered around are rows of trestle tables and benches, all dressed with tablecloths, mismatched tableware and half-drunk bottles of wine.

And I realise I'm smiling.

I walk the perimeter, floating through memories of all of the summers that Ettie and I would take a night off from the café. We'd put on clothes that we hadn't worked in and – armed with our own wine, cigarettes and tablecloth – would choose our table for the evening. We'd chat with friends and get drunk enough that, just for one night, this was the best place to be in the entire world.

Eventually I see The American, perched on a table in the very centre of the covered market. She isn't alone; instead she is surrounded by people laughing, jostling for her attention. They are all united in the way that they are not French. Working here, you learned to spot it, could differentiate between a tourist and an expat. Monpazier has always had a thriving little expat community, mainly retirees who organise social evenings and movie screenings to ensure that everyone would get through the winter socially unscathed. I had thought about going to one once, until I told Ettie and he had looked so disgusted with the thought, I decided otherwise.

I get closer to The American. Her cackling becomes more defined and then I notice the unmistakable redness in her cheeks from what looks like the second bottle of wine.

'Having fun?' I ask.

'Ava!' She greets me enthusiastically. 'Sit down, here, move over!' She beckons me to a seat next to her and then clicks her finger at a face I don't recognise, an older gentleman with a red cravat. He pretends to be irritated but passes over a large glass with a wink.

'Merci,' I smile.

'You're very welcome. We've heard lots about you,' the man replies with a soft Welsh accent. I know my own cheeks have reddened now.

'I'm scared that most of it's true.'

'She likes you. Doris is a good judge of character.'

'Doris?' I look at The American who doesn't look like a Doris one bit. In fact, I don't know what she looks like because I don't know her name, and now it feels rude to ask.

'It's my little pet name for her,' the man says in a stage whisper. 'The poor man's Doris Day.'

I let out a snigger. 'Dare I ask the story behind that one?'

'You daren't.' The American interrupts and shoots flirtatious daggers at the man and thwacks him over the head with a black lace fan for good measure. I don't know why she has one on her, it's barely fifteen degrees Celsius; I am coming to the conclusion that theatrics form a heavy role in her outfits. 'Honestly, Crispy, you're intent on making sure I have no friends left up here, aren't you?'

'I don't mind if you have friends, my dear, just that I'm your favourite.' The man called Crispy pouts over the table at her and she melts a little. I want to ask about his name but he grabs my arm and pulls me closer to him before I get chance. 'We've been friends for so long, at this point it's becoming a hostage situation.' I snort and I notice how his eyes glisten, partly from the lights and partly from the alcohol. 'But I'm glad you've managed to join us, Ava, nice to add a bit of youth to our expat troupe.'

'Oh, I'm not an expat.'

'You're not?' He looks surprised. 'Thought Doris said you were an English girl out here.'

'I am, but not to live. Just to visit.'

'She's a smart girl, unlike us.' The American leans over with the bottle and tops up the wine that is evaporating. 'Wouldn't want you to end up drinking yourself into an early grave like we are.'

'Early grave? Doris, you've been coffin-dodging since the last millennium.'

She hits him with a fan again. This time I can hear it whistle before it's brought down on his shoulder. His wince isn't at all a performance.

'What's good to eat?' I ask the table, desperate to change the subject.

'Not sure. We haven't had the pleasure yet.'

'Let's change that.' I get to my feet and reach for my purse.

'What are you going to get us?'

'Carbs,' I say quickly, and before I can take requests, vault it over to the stall with the shortest line, which happily is a steaming vat of paella.

It is only when I get to the front and Florian is there to take my order that I realise my mistake. Small bloody towns.

'Hi.' Florian wipes his fringe from his eyes with the back of his hand. 'Nice to see you.'

'You too,' I lie. Whilst it looks like everyone who lives in a ten-mile radius of Monpazier is here tonight, I had tricked myself into believing that he may have become some sort of social hermit too, avoiding any signs of life. Instead, he has taken it upon himself to help.

'What can I get you?' He gestures to the cauldron of rice and meat in front of him.

'Three paellas and… do you do bread?' I ask hopefully.

His face screws up. 'With paella?'

I throw my hand in the air. 'Don't worry.'

'Anything else?'

'Actually, do you have water?'

'Yeah, sure.' He pulls out a small bottle and I shake my head. 'More, like five of those?'

'Having a party?'

'Something like that.'

He dishes out the food into steaming containers and then hands them over until we come to an impasse. I don't have enough hands.

'I'll come back...' I start to leave but Florian is already taking off his apron.

'Ava, let me help.' He shouts something to the other man on the stall who looks at me quickly with a small smile and then ushers him off. I realise that rejecting his help would be pretty pointless and just make me look like a petulant child.

'Are you with friends?' he asks as he catches up to me. We weave through the crowd, making slow progress as we near the dancing.

'Sort of.'

'What, they're not your friends?'

'They are... just not what you probably are expecting.'

'Well, it's good that you have some people around.'

'You don't need to worry about me on that front.'

We reach the table, The American and Crispy are deep into an impassioned argument so they don't notice my arrival. The second bottle is now empty and a third has made an appearance. Florian's brow is furrowed, his eyes scanning the table for where my group of age-appropriate friends could possibly be.

'Just set them down here.' I try to give off the impression that he should leave now, but I can see the curiosity eating away at him.

'It's fine, I'll take them to you.'

'This *is* me,' I hiss. It is a sound that grabs their attention and two drunken octogenarians turn to face me, their eyes going from me, to the food and then falling on Florian behind me.

'Oh no dear, I couldn't possibly manage him too,' The American drawls and then the both of them fall about in a fit of cackles.

'Right, food time.' I place the containers down in front of them, add a wooden fork and then open up the water for good measure. I go to take my portion from Florian who has an infuriating smile written large on his face.

'Don't…' I warn him.

'I get why you wanted the bread now.'

'Yeah, let's hope this will do. Thanks for helping.' I sit down on the bench and Florian turns to leave.

'Oh, don't go!' Crispy shouts out through a mouthful of food.

'He's working,' I say quickly and push the paella a little closer to them.

'Florian.' The American suddenly has all of the clarity of someone who has never touched a drop of alcohol in their life and holds out her scrawny hand for Florian to take. 'It's nice to meet you properly, without all the shouting.'

Florian looks sheepish and mumbles a polite 'Enchanté.'

'Sit down and have a drink,' she orders with the authority of a judge. I don't blame Florian who hesitates before obeying. I watch as his eyes pass over to the stall, tries to assess its length, whether he's needed. I look too, see the dwindling line, his colleague methodically plating up without much effort. Florian sits down next to me, hands knotted together, waiting for the questions.

Crispy starts to slur to someone else next to him, leaving Florian to an interrogation.

'So, you're the brother-in-law.' She slides over a wine and Florian takes it, cradling it between his palms.

'Yes… I was.' He nods solemnly. I try to distract myself by chasing rice around the container with my fork.

'You're not any more?'

'Well I mean… I was never exactly a great brother-in-law when Ettie was here, I'm sure she doesn't need me now he's not.'

'If only all family connections were as easy to get out of.' She raises a glass and then watches Florian closely as if inspecting his reaction.

'I should apologise for the other day,' he says, changing the subject. 'We had a bit of a shock, running into each other. I wasn't exactly at my best.' He gestures to me and I nod slowly; it definitely wasn't either of our finest moments.

The American weighs up his apology and then shrugs. 'Ava explained the situation. I think both of your reactions were understandable.'

'I just don't want you to think that I normally chase women down the street…' Florian adds.

'You don't? That's a shame. I quite liked the passion of it all.'

I choke on my forkful of rice.

'I'm teasing you.' The American nudges me and then smiles bashfully at Florian. 'You're quite the thing to look at, you know?' He looks at her startled, as if processing her statement and then, suitably alarmed, looks to me for assistance.

'Easy, girl,' I grin.

'You just have a face that's quite hard to forget.'

'Er, thank you?'

'I've seen lots of faces, you start to know the good ones quickly.'

'Have some water.' I push the bottle towards her.

'Let an old woman have some fun.' She bats the bottle away. 'I'm not drunk, just honest.'

'I'm sorry,' I murmur to Florian. 'Bet you regret offering to help now.' He lets out a stifled little chuckle in response.

'Ava told me you're an artist.' She leans over the table as if she is expecting to see his work tattooed onto his eyeballs.

'Yes.' He nods quickly.

'I love art.' She gestures at her outfit, the colourful kimono and matching headband, with a pout. 'If you can't tell.'

'You should come to Chateau Beaumont on Wednesday,' Florian says lightly, sounding terrifyingly genuine. 'There's an exhibition in the gallery up there, local artists mainly but there's some interesting pieces.'

'How wonderful.' She practically blossoms at the invitation. 'How about it, Ava?' His invitation has caught me off guard; I usually have time to formulate excuses for things like this.

'Come on, darling, it's not like you have any better offers of entertainment in this place on a Wednesday night.'

'Fine.' I sigh, and The American twinkles at my defeat.

The music gets louder, the quartet have added a singer, more people migrate to the stage. The American looks to Florian.

'I like this one.'

'Then we should dance.' He offers her his hand over the table. She makes a girlish squeak and almost jumps from her seat.

'I knew I liked you,' she smiles.

I watch as he guides her through the crowd; he towers over her, and she clings on to him for dear life, but they are smiling and laughing as he twirls her around, pumping her arms to the beat.

'She's right,' Crispy slurs into my ear. 'He does have a very nice face.'

Chapter 11

'YOU'RE ANGRY WITH ME,' The American pouts as I guide the Fiat down the impossibly steep hill out of the town.

'I'm not *angry* with you.' I feel my shoulders relax as we finally turn onto the long straight A road that connects one medieval fortress with another. I hope The American doesn't notice the Sharpie mark on my hand, reminding me to drive on the right. She looks at me with her overdrawn eyebrow raised up into her fringe. I shrug. 'Okay, I'm a little confused perhaps.'

'I thought you two had reached an agreement, an understanding?'

'You saw a man carrying my paella and decided that we were best friends.'

'You're being dramatic. Besides, it's getting us out of the town for an evening. I love an excuse to get dressed up.'

'You're always dressed up,' I scoff, and take another look at her outfit, a lime-green silk gown that she has layered over a woollen turtleneck with enough gold bangles that they take up most of her forearm. She hadn't said anything about my efforts. I hadn't exactly packed for extravagance, making do instead with a striped top and wide-leg trousers with the only pair of shoes I had brought – trainers.

'Is he any good, as an artist?' She changes the subject, steering us away from our first argument.

'He used to be.' I think of the painting that used to sit above a chest of drawers in our bedroom, a portrait of a woman in a bar, with a cigarette in one hand and a whisky in the other. Ettie liked it; he said it was one of Florian's first good ones.

It was a birthday present, from brother to brother, back when money was tight and they were on speaking terms. Before I was on the scene. I didn't hate it, in fact I had always felt some sort of affinity with the stranger, a companionship that came from staring at her in my bedroom for all of the seven years that Ettie and I were together. God knows where she is now.

'Are you any good?' I ask, squinting at a sign in the distance that I faintly recall being the right way.

'What, at painting?'

'Yes. You said you liked art; I assumed you dabbled.'

'Ha!' she splutters. 'I'm no artist. I'm an admirer at best. Blu was my painter, she did enough for the both of us.'

'Blu?'

'Bluette – my friend, the one who owned your apartment.' She says it as if I should know, that she has told me more than she has.

'The tiles?' I think about the splashback in the kitchen. I had confirmed my suspicions the other night, when I should have been in bed, that every single tile was unique, not one repeat; I think I had even seen a small snail on one in the corner. There were the birds too, in the beams in the bedroom. I had noticed them on one of the other nights when sleep just wouldn't materialise. Once I'd seen one it felt like I couldn't stop seeing them. They were on top of the wardrobe, etched onto the windowsill, scattered over the mantle of the door – gorgeous little sparrows that were so lifelike I had to do a double take.

'That's the one,' The American nods. 'Ooh, right here!' she shouts as we almost pass a turning and the car screeches into a dark and unforgiving bend, throwing her towards me a little. When I catch my breath and return the car to a steady pace, crawling up an ever-narrowing road towards an uplit chateau in the distance, I sneak a look at her now unanimated face looking wistfully out of the window.

'You miss her.' I say it in the same way she had said it to me the other day at the restaurant.

She keeps looking out of the window while she answers me quietly. 'Very much.'

The car park is surprisingly full. I go to park down the lane but The American tuts and gestures to her cane. 'Park in one of those bays.' She signals to a disabled space by the entrance.

'I don't have one of those badge things.'

'No one does, just live a little.' She taps the cane on the dashboard until I ferry her into the spot.

I get out, reach for my bag and then go to help her out. She thanks me and loops her arm into mine.

'I just hope he's not one of those artists who just paints vaginas on everything because he saw one once and has to tell the world about it,' she says suddenly. I splutter out a laugh. 'What!' The American lightens up a bit, her thin lips crawling into a grin. 'I went to an exhibition once where the room was just full of naked models, even the waiting staff were in on it. You know, it's very hard to eat a canape from a man with his penis just… hanging there.' She waves her hand around by her knees for good measure.

I don't know what I expected from the exhibition. I hadn't really had time to think about it. I'd imagined enduring a few hours in which The American would see some familiar faces and I could hopefully drink one glass of champagne and sneak off for a cigarette on the balcony. I hadn't expected it to be quite so busy. There were people of all ages queueing for entry, thankfully dressed in varying versions of formalwear meaning that neither myself or The American really stood out.

Once we reach the head of the queue, we're presented with a glass of champagne, a brochure of the exhibition on glossy white paper and directed to a gallery on the first floor. The first few rooms are taken up with some work from other local artists: landscapes of the area, rather sporadic abstracts, the occasional nude although that doesn't deter The American who gives each painting a regimental ten-second glance before moving on.

I've never quite known how to conduct myself in a gallery, not that I have ever found myself in many. With museums it's easy; there's a story through time to follow, with little explanations next to each artefact to help you decipher what you're seeing. With art you're just sort of meant to know what's good. I follow The American's lead but find my eyes chasing around the room, searching for the only other face I know.

The American sees him before I do, she elbows me in the ribs and stares in the direction of a large crowd. I expect to see him on the periphery, a lone wolf skirting around the paintings, I don't expect him to be in the centre of it all. He is animated, his hands waving wildly, grinning as he regales his audience with some story. They all laugh en-masse, the men pat him on the back, the women smile at him softly. I feel like I have landed in a parallel universe.

The American leans in close to me. 'He looks like the life and soul of the party.'

'Maybe they're all friends?' I shrug, and start to notice how the paintings change into pencil sketches on cream paper. At first, they're indistinguishable formless shapes with strange little letters alongside them, the sketches looking like they're in a series, each one changing ever so slightly until the last one forms a full image.

'That's so clever.' The American nods approvingly.

'Is it? It looks like a load of scribbling to me.' I shrug.

'Look closer.' She points at the letters which, at her fingertips, morph into numbers; the lines on closer inspection are angles. It's only when The American turns me to face the sculpture behind me that I realise the framed sketches are exactly that, first drafts of what's to come, the dreams and completely nonsensical ideas to create this thing that exists only in his imagination from a slab of indistinguishable rock.

'They're the plans?' I ask, scared to get it wrong and look even more like an idiot.

'Yes.' She manages to confirm my suspicions. 'It's wonderful.' She stands at the foot of the finished sculpture, a faceless man with a mass of curls, pulling himself out of the raw stone, only his muscular arms and torso managing to make it clear of the base.

'Such talent,' The American says to the faceless man, 'so much time…'

'You can touch it if you like,' Florian's voice echoes from behind us. I jolt and he places a hand on my shoulder. 'Sorry, I didn't mean to sneak up on you.' There's a lightness to him I hadn't recognised before, his eyes sing with it.

'It's fine.' I know I'm blushing.

'Go on,' he encourages The American. 'I think there's always something quite magical about touching it, you know, feeling where it all comes from.'

'It feels wrong,' The American chuckles, but I watch as her hand reaches out and strokes the shoulder of the figure. 'All my life I've been trying not to touch things in places like this.'

'It's not going to crumble.' Florian takes his own hand and knocks on the base. 'If it did it would make my life easier.'

'Go on, Ava, your turn,' The American encourages, but I feel silly now, as if all eyes are on me.

'It's fine,' I object, stepping back, but The American rolls her eyes at my awkwardness.

'Don't be silly, touch it!' She practically launches me forward so that my hand makes contact with the sculpture's hand; it is as hard and cool as I had imagined. I trace my finger over its fingers, the meticulously carved veins on the top of the palm. How anyone starts something like this is beyond me. The imagination and sheer doggedness it must take to turn a formless hunk of stone into art petrifies me, because that's talent, that's creativity. It makes me think of the book I'm not writing, how I have all the material and still can't even get anything down. How I am the epitome of a fraud.

'It's incredible, Florian.' I turn to him with a nod of approval. He is standing back from me now, wearing a pair of tweed trousers and a crisp white shirt slightly unbuttoned at the top. His hands are in his pockets and his hair is gelled back; he looks relaxed, more at home here than I could have ever imagined. Gone is the uncomfortable man I met at the bar the other night, he doesn't have to apologise here.

'I'm glad you two could come,' he says sincerely and The American swaps the statue's arm for Florian's.

'It's remarkable.' She kisses his cheeks. 'What a talent you are.'

'Well, it's nice to take it to people who appreciate it.' He nods at the room. 'It's a big turnout this year, buzzier than usual.'

The American tuts at him, sucking in her teeth. 'You should be in Paris! Not here.'

He shakes his head, sticks out his tongue a little. It makes him look like a kid. 'There are enough artists in Paris. I'll take my chances here.'

'Isn't it wonderful!' another voice choruses into our conversation, a voice that immediately makes my stomach drop and a clammy heat spread across my chest. I keep my eyes on the ground and hope that if I don't move, I might just disappear. 'My son is a very talented man.'

'Mama, I didn't think you were…' Florian gabbles, but she hushes him and continues talking to The American.

'He's always had an eye for detail.'

'And patience I imagine,' The American chimes in. I wonder if she remembers the conversation the other day in the hotel, whether if she just keeps her talking then I can sneak away.

'Of course… you know it's funny, he's always been a very thoughtful, methodical boy, not like his brother, God rest his soul, he was always in such a rush.' I feel myself stiffen at the mention of Ettie, I try to make my exit but as I cut through the little crowd someone steps in front of me, we collide, a glass shatters on the floor. Someone yelps from the noise. I look up, and my cover is blown. She knows it's me as soon as our eyes meet. I wonder if there was ever any use in pretending I wasn't here. She doesn't look shocked; she probably saw me walking around, come to terms with the fact her estranged daughter-in-law is roaming her remaining son's exhibition.

'Ava!' There is venom in her expression, a sort of fixed cabin-crew smile that hides a multitude of poisonous intentions.

'Maxine.' I sort of bob in her direction. This is as far as our familiarity goes. She was Maxine to her face, Madame Grenaud when Ettie and I were alone and ready to trade barbs.

'I did not know you were back.' Whilst her sons had learned to soften their accent when speaking English, Madame Grenaud had not; she wanted to put as much distance between her and 'my sort' as humanly possible.

'It's not for long, flying visit.' I look to Florian who is paler than he was a few minutes earlier. The American is looking anxiously from one face to the other. Even if she doesn't remember, she is picking up on an atmosphere that feels as thick and heavy as soup. I hope that maybe she might fake a faint, distract the crowds so that I can run, but she looks frustratingly stable.

'You knew she was here?' Madame Grenaud directs the question at Florian who practically gulps.

'We met the other day in town.'

I try to assess Madame Grenaud's expression for any signs of irritation but she stays remarkably unmoved. 'How lovely, a reunion.'

'Yes, a bit.' I nod, hoping that if I stick to simple answers, don't overcomplicate anything, then I might be allowed to walk free without too much of an altercation.

'And how special that you're here to see him.' She looks up at the statue and I feel a strange affinity to the poor subject: there he is, trying in vain to escape his rocky prison, and here I am, desperately attempting to claw my way out of this social interaction.

'Yes, it's really something.'

'Well surely you see the resemblance, don't you?' Madame Grenaud persists, her expression sharpening slightly. It is an almost indistinguishable change but when you'd spent a few awkward dinners at her mercy, you learned to prepare yourself for the blows.

'The resemblance?' Florian interrupts, looking equally

bewildered; it is pretty hard to resemble anyone when you're a faceless man.

'Of course, my love, well clearly it's our Etienne.' I notice how she directs the inclusion of 'our' to the two of them. 'The hair, the posture, the metaphor, he would have loved it.' She reaches out to Florian who is stunned into inaction; her hands cradle his face and she plants two kisses on his cheeks.

I could stay, wait for the next blow that she'll have been saving up since she last saw me; it would be the polite, English thing to do, but I don't have much patience for politeness any more. Instead, I turn, walk towards an emergency exit door whilst Florian tries to wrestle himself free.

The exit leads on to a turret which feels suitably grand as an escape option. I perch on the wall, fumbling around in my bag for a cigarette, until it's there, in my mouth, and I can breathe in the bitterness away from everyone else.

I think of Ettie in a way I haven't for a while, as a figure that is tangible, here, next to me, laughing at the situation. He would think it's all hilarious; he always had a way of making his mother look so ridiculous that it became a competition to get her to say the most outrageous thing so that we would have something to talk about in bed later.

'There you are.' The silence is broken by a sheepish-looking Florian, emerging through the door.

'Here I am.'

'I didn't think she was going to come, she never replied to my messages. I would have warned you…'

'You don't have to warn me, she should be here. I'm sure I'm just as much of a shock to her.'

'You don't have to be so nice about it. I know she's difficult.' He perches next to me, gestures for the cigarette and I pass it to him. It's funny, the familiarity we've slipped into now that we have something else to focus on other than the chasm between us. The night at the market had made things easier; it was as if he was an entirely different person to the man I had known before.

'She's your mother, I know better than to agree with that.'

'She's been making an effort recently.'

'Good,' I smile. 'I'm happy for you.' Age must have done a number on me because I genuinely am happy for him. I want her to be better, to at least form some semblance of a functioning relationship with one of her sons. It's what Ettie would have wanted too.

'I know she made life hard for you,' he says to his shoes.

'It's fair to say I was never her dream daughter-in-law.'

He passes the cigarette back to me, and I take the last few drags before it fizzles into a tasteless blur. 'Her dream daughter-in-law doesn't exist, because no one would ever be good enough for Ettie, let alone…'

'Go on… say it,' I tease, 'an English girl.' I put on a sultry French accent and pout in his direction.

'I was going to say someone who made Ettie so happy that his entire life's dream was to just exist with them in that café.'

I catch his eye briefly, nod slowly at quite how lovely that was to hear. I had wondered whether he shared his mother's views, that I was something just holding Ettie back from greatness, but clearly I had misread that. Florian and Ettie had similar values when it came to career plans.

'I'm going to get my passenger and make a quick exit.' I stub out my cigarette and shake the ash off my trousers.

'Don't go,' he pleads. 'It gets more fun, I promise. She won't stick around for long.' He looks almost sad that the night has panned out like this.

'You're very kind, but you don't need your ex-sister-in-law cramping your style.' He smirks but doesn't correct me.

'Sunday then?' he says quickly. So quickly that at first I think he's speaking French.

'Sorry?'

'There's this community gardening project. We meet at ten in the car park.'

'Gardening?' It comes out as a half-laugh.

'Yeah.' He pushes himself off of the stone wall and then gestures to his outfit. 'Do I not look like the type?'

'I'm more surprised that you think I do!' Although, the thought of him in gardening gloves and a sunhat does feel misplaced. I wonder if Ettie could have ever imagined his renegade little brother engaging in something quite so mundane.

'It's an excuse for a gathering. We do some weeding, plant up a couple of things and then there's a lunch at the Salle des Fêtes after. It's fun, quite social. I thought it might be good for you. Unless you have plans?'

I think of my incredibly empty schedule and consider making up an excuse but there isn't much point. He's probably guessed that if my only companionship in this place is with a bunch of geriatrics then I can't really turn down the opportunity for some social contact.

'Fine.' I shrug.

'You'll come?'

'What have I got to lose?'

'A nail at worst.'

'The car park, Sunday at ten.' I nod at him, confirmation that I intend to stick to my word.

I am halfway through the door when he calls to my back, 'It's not him you know. The sculpture. It's not Ettie.'

'Oh I know,' I nod reassuringly. 'It's you.' And I leave him to his turret.

Chapter 12

I MAKE THE MISTAKE of arriving on time. I should have learned by now that 'French time' dictates that you should arrive at least fifteen minutes later than when you are told and I had overestimated the walk. The car park where Florian had instructed us to meet is entirely empty and I will not make the second mistake of being the first one there. Instead, I perch on a wooden bench that looks over the valley and take the diary out of my bag.

The last entry was from after the exhibition. I had scribbled down everything I could have said to Madame Grenaud – all the things that came into my head when sleep wouldn't – and then Florian had inserted himself onto the page; but unlike the last time his name made an appearance, there was less anger, more relief. I try a few more lines, try to pull my focus away from my brother-in-law and onto something safer, the fact I am about to garden for pleasure, how good fresh air really feels, the promise of human contact.

I notice that the car park has started to fill, small groups forming. I wait until I see an old red Citroën CV pull in before I make my way down to join them.

'Hey,' I say to Florian's back as he tries to wrestle a wheelbarrow out of the boot.

He jolts, clearly not expecting the greeting, but when he turns around I enjoy watching the grin appear on his face.

'You came.' He brushes the dirt from his top and leans forward to greet me. The well-groomed artist has been replaced with the Florian I had expected, his suit swapped for some well-worn jeans, a long-sleeved grey top and a fleece.

'You sound surprised.'

'I thought you might have come up with some very plausible excuse.'

'Well turns out there really isn't much to do here,' I shrug. 'Besides, maybe it's the fact I'm bored or that I'm thirty but it kind of sounded fun.'

'You've changed.' He smirks.

'You really don't know me well enough to make a full assessment of my capacity for change. Now can I help?' I point to the wheelbarrow and Florian nods, the grin softening into a contented smile.

'Sure.'

About twenty people begin to cluster around a pile of gardening equipment before a buxom middle-aged woman blows a whistle and everyone forms a circle around her.

She speaks enthusiastically, and loudly, in French. I catch more words now, the dusty connections resurrecting.

She points to people, gesturing to different directions, reaches into the pile of equipment and thrusts trowels and rakes and spades into people's hands.

And then she looks at me.

'Bonjour?' She raises her eyebrows; clearly she hasn't noticed me before now.

Florian steps forward. 'Ava,' he says. And then I translate the words, *Etienne's wife*. I watch as the realisation passes over everyone's faces. I recognise a couple. Customers of the café, acquaintances of Etienne, I had probably said hello to them in passing whilst cleaning down the tables and heading back up to the apartment to wait for Ettie to finish.

'Bienvenue, Ava,' the leader of the gardeners greets me, and then she shouts 'Allez!' deafeningly loudly and the crowd begins to disperse.

I go to follow Florian who is starting towards a scrub patch of dirt at the bottom of the car park with some other men.

He notices me and shakes his head. 'You're up there on planting.' He points to some raised beds by the Mairie.

'Oh!' I stop in my tracks, looking around to see three others heading towards the same spot. 'Cool,' I add, hoping the abject fear of having to speak to some complete strangers isn't immediately obvious.

When I get to the planters, one of the volunteers stands up and turns to me.

'Ava, welcome.' I feel the recognition slip in – the warmth in his face although he has a beard now and carries a little more weight around his middle. Something inside me drops.

'Luc?' I ask although I know the answer. The man in front of me is the closest thing that Ettie had to a best friend.

'You remember.' He smiles.

'Of course I remember.' I reach for him, press a soft kiss to his cheeks. He stands back and takes me in with a genuine curiosity that leaves me feeling a little naked.

'You look well,' he says after a beat.

I try to gauge whether it's a compliment. Luc's face though, the way his eyes deepen as he waits for my reaction, assures me that he is being kind.

'Thank you.' I nod a little over-enthusiastically. 'Yeah I'm doing okay. And you? How are you, the boys?'

'We're well.' He nods and gestures to a woman bending over the flowerpots. I recognise the flash of white in her dark hair; it had made her instantly recognisable. Ettie used to call her the zebra and she had pretended to hate it. They lived in an apartment on the square. When her boys were in bed in the summer we would sit outside the café, baby monitor on the table, working our way through bottles of wine and each other's life stories.

'Angelina!' I call towards her. She looks up briefly, manages a strained nod and then turns back to the soil. I feel like I have been slapped.

'We should start on that one?' Luc points to a bed further away, clearly trying to iron over the awkwardness.

'Yeah sure.'

'How have you been, Ava?' Luc asks as we pick the weeds out of the bed and turn over the soil. It's almost the same thing he had asked earlier but now it's just the two of us I feel pressured to tell him more.

'Getting there,' is all I can manage. 'It's been hard but I'm okay.'

'Did you go back to London?' He looks up at me briefly while trowelling out a stubborn root.

'Yes,' I nod. 'Back with my parents, still there actually.'

'That's nice.'

I look up at him, one eyebrow raised. 'Is it?'

He smirks. 'Well, I don't know your parents but I'd like to think they're nice people.'

'Yes.' I'll let him have that one. 'They are, and cheap to rent with too,' I add, as if that justifies why I'm still there, three years later, rooted in some perpetual Peter Pan existence.

'Are you… with anyone else?'

'As in dating?'

Luc nods. I think of Archie, how I could probably say that I was seeing him, try to mentally calculate whether Luc wants to hear that I am and moving on, or that I'm not and therefore still in deep mourning for my dead husband.

I decide on the latter. 'No, not really.' I throw some weeds into a nearby bucket. I look up at the hunched figure of my old friend at the other planter. She catches my eye briefly and then quickly turns away when she realises I've caught her. 'Is Angelina okay?'

Luc looks over at her and then turns his gaze back to me. He pulls his lips into a grimace and then he lets out a short sigh. 'She is upset that you haven't been in touch,' he says bluntly. A stone that he has been fishing from the soil lands in the bucket with a loud metallic ding.

'Oh.' I feel the statement linger in the air, a heaviness

materialising in my stomach. It wasn't like I hadn't known my sudden departure would raise questions. Part of me also knew that it would piss some people off, but if there was ever a time to be selfish it was in those weeks after Ettie died. It wasn't meant to be permanent; there was a while when I thought I would be back. I told my parents I'd be a month, and then two, and then it was Christmas and we were buying a new mattress for my bed. 'Are you upset with me too?'

'No.' Luc shakes his head. 'I understand you disappearing. It was just a shock when we turned up one day to visit and you were gone.'

'Everything sort of happened last minute.' I start to try to defend myself but Luc waves his hands for me to stop.

'She'll come around.' He looks towards Angelina who is now angrily shoving some seedlings into the soil. 'Eventually.'

We finish the rest of the gardening in silence.

We break for lunch at one. The gardeners gather outside the Salle des Fêtes where someone mans a barbeque and plates of food sit on a picnic table for us to grab. I take one and look for somewhere to sit. I see Luc and consider joining him, but then I notice Angelina next to him and reconsider quickly. I look for the only other face that feels familiar enough to endure a lunch with but he isn't here. I strain my eyes and eventually find him, bent over a bit of ground at the bottom of the field.

I take a second plate.

'You don't do lunch now?' I call and he looks over. His face pulls into a smile when I get closer. 'I thought it was sacred here.'

'I got carried away.' He wipes some sweat off his brow and gets to his feet, hands on his hips surveying his masterpiece of a freshly turned-over flower bed, complete with little rock edging and a spray of small purple flowers.

'It looks done to me.'

'Not quite but I'll do it later,' he shrugs and reaches over for the plate but I whisk it out of his reach.

'What's left?'

'You really want to know?'

'Yeah, what can I say? You've piqued my interest.'

'Fine. Put that down and come here.' He kneels back into the dirt and I copy him. 'Hand me a few big ones, the smoother the better.' He points to a wheelbarrow of stones and pebbles. I do as he says, running my hands through what's left.

'These do?'

He takes them from me and weighs them in his hands. 'Perfect.' He places the largest one firmly into the soil and then takes a second. He sits back, considering something I don't really understand before gently placing the second one on top of the first. He makes minute little adjustments, letting it rock a little and tapping it in one direction or another. I watch how his lip curls up in concentration, how his hands start to move away from the stone but linger close by until he can step away entirely and the stones remain standing.

'A cairn.'

'Ever built one before?'

'No.'

'Ettie and I used to do it all the time as kids.' Something wistful and gentle passes over his face. 'His were always bigger of course, taller, more impressive, but mine lasted.' He beams and when he looks at me, I think I can see an echo of that kid. 'Here.' He passes the third stone to me. 'You give it a go.'

'Really?'

'If it falls, we try again.' He shrugs and moves away so that I can take his place. I take a second rock, try to balance it on the first, but as soon as it makes contact the whole thing topples and falls down.

'Shit. Sorry, I told you I couldn't.' I get to my feet and offer him the stones but Florian crosses his arms. 'Half the fun's in the trying again.'

I seat myself back down on the ground, try the second stone. Every time I take my hands away it tumbles again. Florian had made it look so easy, like these stones were glued together.

'Fuck!' I growl as the cairn collapses for a third time. I expect to feel Florian at my side ready to take over like Ettie would have done, sweep in and correct my mistakes, but he holds back, watching me carefully.

'Would you like a tip?' he asks gently.

'Is it magic?'

'You're being too… rough,' he offers. 'Do you want some guidance?' He hovers a little at my side until I nod. 'Right, do what you did before.' I do as he says. 'Now keep your hands there, and… this is kind of stupid but you need to try to be the rock.' I feel him next to me, the closeness of his body, the warmth.

I rotate the stone a little too harshly and the cairn falls again. Florian sets it up before dusting his hands off and turning to me. 'You need to root yourself to the ground; try crossing your legs.' I copy him, ignoring how the ground is starting to make my jeans damp. I flex out my fingers before starting again, planting the first stone to a flatter surface. Florian disappears from view and then he's there, at my back, a knee either side of me. He's careful not to sit too close, probably equally aware of the fine line between genuine assistance and something much more complicated. He places his hands on top of mine so softly it's like he isn't really there at all, the faintest of touches as he positions them in a way that makes the next stone seem like it's cemented to the one below. He holds me there for a moment, his breaths slow and warm, touching the nape of my neck.

'Almost.' His voice is steady and deep as if in order to make this strange little tribute last he has to speak in a different frequency. 'It helps if you close your eyes,' he murmurs.

'Seriously?' I mutter through gritted teeth and he chuckles into my shoulder.

'It was worth a try. Now take your hands away like this.' I feel the warmth of his fingers leave mine, and then I do as he says until there are two perfectly balanced stones in front of us.

I let out a childish squeak and turn my head round to look at him, meet his grinning face, and I'm reminded of how close we are, of how strange this is.

'Well done.' He swallows back his smile and then moves

away, grabbing one of the plates of food as if nothing out of the ordinary has happened.

'Now do the other one.' He points to the pile of stones.

I roll my eyes but do as he says. It's easier now I know the trick, know how it feels, and the final stone is balanced quickly and without fuss.

'You're a quick learner.' You'd think he had just called me Michelangelo because I am almost giddy with pride.

'Good teacher,' I add and take the remaining plate, taking a seat on the ground next to him and looking at my handiwork. 'So do you like have a *thing* for rocks or something?' I ask, my lip curling up at the edge. 'I mean all the sculpting and cairn building – sounds like you can't get enough of them.'

'Very funny,' he says with a mouthful of food. 'I guess I like how they can't talk back.'

I elbow him in the ribs. 'Rude.'

'Have you… enjoyed yourself?' he asks, and I look back at the crowd for the now-familiar shapes of Luc and Angelina.

'It was interesting for sure.' Florian looks at me with one eyebrow raised. 'My group was just a bit awkward… I used to be friends with Luc and Angelina, that's all.'

Florian rips off a piece of bread and moulds the soft part into a dense little ball between his fingers. 'I know.'

'Oh…'

'They used to ask about you when I moved here. They're regulars at the café now.'

'What did you tell them?'

'The truth.' He shrugs. 'Told them that I didn't have any idea where you were and that we didn't keep in touch.'

'And did you put me in a group with them on purpose?'

'No.' He shakes his head quickly and I believe him. I don't think Florian had it in him to orchestrate some sort of meet-cute with estranged friends, no matter how bad our relationship had been.

We spoon another load of food into our mouths. 'You say you *used to*,' he says.

'Sorry?'

'You said they *used to* be your friends.'

I shrug. 'Angelina's angry that I left without telling them.'

Florian nods slowly paying extra attention to his salad, picking out individual slices of tomato on his fork. 'Do you think her anger is justified?'

I look at him, at the way the humour has clearly evaporated from his face and been replaced by an awkwardness that doesn't suit him. 'Do you?' My voice is colder than I intended it to be.

Florian weighs up my question. 'I don't know. You said they were your friends. Wouldn't you want to know where they went if it was the other way around?'

'So you hate me too? For not telling you where I was?' A pause. A pause that's too long to be explained away. 'Great,' I smirk, put my plate of food on the wall.

'I don't *hate* you, Ava,' he manages to splutter out quickly. 'I get why you did it but it *was* strange. I wanted to see you too, to talk to you, and you just disappeared.'

'I had to, Florian. What was I going to do, stay here?'

'Why is that such a strange thing to do? You lived here for seven years! I know that Ettie was the reason you stayed here in the first place but you're telling me that you had nothing else to stay for, that you didn't make any friends that were worth keeping in touch with?'

The reality of his statement hits hard. How I had realised about five years into my relationship with Ettie that I had become a very different person to who I thought I would be, how I had replaced friends and parties and uni societies for him. I play with my wedding band, spinning it around and around my finger until I feel it tighten. I clench my knees to my chest, rest my head there for a few breaths and then look back at the cairn, focusing on how precariously it's balanced. 'You know, the last night Ettie and I spent together was so fucking unremarkable.' I sniff back a heavy chuckle. 'We closed down the café like normal and then sat on the balcony drinking a bottle of wine with dinner. It was a shit last meal but he didn't complain and it was sunny so it kind of made up for it. Then we fucked and went to sleep.' Florian's face is screwed up in complete confusion as to why I'm divulging this now, his whole body taut and angular. 'And then he died.' I feel the tears stinging the back of my throat. 'He just died. I don't even know when it happened – what time I mean – how long I was lying next to his body, and when I woke up he was fucking gone and so was my life here and everything I knew and I trusted about the world.'

'Ava…' Florian puts his plate on the ground, turns his body towards me. He is probably questioning when on earth this conversation went from jokes about him fancying masonry to this.

'So I left,' I shrug. 'I upped and left because I didn't make sense here. I don't make sense here. Without him I'm just a strange English girl with no friends and no job and no family.' I heave myself up off the ground. Florian tries to grab on to my arm but I yank it away. I turn to him. I'm furious how he can take something good and turn it into this. Furious at him for bringing it all back up to the surface. 'But I refuse to be judged by someone who chose to be absent for all the years Ettie was alive, only to act like the doting brother when he isn't.'

And I walk back home.

Chapter 13

WHEN I WAKE UP, my diary takes the full brunt of yesterday's argument. At first, it's a rant, a stream-of-consciousness narrative lacking in structure or punctuation. I relay his judgy little comment, the look on his face, how ridiculous it was that I had invited him back into my life in the first place but then the cairn made an appearance, how light everything had felt when it was just him and me by that bloody flower bed, laughing, working together to try to understand each other a little bit more, and then there's a strange heaviness, the familiar feeling of embarrassment that sits so closely to guilt. I could have said everything I needed to without bringing up his absence. He at least was trying to make up for the past. I was trying to ignore that the past had ever existed.

And then Sam FaceTimes.

She's in her suitably smart office, all glass, make-up done, hair impossibly smooth and expensive.

'Are you okay?' she asks when I eventually turn my camera on, after clearing my table of any rubbish and slicking down my own slept-in bun with some water. Her voice is laced with concern. When I look at the tiny box in the bottom of the screen, I can see why. I had neglected to take my make-up off yesterday, and most of it is smudged around my eyes making it look like I had spent the majority of my night crying.

'Sorry, it was a late one, I'm fine.' I try to rub off the worst of it, but it serves only to make me look more tired.

'Are you sure?'

'Yeah, honestly, I left my make-up remover at home.'

'I just wanted to check in, see if you had anything to send me yet? Happy to look over a chapter or two?'

'Oh, yeah sure,' I lie.

'Ava?'

'Yes?'

'I've spoken to you every week for the last year; I know when you're not writing. You do this thing with your face.' She tries to recreate my furtive expression and I can't help but smile at my transparency.

'Look, it's been… intense.' I sigh, my hands cradling the back of my neck.

'I bet it has.'

'And I've tried to sit there and write something but…'

'But what?'

'I don't know, it just all feels a bit fake at the moment. People want a book from someone who's guiding them through grief, not someone who is ravaged by it every time something unexpected happens.'

'Oh God,' she sighs. I can see her look in the corner of her screen before getting up, walking out of shot and then shutting the door. I prepare myself for a bollocking, a speech about how there's people waiting on chapters, on how I'm being dramatic and flaky, but instead when she sits down she has this gentle, almost maternal, smile on her face.

'I never took you on as a *grief guru*. In fact, that's what I liked about this whole thing: you didn't know how to grieve, and you were bloody honest about it. No one knows how to grieve, they don't teach it to you in school; people are so bloody terrified of even talking about death it's as if they don't expect it to happen to them. Your blog was exciting because of all that rawness, the anger, the humour, the fact that you don't preach about how to do it; you just talk about you, about things you found hard and how you coped. Now you need to do the same thing.'

'I guess it's just that a lot's happening; I'm trying to process it whilst writing about it, whereas before it was just weird little peculiarities, there was a detachment to it all.'

'Tell me about it.'

'About what?'

'What's been happening.'

'Oh erm, a lot I guess…'

'Just tell me…' she continues and I sigh, comb a hand through my hair and start at the beginning. I talk about The American, about Archie and our phone calls, I tell her about Florian, and she sits there blinking, nodding, cackles when I talk about the drunk octogenarians.

When I eventually finish, when I have wrung out every detail of the last week so that I am out of breath, I realise I have been talking for twenty minutes and I laugh. It's awkward at first, embarrassing even, and then it's sheer relief and shock that more has happened to me this past week than in the past year.

It's only when Sam holds up her phone with the recording button still running that I understand her game.

'You're overthinking it, Ava. You just need to do that, with your words. Stop thinking about the book, the chapters, the audience; it's just a woman on the other side of a screen whose world has been torn apart and you're talking to her.'

I feel the tears stinging the back of my throat. That dull heavy ache that pulls at me until I have to look away from the screen, grab the back of my sleeves and dab at my eyes.

'My first ever like on a post was from this girl – well, woman I guess – but her profile picture looked so young. She didn't post much, but there were pictures of her with a man for a while until he wasn't there any more. In my head, she'd lost him too, like me. She liked every post – I knew because I'd check – until slowly my blog got big enough that it made checking it hard; but, in my head, every time I write something, I think of her reading it.'

'That's lovely.' Sam nods thoughtfully. 'You know when this is all done, we can send her a proof, reach out.'

'So, there's going to be an ending? I'm going to get this thing finished?'

'I've never doubted it.'

'Thanks.' I smile, the emotion turning into a dull warmth of finding a connection you hadn't expected to.

'I think you should go and take a drive somewhere, get out of the village. It sounds a little… close.' She smirks.

'Yeah.' I stretch out my arms and yawn. 'I could do that.'

'I'll catch up next week.' She waves and then we cut the call.

I choose a supermarket forty-five minutes away as my great adventure.

The drive is suitably uneventful; back home travelling anywhere near five o'clock would be considered a suicide mission, but here the traffic jam on my journey consists of a tractor slowing traffic for three miles until it turns off into a nearby farm.

The scenery could be considered boring in comparison to the view from my apartment but its bland tarmac and metal barriers are a welcome change, a return to normality almost. I take it all in, feel a pang of homesickness for London that I have never experienced before. I had drowned myself in chaos back home; it's strange not to do it here too.

I even start to enjoy the simple act of driving on my own, the music turned up too loud, the way I can trundle along as fast or as slowly as I like, that strange knowledge that I could turn my car down a road I had never been down and end up somewhere entirely different. I could, if I wanted to, disappear entirely.

The first real sign of humanity, real humanity, is an advert for McDonald's. I follow the sporadic signage until I'm ordering a burger, some chips and a Coke. I make it to the car park, unbuckle my belt and scroll through my phone. The 4G is strong here and my Instagram floods back to life. I ignore the grief account, look instead at my personal one, binge on the lives of old uni friends, cousins, my estranged aunt who is ranting on about her dead hamster. I take it all in like a drug, let the inane pointlessness of it all sweep over me and feel myself be carried away in a doom scroll of epic proportions until the last chip has been consumed and the straw gurgles at me that the cup is finally empty.

I drive to Leclerc. The building is probably bigger than the whole of Monpazier itself, with its garish white metal cladding and blue neon lettering. I take a trolley for good measure.

Inside is another world: fluorescent lights, screaming children, dozens of brands of the same product all stacked to the ceiling, and it feels strangely wonderful. Something that was such a chore back home, to head to the big ASDA, was my idea of a dream escape today.

Money is a concept I ignore as I glide through the aisles, picking whatever takes my fancy: biscuits I used to love, cheap cheese that the artisanal market stalls don't sell, some freezer food, cleaning supplies. I lose myself in the wine section, adding bottles of red, white, crémant and cava, wondering if it's humanly possible, let alone safe, to consume this much in the remaining three weeks of my trip, but adding it to the trolley anyway because it's so disgustingly cheap it feels wrong not to. The clothing section wastes another half an hour. I find a leopard-print silk scarf with neon green edging and buy it for The American; she'll appreciate the effort.

Finally, I find myself in the beauty aisle and add face masks, eyebrow tint, make-up remover and nail polish to the trolley, curating a list of things that can fill up an evening and make me look less like a dishevelled pity parade. It's times like this when I appreciate being a woman with the multitude of things we can buy and do to distract ourselves for an evening.

When every aisle has been plundered and the trolley wheel has started to squeak with the weight of my impulse spending, I admit defeat.

It's dark when I leave the car park. The familiarity of the roads leaves me along with the thrill of driving on my own. Instead, the sparse traffic has been replaced by large, unyielding lorries with headlights so bright I am momentarily blinded, and I resort to a 'point, shoot and pray' method that leaves me gripping the steering wheel so tightly my palms sweat. I try to distract myself by picking at some sweets and turning the music up so loudly that I can feel the bass through my feet.

I am grateful to turn off the A road, grateful to swap the lorries for the occasional car overtaking me, these routes so engrained into their day-to-day lives that they have no qualms about driving at sixty around a single-track blind bend.

When I finally see the small beacon of Monpazier, the yellow streetlights, a halo on the hilltop, I feel like I can breathe. Ten minutes and I can be there. Ten minutes and I will be standing on my doorstep with the daunting realisation of how I'm meant to be getting a boot-full of wine up the—

I hear the hit before I register what's happening. There is a thud, the crack of glass, the screeching of the breaks, my detached screaming as the car pirouettes on the road, tyres burning on the tarmac, bottles smashing, until everything comes to an eerie silence.

I sit there panting and then when my senses return, I turn off the engine, yank the keys from the ignition and throw myself out of the car. I run to the front, where a deer is slumped, bloodied and limp in a ditch.

The car is facing the wrong direction, the windscreen cracked, a large, deer-shaped divot on the bonnet.

It's almost like my own father has taken control of me. Without thinking I locate a warning triangle, put on a fluorescent jacket, wrestle on the hazard lights and then I slip myself down the bank, catching my breath in the irrigation ditch on the other side of the road.

I reach for my phone and pause because there's no one to call. No one that can help. There's no Ettie any more to rescue me, no point in calling my parents, no point even in calling Archie, although I'm sure he could say something that would make the situation a little easier to deal with. I scroll through my contacts, down to the F, down to a number that has only ever been in my phone for the direst of emergency, a number I had only ever dialled once before.

I don't want to do it.

Yesterday is still all too raw: the look of devastation on his face when I pointed out his hypocrisy is still branded into me but the memory that lingers hotter and longer is the feeling of his hands on mine, his closeness, his softness. I look at the bashed-up car, turn the phone over in my hand, try to work out how long a walk it would be. I yell out in frustration, a frayed and guttural sound because I know I have no choice.

'Ava?' Florian answers after the second ring. He sounds as confused and worried as he had done the time I told him his brother was dead.

Chapter 14

FLORIAN ARRIVES FIFTEEN MINUTES later. He pulls his car up behind mine and then before he even looks at it, he searches me out. I wave limply in his direction and then he's in front of me, hands on my shoulders forcing me to look into his eyes as he asks me whether I'm hurt and what happened. I point at the body of the deer that hasn't magically regained consciousness and feel the guilt creep in.

Florian leaves me his coat whilst he inspects the rental and then he grabs his phone and starts to make a couple of calls, talking enthusiastically in French to whoever's on the other end.

'Someone will come to get it tomorrow.' He puts his phone back in his pocket. 'Nothing else we can do tonight, so you should probably come with me.' He leads me to the passenger seat of his car. I get in and I'm immediately smothered with nostalgia at the smell, the warmth and the poorly sprung seats. I sit there, paralysed, as he starts to load the shopping from my boot to his.

'You may have lost some bottles. Managed to save about half,' he says, his breath slightly ragged from the exertion of my retail therapy.

'Sorry?'

'The wine, still enough for a very good night though.' I think he's making a joke, trying to lighten the mood, but I don't have the emotional resilience to even pretend like it's amusing.

'Thanks.'

'You okay?' he asks, as he slips into the driver's seat, starts the ignition. The car hiccups into life, the whole thing trembling beneath me.

'I'm fine,' I nod.

'It's just that you're crying.' He reaches into his pocket and pulls out a handkerchief that is covered in paint. He winces at it a little, but I take it pretending not to notice.

'Am I?' I catch a tear with my finger. 'I just can't believe I killed something.' The words catch in my throat.

Florian looks at me warily. 'I'll take you back to mine.' He moves the car off before I can object, not that I think I would. I don't really care where I go at this point.

He fiddles with the radio, and voices fade in and out of a background of permanent static. He keeps his eyes on the road and I watch his lip curl in concentration as he rotates the dial, trying in vain to find something that might fill the silence.

I decide to fill it for him.

'Thank you for getting me.' My voice is almost as weak as the radio signal.

'It's fine. No trouble.'

'It's just, after what I said yesterday… I'd understand if you hadn't.'

His hands tighten on the steering wheel. 'I wasn't going to just leave you there, Ava.'

'I guess I'm trying to apologise,' I wince and watch as his face softens, his eyes still locked onto the road in front of him.

'You don't need to—'

'I do.' My voice is stronger now. 'I shouldn't have said it; Ettie wouldn't have wanted me to have said it.'

'Ettie isn't here. You can say what you like.'

'And I would like to apologise. I know what I did was wrong, leaving I mean. I feel bad about it. Probably why I've put off coming here for so long, but I don't think I ever really knew why I did it until yesterday, until it all just came out.'

'I understand, Ava.' He looks at me then – allows his eyes to move from the road and onto me. 'And I mean it when I said you don't have to apologise. What you said, it makes sense, you make sense a little more now.' The sentiment hangs in the air between us. I don't know exactly what he's referring to, whether my tantrum means he now understands what a nutcase I am, or whether he actually did hear me, understand me, take the time to think about the words I hurled in his direction. I'm not used to being so easily read. He shrugs. 'So shall we just move on?' I feel my lip pull up at the edges, grateful for this man's insane ability to navigate emotional turmoil with a quick gear change.

'Yes.' I nod earnestly. 'Yes, let's do that.'

The car trundles up the road until he indicates off a gravel track to a small stone house at the base of the hill. There's a light on in the window and the smell of woodsmoke: the promise of a fire and somewhere warm.

'I haven't had a chance to tidy up,' he says apologetically, letting himself out and then coming quickly to my door. He offers me his hand and I take it.

'I'm sure it's fine,' I placate and watch as he opens the boot and stands there looking at all of the bags. I swoop in, reaching for my rucksack and a bottle of wine. 'Rest can wait.' I go to shut the boot but Florian holds his hand on it; he grabs a bottle himself.

'Better safe than sorry.'

Chapter 15

WHILST HE CLATTERS AWAY in the kitchen, I launch myself onto a sofa that almost swallows me in its softness and take in the details. There are things everywhere but there is some organisation to the chaos, and it feels like everything here has been chosen carefully for its usefulness first and its appearance second.

There's another sketchpad on the table already open onto a page with a half-drunk cup of herbal tea next to it; this was what I had interrupted with my phone call. I know I shouldn't but I can't help myself: I swipe away the charcoal and pencil shavings to reveal a perfect replica of the cairn from yesterday with two sets of disembodied hands hovering nearby. The breath catches in my throat, knowing that he's been thinking about it too, drawing it out whilst I've been writing it down. It's the first time I've felt sane in the last twenty-four hours.

'It's not much but I need to do a shop,' Florian announces, and I am grateful for the warning so I can sit back, occupy my attention by pretending to look at the pictures on the wall instead. He places a large board of bread, cheese and figs in front of me and then he roots in his pocket and pulls out a corkscrew from his keys, uncorking one bottle of red wine and passing me a large glass. Then he sees the sketchbook. He clears his throat before hurriedly tidying it away into a drawer. 'Told you you'll have to excuse the mess,' he adds with an awkward chuckle.

'It's not messy at all,' I lie, the image of the cairn and my hands, *our* hands, stuck on a loop in my head. 'Thanks for the food,' I add, reaching immediately for a large chunk of bread and starting to pull it apart, grateful for something to do with my hands.

We fall into an uncomfortable silence and it's strange because not once since the day that I ran into him have we struggled to find something to say to each other.

He turns and adds a log to the fire, spending too much time poking at it until I can hear it start to roar back to life. I turn my attention to his décor choices. Archie's flat looked like it was something out of the development brochure and I'm pretty sure that he walked into it one day fully furnished and said he would take the lot. The paintings on the wall were therefore modern, bland and either graffiti or pop-culture based: it was a step up from a replica Banksy poster in a teenage boy's bedroom but I knew they were there because there should be something on the walls rather than because he actually liked them. Here, in Florian's house, there is less refinement; the walls are covered with mismatched picture frames nailed up in no particular order with layers of dust gathering on the mounts. There's no attempt at unification: postcards are placed next to polaroids, next to pictures of statues, letters, oil paintings, a couple of life drawings, a concert poster. And then something catches me off guard: two little boys with toothless grins stare at me in black and white. They're both shirtless with skinny chests, one slightly taller than the other, both grinning with dimples in their cheeks, sea-soaked curls and freckled faces.

I get up, take my glass of wine and get closer, take them in.

'We were cute, weren't we?' Florian says, standing next to me. The smoke from the fire is pressed into his shirt, his closeness brings me back to yesterday, the feeling of his breath on my neck.

'Dangerously cute,' I agree quickly and return to the safety of the sofa. 'I've only ever seen a handful of pictures of him as a kid.'

'That's because there aren't many. Difficult to take pictures of your kids when you aren't even in the same country,' he shrugs. 'The au-pair took that one on the beach at Île de Ré.'

'Do you have any others? Of Ettie?' I ask.

'Erm, a couple, sure.' He heads over to the bookshelf and pulls out a dusty little album and passes it over. He watches me take in the pages: the christening pictures where even Madame Grenaud looks happy, the obligatory bath photos, the first day of school, a couple of birthdays, Ettie looking older and older in each one, more like the man I eventually met until there aren't any more. None of the café, none of the occasional Christmas, none of the wedding – none of us at all. I don't know why I'm disappointed, I wasn't expecting there to be; but there's a finality in it now. There won't be any more pictures of him.

'I feel like I never took enough,' I say sadly, setting the album aside and replacing it with another hunk of bread. 'After seven years of being together you kind of stop thinking you need to capture every moment. The last one I have of us both was a whole year before he died.' I watch Florian stiffen, his hands folding up to his chest. He is looking at me carefully, eyes narrowing, and then something breaks: he unfolds, marches over to the fireplace and grabs a tattered old book from the mantlepiece. I watch as he pulls something out of the cover. He doesn't look at it, instead he slumps himself into the chair next to me and passes it over into my hands.

I stare at the two brothers, older in this picture. It's lovely at first, seeing them again, grinning almost identically to the way they had done in the old picture on the wall but with more lines and stubble on their faces. Then I notice something that makes everything inside me feel heavy because in this picture, Ettie is wearing a jumper I bought him the Christmas before he died, after he had told me he wanted nothing more to do with Florian.

I look up at Florian who can't quite meet my eye.

'The other day at the café when you said that I hadn't seen Ettie for months before he died, well that wasn't entirely true.'

'But…' I start, but my head feels foggy. I don't know where to begin, how to unravel it all. 'I need more wine.' I reach for the bottle but Florian already has it in his hands and he is pouring us both large glasses.

'I had no idea you didn't know until the other day. I thought he might have said something.'

'Why didn't he tell me? Why lie?'

'I don't know, Ava.'

'But the money—' It slips out.

'What money?'

'The night he took you back to Bordeaux, he took the money out, gave it to you?'

'No he didn't.' Florian looks mildly horrified. 'Ava, Ettie never drove me back to Bordeaux. He took me to rehab.'

'Rehab?' I try the word on my tongue.

'Yes.' He looks similarly uncomfortable at the mention of the word. 'Ettie was the reason I got clean. After I turned up at your door, we spoke. You'd gone to bed and Ettie found me crying on the balcony. I knew things were bad, but I don't think I realised how bad until I saw the life that you guys were living and it felt so far out of my reach, that kind of safe normality, and it all hit me. Ettie listened, listened as I poured my heart out, and then the next morning he told me to get in the car. He drove me here.' He points to the picture on my lap. 'The place I went to was expensive. He paid for it, but it was always a loan. He told me that the next summer I was going to work for him at the café, do a season to pay you both back.'

'But why didn't he tell me?' My voice comes out strained. 'Why let me believe that you'd taken the money to… carry on?'

'I don't know.' He shakes his head. 'I guess that maybe he didn't want to get his hopes up.' Florian sighs. 'I'd gone sober before, failed miserably, and each time it got worse. Maybe he was waiting to see if it really worked. Giving your money away for his brother to go to rehab is one thing; for it to fail is another.'

I let the truth wash over me, a truth I never thought I would have. 'But it didn't fail?'

'No… it didn't.' He smiles. 'This one worked.'

'But you said he never knew you were sober, that you never got to apologise.'

'*You* said that Ettie didn't know I was sober; I never corrected you. As for the apology, I said sorry to him many times but it wasn't the kind of apology I needed to say. Those ones are formulated much later, when your life has moved on so much you can really look back and see who you left in your wake.' He takes the picture from my lap, studies it with a soft smile on his face. 'This was my last day. He picked me up to drive me to the station but we stopped at the beach on the way, the beach we came to when we were kids. It was nice, being together again. It felt like the end of something and the beginning all at once. And then you called me eight days later.' He clears his throat. 'And that was that. He was gone.'

'I never knew.' I reach out, take his hand in mine and squeeze it. I look down at the picture, at Ettie's face, and notice how happy he looks, how relieved. 'If I'd have known I would have reached out more, after Ettie I mean. I wouldn't have gone back to London without saying anything…'

'I know.' He squeezes my hand back. 'But I kind of like the fact that you didn't really know me then. I like the fact that you get to know this version of me. I like him much more.' I see the bashful pride on his face, how calm he looks now that the whole truth is out there. I think of all the horrific microaggressions I used to harbour for him – the anger, resentment, pity – and I hate myself a little for it. That underneath the old Florian was just Ettie's little brother, the man sitting next to me now.

'He's growing on me.'

Florian smiles to himself and then clears his throat. 'Well, here's to you surviving your first hit and run.' He gets to his feet in order for our glasses to touch and then stays standing. 'Can I show you something?' He looks nervously at a door in the corner.

'That sounds ominous.'

He grabs two coats and throws one at me and heads to a door at the back of the house, grabbing the remainder of the bottle of wine on our way out. It leads to a cold, stark little passageway that he takes me down until we get to another door.

'Now, it's not finished, so don't judge it too harshly.' He reaches into the darkness of the room and flicks the switch, sending iridescent light streaming onto every cement surface. In the middle of the room, standing around 10 feet high and around 5 inches diameter is the statue, white and speckled with glinting flashes of alabaster. It takes a while to adjust to the sheer size of it, the ridiculousness of this sculpture in the middle of the shabby studio, where plaster is splattered on every inch of ceiling and skirting and floorboard.

I step towards it, reach my hand out and run it along the base. There are birds in all different stages of flight and size, skimming the surface. Flowers trail up to the calves of the central figure: a woman, holding in her hands a pomegranate as her hair falls around her shoulders like seaweed, so smooth and fluid. I move around it, my fingers tracing the indentations he has so delicately carved out. I follow the line from where her bare palm reaches for her counterpart across the rock: a man, cowering below, prostrate, his face pained, whilst around him the flowers turn to strangling weeds knotting around his thighs, but still his hand reaches with such determination towards hers.

I turn my gaze to the sculptor who stands watching me take it all in. His arms are clutched around his body, his feet tapping out an unsteady beat.

'It's beautiful, so beautiful.' It comes out as a soft murmur.

'You like it?'

'How could you not?'

'You get the reference?'

'Now with my limited ancient knowledge, I'd say she's Persephone?'

'A+.'

'But him?'

'I wanted to look at the story from Hades' perspective. Whilst everyone celebrates Persephone's ascendence back to the living for half the year, I imagined Hades, rooted in the Underworld with all the things that are doomed and dying whilst she lives and flourishes without him. He gets his love, for a while, but knows that she will always have to leave him. Whilst Persephone thrives, Hades dies.'

'One forced to die, the other forced to live. Why does that sound familiar?' I manage a wry smile as my fingers retrace the point where the couple's fingers touch.

'It's not about Ettie,' Florian says quickly, his voice suddenly sharp.

'Okay...' I hold my hands up, jokingly at first, until I realise that Florian's voice isn't softening; instead his head turns to me, his eyes pointed.

'Ettie's death isn't something I'm ever going to make art about. I can promise you that.'

'Why not?'

'At the very least it's a bit obvious, at its worst it's sleazy, you know – making money from something so tragic.'

'I don't know...' I go to defend myself, as if it's a personal attack – and I guess it is, because that's exactly what I'm doing, isn't it? Florian agrees with the troll in my Instagram comments who told me I was an opportunist who only got my book deal because my husband snuffed it.

Florian takes a gulp before clearing his throat, not letting me finish my point. 'You know when it first happened, I was living with this guy and the second thing he said to me after the obligatory, "I'm sorry," was some shitty comment about how I could make a series of sculptures about it.'

'Well yeah that feels a bit callous but—'

'I don't think I've ever been so angry. I kicked him out; we haven't spoken since.'

'Right.' Everything tightens. I think of the book, the blog, the trip and suddenly I'm aware that everything I have told him about me being here is ultimately a lie. A lie that if I try to explain will now probably end with a similar excommunication.

'Wouldn't Ettie have liked it though?' I take a breath. 'I mean he liked art, he liked us, if it made your life a little more comfortable, then he would want that, wouldn't he?'

'Pfft.' He rolls his eyes when he says it. 'I'm not a sell-out. I would rather die without selling any of my work then make it big whilst profiting from Ettie's death.' He shakes his head, a look of sheer disgust writ large on his face.

'Right.' I clear my throat and haul myself up onto the counter and sit with my legs dangling, wondering if there is a particular way I could word my confession about my blog that would make him see sense, make him not hate me. Florian hands me the bottle and then pulls himself up next to me. We sit in silence, let his anger dissipate.

'You said the other day about knowing that other statue wasn't Ettie,' he says quietly, his voice returning to the Florian I know, the thoughtful, reflective one.

'Yeah?' I sound apprehensive, aware of the implications of a throwaway sentence I had made to end our conversation.

'But you said it was me?'

'I thought it was obvious.'

'How?'

'Oh, come on, a man pulling himself out of a formless object, isn't that just what you do? Pulling art out of nothingness. I thought it was all a bit meta.'

He smirks into his lap, ruffles a hand through his hair. 'I'd never thought of it like that.'

'No?'

'No! I just had the idea one day, chiselled away until it looked half decent.'

'You make it sound so easy.'

'It is and it isn't. Sometimes it's the easiest thing in the world. Other times it feels impossible.'

We let the statement grow stale in the air, feel it swell and warp and change into something with a hundred different meanings.

I grab the bottle from his hands, take two large mouthfuls and then sit there whilst the taste sits on my tongue, growing bitter and vinegary.

'You know I hate him for leaving me sometimes,' I say to

the statue. It feels like a confession, my voice strangled, quiet. Florian stiffens next to me. 'Like I *properly* hate him and I used to think it was just grief, but it's not. It's rage… it's… fury at how unfair it all is. Why did he have to go and fucking die and leave me to do this on my own?' It's all too honest, I know; stuff like this is usually reserved for the diary but after listening to Florian be quite so open and sincere about his feelings it feels wrong to not give something back, to make us feel like we're on even terms again. 'I used to have someone who was always on my side, even when I was stupid and childish and wrong and I don't have that any more. It's just me and that's fucking terrifying.' I wipe away the wetness that is pooling in my lash line with the back of my hand, and manage an exasperated laugh at how pathetic I sound. 'God, I'm drunk, I need to go.' I slip off the counter but Florian's hand reaches out, encircles my wrist and grips it firmly.

'Don't.' He shakes his head, his own eyes red-rimmed and watery. 'I'm on your side.' He says fiercely. 'I can't do much, I can't take back the past, but I can promise you that I am on your side.'

I look at him properly, take in all of those features that feel so dangerously familiar, so within touching distance and so far away all at once.

'You really do look like him sometimes.' I reach my hand out and it hovers inches from his face. 'Can I?' I ask and when he nods gently, I trace my fingers over his jaw, the sharpness of his stubble, the softness in his cheek, the divot in his chin. I lean against his knees, half expecting him to pull away but he doesn't. He stays there, watching me close the distance between us until I can feel his breath on my lips. He closes his eyes and becomes as formless and motionless as his statues.

I kiss him.

His lips are hard and unmoving against mine. I stop. Pull away. A heat that, moments ago, flooded through me comes to rest in my face, a deep-seated shame that I can't shake off. It's so tangible that for a second I think that if I close my eyes and try hard enough there is a serious way I can go back in time and stop myself from being such an idiot. He pushes a piece of my fringe behind my ears.

'It's fine…' he says before I can start apologising.

'Oh God.' I cringe into his palms.

'Ava…'

'I'm so sorry… honestly, I don't know what happened. I just… the wine? And I'm so…'

'Ava, look it's fine.' He hushes me, his fingers stroking my cheek. This isn't how you react when your sister-in-law kisses you. Not that I'm sure it's happened that much because most people aren't raging idiots who confuse kindness with an invitation to snog them. But no, I'm pretty sure that you don't stroke the cheek of someone you didn't kiss back; it's too gentle, too intimate. He lifts my chin so that I have to look him directly in the eye and I feel the naïve fluttering of hope. He leans forward and presses his lips into my head, the kind of platonic kiss that a priest bestows on a member of the congregation. 'I know you just wanted to kiss him again.'

I try to ignore the deep, swelling disappointment that is dangerously close to suffocating me.

'Yeah…' I nod, a little too enthusiastically. 'Yeah you're probably right.' I step away and try to ignore how cold my body feels without his closeness there, how that chaste forehead kiss now feels like a brand. 'I should go home.' My voice cracks with false civility, trying far too hard to turn myself into the cool girl who won't be re-running this moment in my mind thousands of times before I eventually can go to sleep. I push some hair behind my ears and turn towards the door of the workshop.

He doesn't stop me.

Chapter 16

'WHAT ARE YOU DOING this weekend?' I ask Archie, stirring my tea a little too vigorously so that it slops over the side of the rim and splatters the cover of the diary on the coffee table. When I got home and started writing, the words wouldn't come, like I couldn't actually formulate the sentence 'I kissed Florian', so I skirted around them, lying to the only thing that I have sworn total fidelity to until I had drained one of the remaining bottles of red in the apartment and finally gained the courage to admit to it. And then, in a drunken haze, I kept writing until I admitted something so concerning that I had slammed the diary shut and promised to never reread it.

I root around for a tea-towel to dry the worst of the spillage off.

'What – the weekend in three days?'

'Yes.'

'Erm, nothing much… why?' He sounds concerned, drawing it out. I can't tell him the truth, can't let him know that last night I tried to snog my brother-in-law and I'm now looking for any excuse to not have to face that fact. After I had made the largest fuck up of the millennium I left, walked the two kilometres in the cold and dark as some kind of atonement. I would have taken self-flagellation over re-running every detail, groaning at the embarrassment, wondering why I appear to be set on permanent self-destruct mode.

'Come over.'

'To France?'

I pause. 'Yes.'

'Are you feeling okay, Avie?' I'm not a fan of this new nickname; it's pretty useless. It doesn't shorten my name, just changes it. I think it's meant to be a joke but I never pulled him up on it before, and to do so now would make it 'a thing'.

'I'm fine, just think it would be nice; the weather's meant to be good, hot even.'

'Well, I do have some days in lieu? I could see if I could use them up? It's quiet at the minute. Could put a couple of days either side – long weekend?' I register the fact that he is framing everything as a question, his voice lilting at the end, ready for me to pounce on him, to tell him no, that he's got the wrong end of the stick.

'So, you could maybe come Friday? That would be amazing!' Three days. He could be here in three days. That means I only need to get through the next 72 hours and then there would be a distraction, someone else I could focus on.

'It would?' He sounds sceptical.

I sit on the corner of the sofa, one hand clinging on to the tea, the other on the phone. 'Yeah, of course it would.'

'Yeah, I mean— I just thought—'

'Thought what?'

'It doesn't matter. I'll text my boss and if it's all cool, I'll book a flight for later. You have a car there, don't you, so you can pick me up?'

I think of the silver Fiat probably on the back of some tow-truck on its way back to the airport by now to be inspected. 'Oh erm, no… long story – no car at the moment.' I hope he doesn't ask anything more. 'There's a taxi company, I'll get one to pick you up.'

'Okay. Wow, not what I thought this call was going to be about.'

'What did you think it was going to be about?'

'I don't know, more gossip about Florian I guess.' My stomach twists at his name. I see his grin, his body sitting on the counter, his look of total disappointment when I kissed him, the fact I will never be able to take it back.

'Oh no, same old on that front, haven't seen him since we last spoke.' It's worrying how quickly the lies come.

'Okay, well maybe I can meet him when I'm there?'

'Yeah maybe!' I don't push the subject.

Archie eventually hangs up after once again asking whether I was being serious. As soon as his voice disappears, the regret kicks in, the kind that slaps you immediately after you make a bad decision. He sounded so shocked, that even though I had worked hard to build up this wall that made boundaries clear and uncrossable, here I was opening a door, letting him in and the possibility of more. I try the radio, let it buzz into existence until it crackles out its latest rendition of a new Europop hit. I try to start prepping something for dinner but keep having to triple check every detail on the recipe because as soon as I look away from my phone, I forget. After my second attempt at caramelising onions begins to char, I throw it away, pan and all.

Even though the thought of running into Florian is sickening, I need air. I need to do something other than sit and marinate in the shame, so I grab my jacket and head out onto the street. I skirt the edge of town, just to make sure I don't see him, and eventually wind my way towards the hotel.

'Hi.' I smile at the receptionist who barely glances in my direction. 'I'm looking for someone... a resident.'

'Name?' she asks.

'Oh.' I pause, remind myself of the stupidity of the whole situation, that in all the conversations we have had, how she is the closest thing I have to a friend and I don't even know her name. It feels strange to ask now, that if I do she'll realise how fragile this whole relationship is and I can't lose any more of the limited friendships I have. 'I... I don't know.'

'You don't know their name?' The receptionist looks up at me then, one eyebrow raised, her mouth working overtime on some gum.

'*Her* name and no, I don't. She's American, about this high.' I gesture to my chin. 'Old, a bit... mad looking?'

'Ava?' I turn to see The American, this time wearing a cerise-pink trouser suit, sitting in an armchair by the window.

'Found her.' I manage to flash the receptionist a smile before making my way to the other armchair and slump myself down with an exasperated sigh.

'Well, I hope the police never ask you to write my description for the paper,' The American chuckles.

'Sorry.' I cringe a little. 'I've had a day of it.'

'Here, you better take this.' She hands over a tumbler and I receive it without asking its contents. 'You look like you might need it more than I do.'

'I fucked up,' I say into the glass and then take half of the liquid into my mouth. Brandy. I want to spit it out but I'm committed now and gulp it back against my better judgement.

'What now?'

'You're going to think I'm mad. *I* think I'm mad.'

'It takes a lot for me to call someone else mad, my dear.'

'Last night I… God I don't think I can even say it out loud.'

'That bad eh?'

'It's worse than bad.'

'Well, now I'm intrigued.'

'I…' I look around for signs of him or any familiar face that might be lurking in the foyer. When I'm satisfied that we are clear, I lean forward so that there's barely a foot between us. 'I kissed Florian.'

Her cackling laughter is so loud that all the other guests turn to look at what could possibly be that funny. She is laughing so hard the exertion looks like it's physically painful.

'That's the best thing I've heard all year.'

'The best?' I wonder for a moment if she has actually heard me. I had expected to be berated, chastised; I hadn't expected her to find this all quite so hilarious.

'Honey, gossip is in short supply here, we've got to take a win when we can get some.'

'This is not a *win*,' I hiss at her and wait as the other guests start to lose interest, their heads turning back to their own business. 'Not in the slightest, this is the worst thing I could have ever done.'

'Oh, Ava darling.' She reaches out, her hand stroking my knee. 'It really isn't that bad. So what, you kissed him. It's hardly nuclear war.'

I shake my head at her. 'He's my brother-in-law.'

She straightens up a napkin on the table. 'You said yourself you don't know what you two are to each other now that the in-law bit is slightly redundant.'

'Semantics don't matter.'

'Semantics are all that matters.' She leans back in her chair, surveying me; when she's satisfied she inspects a bangle on her wrist. 'Did he kiss you back?' My mouth goes dry remembering how his lips felt, how humiliating it had been being rejected like that.

'No.' I shake my head. 'No, he didn't.'

'Ah, so that's why you're so mortified.'

My forehead ruches so hard, I can feel the lines appearing. 'What?'

'Well, it would be different if he kissed you back, wouldn't it?' she challenges. 'You both would have something to feel bad about. Now you're wondering why you got the wrong end of the stick.' She says it so succinctly, it feels like I've been punched. But she's wrong, that isn't why I feel bad; I feel bad because I kissed the one person on this planet I shouldn't have. 'To be honest, I'm surprised…' she adds, more thoughtful now. 'I thought it might be the other way around.'

Everything stops. I look up at her quickly, trying to read the strange look on her face. 'What do you mean by that?'

'I don't *mean* anything by it, just that when you get to my age you notice things, things that younger, more naïve, people don't.'

'I'm not naïve.'

'Of course you're not.' She pouts and then goes back to eyeing me up and down as if there might be something she has missed. 'What are you going to do about it?'

I snort. 'Avoid him until I have to go home.'

'Well, judging how you possess an innate ability to "bump" into each other, I'm pretty sure that won't work.'

'Well Archie's going to come over.'

'The man from London.' She says it dryly, one eyebrow arching up into her hairline.

'Yes, the man from London.'

She dusts off some imaginary crumbs from her skirt as if she's bored. 'And what will you do with him?'

'The things I clearly need to get out of my system,' I shrug. 'Besides, he's nice, sensible; you'll like him.'

'*Nice and sensible*, words that send every woman's heart a flutter.'

'Oh stop it!'

'And by having Archie out here, your feelings for Florian will just disappear?'

'I don't have any feelings for Florian.' I say it flatly, because I know if my voice wavers a decibel, she will not believe me. 'He just looks a bit like Ettie. It was all just some confused misplaced affection – Florian said so himself. He… he said he knew it was about Ettie and not about him.'

'Did he? Very big of him.'

'Yes, well…' I lean back in my chair, fold my arms into my lap. 'He was very good about it to be honest.'

'So, Ava.' The American adjusts herself and looks me square in the face. 'Why are you here, clearly mortified, looking like you've been caught with your knickers down? It's a kiss, Ava. By the sounds of it you've managed to justify it as some strange form of grief, Florian doesn't sound too bothered by it, and you have your lover coming over to keep you company?'

'I don't know… I just feel…'

'Feel what?'

I'm growing petulant. My shoulders have slipped so far down the wing-backed chair that I am almost lying horizontal. I throw my hands into my hair. 'I don't know. I just feel…'

She holds my gaze a little too long, eyes narrowing, waiting for me to add something else, and when I don't she sighs. 'Well perhaps you can work it out over the weekend, I'm going to Toulouse.'

'What? Why?'

'Florian's exhibition the other day made me think about some friends I lost touch with. I have a taxi picking me up any minute.'

'Oh.' I don't want her to go. Not when Archie is here; I was counting on her as a distraction. She has become my kind of social stabiliser.

'But you'll be fine of course. Sounds like you've got enough things to keep you busy in the meantime.' She goes to get to her feet which means I feel like I have to do the same.

'Yes… well…'

'And, Ava, when you finally figure out why you are beating yourself up, you might want to write it down in that book of yours; I'm sure it could prove very enlightening.'

Chapter 17

ITIDY THE APARTMENT from top to bottom, change the sheets, dust the shelves, open the windows to let the warm spring breeze in. I guess it's a cleanse of sorts, one of those things spiritualists on Instagram warn you to do before you get stuck with another ten years of bad luck. In my head, the deep clean means that if I make the place look like the home of someone who has their shit together then it might eventually come true.

By the time the buzzer finally goes at three o'clock I have been sitting on the sofa, waiting for an hour and a half. I practically fly down the stairs.

'Hi.' I smile as I open the door onto Archie. He looks so wonderfully familiar: his face, tanned, clean shaven, his eyes bright and glistening.

'Hi.' He has that smile tattooed onto his face, the knowing one, the one that feels like it's our little secret, that in that moment we both know why we are here.

'Hi,' I say again as he bites his lip, bridges the distance between us.

'We've done that bit already.' He chuckles and then kisses me, re-writing the last time my lips touched someone else's, returning me to comfortable territory.

I don't notice the steps up to my apartment this time, there is a delightful knot in my stomach that distracts me. When we reach my front door, I look back at Archie, lugging his bag behind him.

He screws his face up a little at me, looks down. 'What?'

'I just can't quite believe you're actually here.'

'Yeah well, needed a holiday.' He winks.

He sets his bag by the door and surveys the apartment, hands on his hips, inspecting each and every corner.

'It's cute,' he shrugs. 'Bigger than I thought it'd be. Could do with a bit of modernisation in places.' I feel a little surge of protectiveness inch its way up my spine.

'No it doesn't! Not everything needs to be white and grey and shiny.'

'Alright, alright, didn't mean to touch a nerve.' He reaches out for my hands; I hold them close to me until he has to physically untangle them, and then we're standing there palm to palm, looking at each other, that same knowing grin occupying his face.

'What?' It's my turn to look confused.

'I've missed you.' He reels me in until there's only a few centimetres between our heads. The guilt floods in, because I know that he means it and I can't say it back. But here he is, just off a flight, without a second thought, all because I asked him to. I've forgotten how handsome he is, how his smile is so entirely infectious, how he drips with security and comfort. He guides my hands around his neck and I let him mould me into him.

I kiss him again before he can say anything else. He tastes fresh, like he's got through half a pack of chewing gum in the taxi here. I press my hips to his, start to pull at his shirt but he laughs at me, shaking his head.

'Not yet.'

'Oh, come on!'

'We have all weekend.' He pulls away from me, his hands held up in the air. 'We should at least get dinner first.'

'Why?' I try again, reach for him, stroke his cheek. He looks like he might fall for it for a moment, reassess his priorities, but he stands firm.

'What's got into you?' He's laughing but there's an edge.

'Nothing. I just missed this,' I rephrase.

He takes the smallest step back, assesses me. 'Me or the sex?'

I falter. 'Am I allowed to say both?'

He swallows hard and then shrugs, his hands squeeze me and then he reanimates.

'Let me have a shower and then I'll take you out for dinner, wherever you want. You can show me around and then we can grab some drinks, come back later, and I promise you can do whatever you want with me.' He winks as he says it and then reaches for his luggage. 'Which door for the bathroom?'

'Through that one and then left,' I point, and when the door closes, I collapse into the sofa slightly deflated.

I pick L'Auberge for dinner, it fits the bill as somewhere that is quintessentially French and also a place I never visited with Ettie. I appreciate that I'm not cheating, that walking through the place Ettie and I met is no worse than the handful of times I've slept with Archie before coming here, but the boundaries are blurring.

We leave half an hour early to amble through the town, picking out the top five things to see in Monpazier, which other than the covered market, church and general quaintness, consist of a pretty fountain and an apparently cursed gargoyle.

When we emerge from the dank nave of the church and back into the quickly fading evening light Archie nudges into me. 'I can see why you fell in love with the place.'

'Pretty, isn't it?'

'Could be the setting of a Disney film.' He doesn't sound particularly pleased with that statement.

'Yeah, but I mean the charm wears off after a while.' I play it off.

'It's a far cry from Hoxton, that's for sure.'

'They each have their appeal.'

'Maybe you could show me where you lived, before…' he asks slowly. I feel everything tighten at his request: my shoulders, my stomach, my palms.

'We'll be late for dinner.' I try to placate him, put on my best fake smile and hope that he might get the hint but he shrugs.

'We have ten minutes, besides I'm sure they'll hold it.'

I look at him, his soft, wide eyes, the way he hunches over slightly to try to look me squarely in the face. 'You really want to see it?'

'Yeah, I do.'

I look at my phone, knowing that it is way past closing, that my chances of running into Florian are as slim as bumping into him at the supermarket, which still feel strangely far too high. 'Okay.'

We round the corner and come to a stop at the edge of the café. It looks almost skeletal now, with the chairs and tables all safely packed underneath the arches waiting to be laid out again tomorrow. The only signs of life are in the warm-yellow lights emanating from the apartment above. I feel the lump in my throat and swallow it back.

'So... this is *the place*?' He asks as if it's more than it is.

'This is the place,' I repeat and check his face for any signs of disappointment that the most interesting thing about me is a rather bland, dilapidated building in the arse end of nowhere. 'It's a bit livelier in the day of course, when the tables are out and there's... people.'

'It's exactly how I imagined it, Avie.' Then there's something warm and firm in my hand, and I look down to see Archie's hand. He gives me a reassuring squeeze. It feels comforting and alien all at once.

Archie doesn't let go of my hand until we get to the restaurant. Something has come over us, a strange familiarity that goes beyond the handful of times we have slept together. I imagine what we look like through other people's eyes: a couple perhaps? Two people who are happy and content in each other's company and I don't hate it. I like the feeling of being *with* someone again, someone who makes it all so bloody easy.

When the waiter comes over with a pad and pen, I go to look at the menu but Archie whisks it away. 'The Pécharmant and two menu du jour.' He phrases it so lightly, the same gentle smile on his face, like he hasn't just ordered on my behalf without even so much as checking that I'm not deathly allergic to something.

Something writhes inside me; I'm angry and I don't really know why because Ettie used to do this all the time.

'Did you just order for me?' I ask when the waiter disappears. Archie's face doesn't falter.

'I thought we'd go all out. My treat.' He shrugs but when my face doesn't fall back into submission and I don't start uttering adoring thanks in his direction, his brow twitches. 'Do you not like it? You can order something else if you want?'

'It's just…' I start to say how, in that moment, I felt like a kid again, like someone who couldn't be trusted to make the simplest decision; but I pause. There are many ways this conversation can go, and only one of them leads to a nice evening with the possibility of some uncomplicated and distracting sex. 'It's fine, it sounds lovely.' I deflate. Drink down a glass of water instead.

'How are the chapters coming along?' he asks over our main course, a duck breast smothered in sauce.

'It's starting to come together,' I shrug. I think of the three pages I managed to write last night; it might make anyone else baulk at my lack of productivity, but it felt like something had switched. Kissing Florian had cleared the creative block, maybe because I wanted to do anything other than think about him.

'Getting a bit more used to the place again?'

'Like riding a bike,' I say, still chewing a piece of fatty meat. 'After a while you slip back into the way of things.'

'And The American, will I run into her?'

'Unfortunately not, she's visiting some friends.'

'That's a shame.' He takes a sip of his drink before leaning over the table towards me. 'Please tell me you at least know her name by now.'

I push some hair behind my ear. 'Well, not exactly…'

'Seriously, Ava?'

'It just hasn't come up and it feels so stupid now that so much time's gone on!' I raise my hands in defeat. I have mulled over the name that Crispy gave her more than I care to admit. I wondered if it was short for something – Dorothy maybe – but that didn't suit her either. Maybe it was a code that only those over the age of eighty would truly understand. 'I don't think she even realises,' I shrug. 'I mean it's not like it matters; we seem to have muddled through just fine without knowing details.'

He smirks. 'Oh yeah, silly little details like your best friend's name.'

'She's not my best friend,' I say defensively. I go to name someone else, but I come to a rather depressing conclusion – there isn't anyone. There are friends, sure. There are people that used to hold that mantle until my life got complicated, but in terms of a figure to whom I would divulge my deepest, darkest secrets – well, there's her. And I don't even know her name. 'Shit. She's my best friend.' I clasp my head in my hands.

Archie looks rather gleeful at my discovery until he takes a swig of his drink and turns his attention to a rather stubborn hangnail.

'I'm assuming I'll get to meet Florian at least.'

'Oh.' I recover my hands, chase a stem of asparagus with a fork, thinking of the perfect excuse as to why I will be attempting to keep Archie and Florian as far away from each other as possible. 'You know, he's pretty busy at the moment. I don't see him that much anyway, always been a case of running into him rather than planning anything.' I mean it's not a complete lie, at least half of my meetings with Florian had been incidental at best.

'So, no one wants to meet me?' He puts on an exasperated pout and I roll my eyes at his performance.

'Rather I've put them all off.'

'Well, there's only so much time we can spend in the apartment surely?' he asks, his eyebrow raised into his fringe. I feel the heat returning to my cheeks.

I spear a final cube of potato into my mouth. 'No comment.'

Archie throws down a chunk of notes and then when I get up from my seat, it's like he sees me again for the first time. I watch him watch me, curious at what exactly is so worthy of his attention.

'You know you look good, like really good.' He shrugs on his jacket.

'Do I?' I look down at my very unexciting outfit; I mean yes, I had shaved and washed my hair and put on make-up but I still feel the opposite of attractive.

'Yeah, I mean you just look different than when you were back home, not that you're not pretty there, it's like you suit being here, in this place.' He fights for clarity, desperate not to turn a compliment into an insult.

'You make it sound like a bad thing.'

'No!' He gabbles, 'no not at all, I just... God my chat is pretty shit tonight.' He laughs at himself. 'Let me try it again.' He reaches for my hand and I let him take it, threading my fingers with his. 'You look beautiful, I'm lucky to be here,' he says sincerely. I press a kiss into his cheek and we linger in the closeness. His hands move to my arms and he squeezes gently, a sort of embrace for people who weren't going to be big on public displays of affection.

And then we walk back, taking the quick way this time, straight back to the apartment.

Chapter 18

ARCHIE LINGERS IN THE entryway, his eyes tracing over the details of the apartment again, as if he never quite saw it the first time we were here. 'What's with the birds?' His eyes are drawn to two little blue lovebirds painted on the beams.

'I don't know. Guess the old owner was a fan,' I shrug.

He sniffs. 'Bit odd, isn't it?' He catches me frowning in his direction. 'Sorry,' he adds. 'I don't know why I'm being so… weird,' he says quietly. I go straight for the cupboard to retrieve one of the surviving bottles from the deer hit and run, doing everything in my power not to think of Florian.

'You've not been *weird*.' I try to play it off but he shoots me a look that lets me know I'm a shit actor. 'Okay maybe, but this whole thing is weird, you out here with me. It's not a two o'clock "you up" text after the pub.' I uncork the wine and pour us two large glasses, hoping that by the time he finishes this one he might be acting slightly more himself.

'I'm glad it's not that. Glad that this is more than that now.' He falls back into the sofa with a sigh, taking a large gulp of the wine. 'I guess it just feels a bit odd, me being here, in this place, with him…'

'Who?' I take a large gulp myself. 'Ettie?'

He cringes at his name; I know he doesn't want to bring this up now, but something is compelling him, his conscience perhaps, something I clearly don't have. 'Yeah. Don't get me wrong, I know that if he was still here then you and me wouldn't even be a thing, I'm aware of that. It's just odd, isn't it? Like normally you date girls who've been cheated on or broken up with, not girls who have had this dream relationship with this perfect guy.'

'He wasn't perfect.' I sit next to him on the sofa rubbing a point in my head where a persistent little ache was beginning to form. I hadn't expected to get into this so quickly; I wanted sex and I wanted to drink and be normal. I didn't want deep, meaningful conversations about my dead husband, especially when the last one led to me practically snogging his brother.

'Yeah, but he was perfect for you. If he hadn't...'

'Died.' I fill in the gaps for him.

He looks at me, his eyes wide with alarm at the word and then they soften when my hand reaches out and strokes his cheek. 'Yes.'

I move closer to him, his arm weaves its way around my neck. 'But he's not here any more, Archie.'

'No.'

'And you are.' My hand finds its way to his knee.

'Yes, I am.' He turns to me, the gap between us diminishing by the second. I reach my hands around his shoulders and swing my legs around so that I'm straddling him. He sighs with relief, happy that we have returned to the territory we are comfortable with. He flexes his hips, moving me closer to him, his thumbs hooking themselves into the back pockets of my jeans.

'And I like you, Archie,' I say as I loosen the top button on his shirt. 'But this doesn't work if we overthink things. If we spend too long questioning what *this* is then we kill it.'

'But it's... this is more than sex, isn't it, Ava?' It comes out as a long groan, as if he doesn't really want to say it but knows he doesn't have a choice. I feel an unpleasant heat start to spread around my body, crawl its way up my back. I can't have this conversation now, at least not when I'm sitting on his lap.

'It is. Now do you want to watch a film... or sign some sort of pact or... exchange a blood vow?' I pretend to leave but his hands secure me against moving, pulling my hips deeper into his. I let out an involuntary little groan.

'No.' He shakes his head emphatically. 'No, I do not want to do anything else than this, right now.' He kisses me. It's gentle at first, soft and sweet, but as I start to move against him, sinking into his lap, the kiss grows harder, faster, more desperate.

He reaches underneath my top and tugs at my shirt until I pull away and he strips me of it. He clumsily works at my bra, he always struggles with this bit; after tugging at the clasp for a while he grows frustrated but when I go to attempt it, he shakes his head and yanks at the fabric. I hear the material tear.

'Did you just break my bra?' I push myself off him a little. He isn't the sensible Archie any more; he is a sweating, panting stranger below me.

'Oh shut up,' he chuckles, taking my breasts in his palms and rocking me forward so I'm back where he wants me, back where I want him, with only our jeans between us. 'I'll buy you five more.' He peppers my neck with short, sharp kisses stretching from my ear to my collarbone, his thumb brushing my nipple, and I groan, louder this time. I start to unbutton his jeans and when I reach the last one, see his white boxers, I try to slip my hand underneath the fabric but he stops me.

'Not here.' He shakes his head.

'Oh come on…' I object, gesture to the perfectly good sofa that would serve any purpose we would require, but his face isn't budging. 'Seriously?'

'Seriously,' he echoes.

'Square.' I roll my eyes but get to my feet anyway. I don't want to argue, I just want to keep this going. This is what Archie and I do best, the safe ground that both of us know. If we lose momentum he might stop again, decide that he isn't doing this unless I wear a promise ring. I pull him to his feet and lead him through the door to the bedroom. He winds me back into him; he's only slightly taller so it isn't any effort to kiss him and we do. We take our time, trying to recapture what we had on the sofa, that immediate urge to be everything to each other, but it's different in here, things slow down. His kisses are long, slow. I let him undress me, peeling off my jeans until I'm standing there in my knickers, the good pair. His hands trace down every inch of my body until he's pressing me down onto the bed, my arms thrown up around his shoulders. He takes his own jeans off, tugging at them until they get slightly stuck around his ankles and he has to kick them off. He looks at me slightly apologetically for the disruption of the mood but I take his face in my hands, kiss him long and hard, until I realise that he has managed to manoeuvre my knickers off of my body. He takes one last look at me, his head cocked to one side. I manage a smile, a nod of my head and then my hands reach for him.

Chapter 19

THE SUNLIGHT FILTERS THROUGH the curtains, casting intricate lace shadows on the wall and over Archie's body. I trace them into his abdomen, tiny impermanent tattoos. He's not asleep; instead his own fingers are brushing over my shoulder but we're not moving.

'It's strange,' Archie says to the ceiling. 'I'm sort of waiting for you to tell me you've got to go.'

I let the comment hang in the air, think of all the times he played it cool, acted like I was doing him a favour by leaving as soon as we were finished, until he stopped, until he did everything other than actually saying that he wanted me to stay.

'I can if you like.' I sit up in bed, pull the covers to my chest and try to slip out.

'Oh no you don't.' He reaches for me quickly with a grunt, both hands clasping around my waist and pulling me back to the bed with a thump. I shriek – it feels strange to laugh quite so early in the morning, before the coffee, before warming up for the day. We stay there, his arms cocooned around me, his warmth, the sleep still in my eyes, and he presses his lips to my neck in a long, languid kiss. I take it, take him all in.

'I want this,' he says quietly into my ear. 'I want this, all of the time.' I feel an ache in my stomach, a momentary chasm of sadness that disappears when my rational brain kicks in. This is Archie: gorgeous, talented, safe Archie. There's nothing to be sad about. Here he is, wanting me.

'It won't be like this all the time,' I reason, the frustratingly logical spoilsport coming out. 'We'll only get a handful of nights like *that* and mornings like this.'

He sighs, goes back to pressing his lips into my neck. 'I guess I don't really mean the sex and the lie-ins,' he murmurs. 'I mean you, Avie. I want you.'

'Why?' I scoff. I sound mildly irritated and I don't know why; any other girl would be swooning. I should be swooning. I pull away from his arms and look at him, tugging the covers up to my shoulders as if last night hadn't happened.

'What?'

'Why do you want me, Archie? You could have anyone, girls must be throwing themselves at you. Why on earth are you here, putting up with me and my baggage, wanting me?'

He lets out a frustrated sigh and looks up at the beams in the ceiling, biting the corner of his lip so hard it starts to blanche. When he has gathered himself, he looks at me with a clarity that is terrifying: all of his features sharpen, the whites of his eyes are brighter, the green of his pupils practically radiating. 'You really don't get it, do you?'

'No, I really don't.'

'That night when I met you, before I knew who you were and what had happened, you looked so out of place there was this sort of halo of sadness around you and it didn't suit you one bit because you don't look like a person who should be sad. And those first few times we hooked up, you came to me this kind of despondent flight risk, but then when we were together, there were these... glimmers of happiness.' His hands wave about in the air a little and he smirks as if he knows how poetic he's being, how uncomfortable this is for both of us. 'It was like I could kind of help mend you in some way, and I wanted to. I never knew the person you were before you lost him, but I see echoes of her sometimes.' He is picking his words so carefully, so gently, I wonder if he has thought about them before, practised them, maybe even written them down somewhere. My throat starts to ache with a lump of emotion and I have to swallow it back to regain control.

I unwind his hands from my torso. Turn my body so that I'm looking in his eyes, which are glistening in the corners. 'Avie, what I'm trying to say is, I want to be a part of your life in a way that isn't like it is now…'

My hand strokes his cheek. 'I know and you've been so good and so fucking patient and I don't deserve it…'

'Of course you deserve it,' he persists.

'I…' I shake my head. I could tell him everything now, lay everything on the table about Florian, about how complicated this whole thing is, the reason why Archie is even here in the first place, but he looks so bloody hopeful that I can't bring myself to do it. 'I just need a bit more time, Archie.'

He falters. 'But you do want it too don't you, eventually?'

I think of last night, being a couple again, how easy it made things, how the world was built around not being on your own. Mum will be ecstatic, the conversations about dating will stop, there'll be someone to go to dinner with, or pick me up from the train station, I could split rent, move somewhere new, start again. I won't end up kissing my brother-in-law because he showed me a basic level of kindness. I won't be alone.

'Yes,' I say earnestly. 'Yes, I want it.'

His happiness is intoxicating, the look of relief on his face contagious. For a moment I wonder if I've agreed to marry him. I slip out of the bed and stetch out my limbs that have been contorted into positions they hadn't been in for a while.

'Where are you going?' He lies back in the bed, arms behind his head watching me.

'Oh, running away.' I shrug, reach for my pants and throw his shirt on over the top for decency in case someone catches a glimpse through a window.

'I'll take mine black with no sugar,' he shouts after me.

I turn the radio on. The apartment is warmer than it has been; it's meant to be the first properly warm day of the year – a spring heatwave – which has caused some more protests about climate change but I'm quite glad I can at least be here to enjoy some sun.

I fill the percolator and place it onto a burner on the stove. The buzzer goes. It's strange for a Saturday; no one buzzes for me apart from The American. However sometimes people read the names wrong on the interface, so I press the button to the main door regardless and start preparing some eggs. I turn the radio up, dance around as the coffee boils and the eggs start to whiten in the pan.

I feel like my senses have ignited. I feel everything, notice the cobwebs in the corner, a new little watercolour sparrow on the side of the fridge, how much the basil plant has grown in the corner. What I clearly don't notice is the knocking at the door, the person calling my name. I only notice when it's too late, when Florian Grenaud is standing in an open doorway grinning wildly at me dancing in my underwear.

'Fuck!' I scream as I notice him. I look down, realise my predicament and turn to the wall, furiously buttoning up the shirt until it covers most of my modesty. 'What the fuck, Florian?'

'You buzzed me in!' He holds up his hands and when I turn back around, he keeps his eyes fixed on the floor.

'I thought it was a mistake.'

'I've been knocking for a while; I rang you too.'

'Yeah, well I've been… busy.' I look around at the kitchen, rush to turn the radio down.

'I can see that.'

'What are you doing here anyway?'

He shuts the door behind him, aware that whilst I haven't exactly invited him in, we're probably past pleasantries now.

'I haven't seen you around.'

'Not a coincidence,' I answer back quickly and push the second cup out of view.

'I'm not here to bring it all back up again, it was… well it was what it was, but I've started getting quite used to seeing you around, I might even go so far as to say I enjoy your company.'

'Well, that's great.'

'Come down to the river tomorrow with me.'

'Sorry?'

'It's meant to be hot, you have no transport, thought it might do you good to get out.'

'Oh, that's kind but I'm busy…'

'Busy?' He gestures to the radio, to my outfit and the dance party for one he had interrupted. 'Sure you are.' He smirks into the floorboards just as there is movement from the back of the room. We both look up, startled, as a man in his boxers walks from the bedroom into the lounge. I stand there aghast watching both men take in the situation. Archie's eyes fall on Florian, confusion rippling through his features. It's almost the same look on Florian's face mixed in with something a little edgier.

'Hi?' Archie greets him warily, skimming around the apartment to my side. His hand reaches around my waist and rests on my hip. I look at Florian whose eyes fixate on the connection, the familiarity.

'This is Ettie's brother, Florian,' I fill Archie in.

'Oh!' He holds a hand out to Florian who looks at it a little cautiously before taking it and is then shaken vigorously by Archie. 'Sorry, mate, you're not what I expected.'

'Sorry to disappoint.'

'Not at all. As you can probably tell we weren't expecting visitors, would have maybe put some clothes on,' he laughs, gesturing to the both of us. Archie doesn't care about the fact that he's in his boxers; I mean he doesn't exactly have anything to worry about on that score anyway but he does hover over me, making me feel a little more exposed than before.

'I was just popping by, but I'll leave you to it.'

'Florian was inviting me to the river tomorrow, but I said we were busy.'

'We can go,' Archie says casually and reaches for the coffee cup on the side.

I pivot. 'What?'

Archie shrugs. 'Not like we have plans and it's meant to be hot, isn't it? I mean, if you don't mind me tagging along?'

Florian doesn't look as alarmed as he should, instead he manages to play it off coolly. 'Uh, no sure.'

'Didn't bring any trunks though.' Archie grins widely.

'You'll be fine in those,' Florian gestures to Archie's boxers. 'Although Ava might need to bring something else.'

'Yes, thank you,' I snap at him, but Florian's lips have curled up in a little grin at his own comment. It quickly vanishes when he looks back to Archie, perhaps realising what he has just agreed to.

'I'll pick you up tomorrow at eleven.' He turns to go. 'Nice to meet you...'

'Archie,' Archie fills in the gap.

'Archie,' Florian confirms and then leaves.

Chapter 20

WHEN FLORIAN COMES TO collect us, half an hour later than planned, the waitress from Fromages et Vins is sitting in the passenger seat. I stall a little, wondering if I've missed something, whether their arrangement was something more than I had assumed.

'Hi.' I try to hide the tone of surprise from my voice when I reach the car with Florian and the pretty blonde girl deep in conversation.

'Bonjour!' She beams at us.

'Ava, you've met Inés before, haven't you?' Florian gestures to her with a little flourish.

'Briefly.' I manage a strained smile. 'Hi.' I kiss her cheeks as she gets out of the car to let Archie and me in the back.

'We're only there for the afternoon,' Florian says curtly as Archie heaves half the contents of our fridge into the boot.

'Well, *be prepared* and all that,' Archie beams, clambering into the back of the Citroën. When I slot myself in the seat next to him, his hand reaches for mine in a lovely, automatic sort of way. I thread my fingers through his and notice him looking at my wedding band. It's caught his eye before even though I know he would be mortified if I called him out on it. I understand his curiosity about whether it's going to be a permanent feature on my hand. It's a question even I don't know the answer to yet.

The drive is as uncomfortable as I had anticipated. The only one daring to ask questions is Inés, who points out features on the drive that Archie might find interesting. She is sweet, chatty, a kind of human personification of sunshine, and therefore the complete opposite of who I imagined Florian to be into.

He doesn't make polite conversation. I can see the profile of his face occasionally in the rear-view mirror. He is rigid, his jaw clenched, hands clasping onto the steering wheel until he looks up, catches me staring. I don't look away. If he wants me to feel bad about bringing Archie here, then I won't. His forehead ruches, his hands slacken and then the car wavers slightly. Inés makes a protest in French and the car straightens. Florian's eyes drift back to the road without uttering an apology and I take my win.

When we reach the town of Castelmoron-sur-Lot, with its artificial beach on the river, it feels like a relief for all involved. Florian parks the car under a cement bridge in the shade. He and Inés have packed lightly in comparison to us: a small canvas tote between them with a towel each and a packet of cigarettes, and it makes me feel like a complete tourist. We find a spot, semi-shaded and slightly away from the melee of screaming children and overconfident teens launching themselves off the diving board. Florian takes his towel from his bag and slumps himself down on top of it, immediately reaching for a cigarette whilst Archie busies himself with wrestling a picnic blanket into submission. Inés and I stand there for a moment then she strips into her bikini, her body slim and toned with actual abs. I decide against taking off my shirt and instead shed the rucksack and grab four beers. Florian gestures for me to pass them over and swiftly beheads the caps with his lighter.

'There you go.' Archie presents the blanket as if it's something much more than it is, but I sit on it appreciatively, passing him his beer.

'Cheers.' I try to break the awkwardness by clinking the bottles together but Florian abstains. Instead, he strips off his shirt and lies horizontally on his towel, sunglasses hiding whether his eyes are closed.

'This is nice.' Archie takes a sip of his beer. He kisses my cheek, and I suddenly feel very aware of every part of my body, everything feeling frustratingly forced.

'Yeah, it's lovely,' I lie. This is possibly the worst thing we could have ever done.

I start to put on my sun cream and offer it around as a sort of peace offering to show that whilst I don't particularly want to be here right now with these people, I don't want them to get skin cancer either. Archie looks at his already dark skin and wafts it away and Inés screws her face up at the bottle as if she's never heard of it. Florian ignores my offer entirely.

'Fuck, it is hot isn't it?' Archie says. I notice the sweat on his forehead.

'Get in the water then,' Florian says sharply, interrupting his own apparent vow of silence and Inés and I turn to him abruptly.

Archie surveys the wide stretch of slightly brown water about ten feet away. 'Is it… clean?'

'It's a river,' Florian says curtly and I can see Archie weighing up whether that was an answer to his question or not. 'The water flows, you'll be good.'

'I'll come.' Inés jumps up enthusiastically.

Archie shoots me a pleading look. 'Ava, you coming?'

'I might sit this one out for now, sun cream.' I gesture to the milky sheen on my skin. Archie raises an eyebrow in my direction. I'm not completely sure when I became the exact embodiment of my mother, but clearly that little transition had happened without me realising.

'Florian?' Inés asks hopefully.

'I don't swim,' he says into the sand.

'Looks like it's just us then.' Inés gestures to Archie to follow her and he does, slightly begrudgingly, down to the shoreline.

With Florian still face down on the sand, I take the diary out of my bag and turn to a fresh page. When Archie was here, I couldn't easily write in it without him asking questions, and they were questions I really didn't have the answer to.

I try to push out the sounds of the kids screeching and the cars travelling over the nearby bridge. I write about the sad little look on Archie's face when he asked whether I wanted him the same way he wanted me, the thought of not being alone, the opportunities, how normal I'd be, how lucky I'd be. I write about him ordering for me at the restaurant, about how Ettie did the same, about how the old me feels like a totally different person to this current version. That I like this one a little bit more. I write about Florian finding me in my underwear, how I felt more comfortable in that short and incredibly uncomfortable interaction than I have done all weekend with Archie. And then, with that final damning realisation, I slam the diary shut.

'Do I get to ask you what's going on now?' Florian asks. I look around guiltily to see him propped up on his elbows watching me. I feel caught out, wait for the onslaught of questions about the writing, the diary, the entire reason I am here.

I slip the diary back into my bag and turn over, sit up and shield my eyes from the sun. 'You can ask…' I try to play it off.

'Good, what's going on?' he says again. 'Who is *he*?' He gestures to the water where Inés and Archie are swimming out to the diving platform. I feel a gentle relief fall over me. I can handle questions about Archie; he is much easier to explain.

'A friend.'

Florian scowls. 'A friend you're sleeping with.'

'How very astute you are.' I smile sarcastically at him and watch Florian writhe a little at my admission. He starts to play with the little leather bracelet on his wrist, plucking at it absentmindedly whilst he looks again at Archie swimming a few metres out, totally unaware of the conversation currently happening on shore.

'When did you invite him out?'

'Bloody hell, Florian!' I whip my sunglasses off and stare at him, hoping that he might get the message. 'What about her? You don't hear me interrogating you about your fucking sex life.'

'Just tell me.'

'The day after we…' I stop, correct myself. 'The day after *I* kissed you.' My response satisfies him. He lowers himself back down to his towel, lighting up another cigarette, and points at the rucksack for a beer. I swear under my breath but still root around for the bottle.

'He's a nice guy, Florian. I'm sure you'd like him if you were just a bit nicer to him.' I hand over the beer; our hands brush involuntarily, and I snatch mine away quickly. Florian smirks.

'I am being nice to him; I drove us here, didn't I?'

'Yes, and pretty much spent the entire forty-minute drive in silence.'

'Maybe it's the language barrier, perhaps my *niceness* doesn't translate well.'

'We've never had that issue before today.'

He looks over the top of his glasses at me. 'Maybe you just understand me a little better.'

I roll my eyes and then fix them on a cloud that I hope might shield the sun for a moment and give us a break from the heat that feels far too intense for early May. 'I don't think I understand you at all.'

Florian lets out a sharp exhale of air. I ignore it, choosing instead to search again for Archie who is now sunbathing on the platform.

'Is he your boyfriend? It must be serious if you've brought him all this way.'

'No,' I say quickly, all my coolness and mystique evaporating. 'I mean we're dating, that's all.'

'Does *he* know that?' Florian gestures to the picnic blanket with a sarcastic flourish.

'Of course he does.' My eyes return to the river where Inés pulls off an impressive dive.

'She's peppy.' I don't like how bitter I sound.

'Well, I just figured it might save a little on the awkwardness if it wasn't just us three like some strange little ménage à trois.'

'Ah, that's why you bought a gorgeous young girl to the beach with you, how wonderfully considerate of you, what a hardship.' I catch his eye then, the same wry smile he has mastered reappearing in the corner of his lips. I know that my own lips are pulling up into the same little grin even though I try to wrestle them back under control. 'Fuck I'm warm,' I groan, downing the last of my beer.

'You should take your shirt off,' Florian shrugs.

'Sorry?'

'You're wearing a swimsuit, so wear your swimsuit. No point coming down here if you're going to just sit here in all of your clothes.'

'You're *fun* today.'

'What, hasn't "monsieur picnic blanket" seen you in your bra before?'

I sense an opportunity. It's childish, slightly pathetic, but it's there and I know it might make Florian at least blush. 'Not really no, they don't tend to stay on very long around him.'

I enjoy that his lip twitches before he regains control of his apathetic frown. 'Well, don't worry about me.' Florian holds out his hands, his voice a little louder than before. 'I couldn't give a shit what your tits look like.'

It feels like a challenge. I get to my feet, work at the buttons on my linen shirt and then strip the fabric clumsily from my shoulders until I'm there, in front of him in my bikini top, praying that everything is still fastened into place. I finish my beer, drinking it down to its dregs and then I toss the bottle in his direction. He catches it with his fingertips and he looks up at me, bemused, until I can feel his eyes roll over me. He takes me in, inch by inch, and then his face falls a little. For a single guilty moment, I'm upset. But I look at him again, closer this time, and realise that the look writ large on his face isn't disappointment, it's something else entirely. I falter, feel the heat in my cheeks, feel something else snake down my body until I realise quite how wrong this is. Florian seems to notice it too; in a quick movement he rolls over. I clear my throat, the confidence vanishing. I look over to the water, where Archie is bobbing around entirely unaware of what's just happened, or not happened. I hurry to the shoreline, let the cold water dull the heat and wade over to Archie, who wolf whistles his appreciation. When I get close, I throw my arms around his neck, weaving my legs around his waist.

'Hey,' he croons as I kiss him, his skin cool and wet and his touch is not laced with any other intentions than to be exceptionally nice to me.

'Hey.'

'What about your sun cream?' he jibes.

'Fuck it.' I shrug and kiss him again. When I cast a glance back to the beach, Florian is still lying face down in the sand.

We switch between swimming and sunbathing until the light fails and everything begins to chill down. We start gathering our things, Florian and Inés standing by the car smoking yet another cigarette whilst Archie and I squish down the picnic blanket on top of all of the food we never ate.

When we finally clamber into the car and Florian begins to point the Citroën in the direction of home, Archie clears his throat. 'You guys should come for dinner.'

'Tonight?' I hear the abject horror in my voice and try to tame it back. 'Sorry, it just feels late.'

'Yeah! Why not?' Archie shrugs. 'It's my last evening when I can have a few drinks. I'll cook, my treat,' Archie persists.

'I don't have any plans,' Inés smiles.

I try to catch Florian's eyes in the rear-view mirror like before, but he doesn't reciprocate. Instead, he nods. 'Yeah, fuck it. Why not.' Florian throws away the comment as if it's nothing, as if he says yes to random dinner party invitations all the time.

I look at Archie, how bloody blind he is to what he's just walked into. I remember then, how sometimes it's so much easier to be single, how you never had to factor the wild card of someone else into your daily decisions. You can only blame yourself when you manage to fuck things up.

Chapter 21

I LEAVE ARCHIE TO the shopping whilst I focus on readying the apartment; I figure that if I can at least control the ambience of the evening then we might all be able to get out of this relatively unscathed. I pull the table away from the wall so that it can almost comfortably seat four people and then rummage around in the armoire for four placemats and plates that are at least roughly the same size. The one thing this place has in abundance is wine glasses; yes, not a single two match but once I have given up on uniformity a sort of unique charm settles over the table. I add my mint and basil plants in place of actual flowers, fold up some linen napkins and when Archie comes back into the room laden with bags from the supermarket, he looks suitably impressed.

'Wow, Avie, looks great.' He pecks me on the cheek.

'I just wish you'd maybe asked me before inviting the others. I had hoped for a repeat of last night… and the night before.'

Archie starts to unload the shopping onto the counter. 'To be honest, I didn't think they would actually say yes, I got the distinct impression that he wasn't my biggest fan.'

I light the candles. 'He was in a bad mood.' I don't know why I'm leaping to his defence. He *was* in a bad mood; more than that, he had been a bit of a prick, and yet here I am, telling Archie that he's imagining it.

'He did invite *us*, didn't he?' Archie stares into the fridge for a little too long. 'Well, I guess he invited you, he didn't know I was here.'

I feel a coolness settle over me. 'Your point?'

Archie turns round, frowning. 'He wasn't in a shit mood because I came, was he?'

I laugh. Well, I guess it's more of a manic cackle. 'Don't be silly.' I trim a rotting leaf from the basil. 'Besides, he bought Inés.' I bring the water jug over to the sink, aware of how flat my voice sounds and I hope that Archie isn't astute enough to notice. Florian had bought another woman, a woman who's beautiful and lovely and uncomplicated. And the fact he hasn't even mentioned that he's been seeing her, or bought her up in conversation makes me so pointlessly angry because haven't I done exactly the same thing with Archie?

'I guess.' He throws an onion in the air and catches it behind his back with a slick movement.

'Well look at you.' I wind my arms around his neck, kiss the exposed skin around his collar. 'What a talent.'

'You're a lucky girl.'

'Hmm.'

He pretends to look a little bruised at my lack of affirmation but gets distracted by the radio that I had recently discovered doubled up as a cassette player. 'Hey, this is a good song!' After reminding myself how a cassette actually worked (with some help from Google) we now had three albums we could play on demand. Two were French – Serge Gainsbourg of course, and Francois Hardy – the final, slightly more worn, tape was one I recognised from my mum's collection, *Tapestry* by Carole King. As the music had started up, I felt the whole album came back to me, song by song, until I am eight again and sitting in her car as she drives me to school, singing at the top of her lungs.

'Maybe we should...' He starts to sway me from side to side; I protest, try to pull away, but he clamps on to me harder until he starts to spin me around and we're laughing, really laughing, and it feels so bloody good to not have another evening eating dinner on my own.

We are interrupted by the buzzer.

'Just drink through the socialisation.' Archie refills my glass and sends me off to let our guests in.

*

'Hi.' I hover awkwardly at the apartment door before Florian quickly launches into his precise greeting. I think we could be active enemies and still we would be polite enough to kiss each other's cheeks.

'Evening.' He manages an emotionless smile.

'Ava, bonsoir!' Inés bombards me with a bouquet of flowers and a bottle of wine. She looks beautiful, wearing a little pinafore dress, her grown-out bob pinned back with a bow. Her angular features making her look like something out of a 1960s fashion magazine. Florian, in his familiar jeans and plaid jacket combination, looks so plain in comparison it's as if they exist on entirely different planets.

'It is so beautiful here.' Inés parades around the space, taking in the books, the view, the table. 'Don't you just love exploring places you never even knew existed?' She smiles at Florian who nods quickly and then turns to the counter where Archie is now cooking something with a worrying number of pans. I stall, wondering whether I need to be there to play referee or to just make sure Florian behaves, but Archie laughs. It's his real laugh, his shoulders sort of tremble with it, and then Florian looks a little more animated, talking in more than just monosyllables.

'Florian says you're only here for a month.' Inés jolts me back into reality, her fingers brushing through the volumes on the bookshelves.

'I was, only about a week left now.'

'That's a shame. It's nice to have some younger people around the place.'

I perch on the arm of the sofa watching her take in my home. 'Are you from here, I don't remember you before?'

'My grandmother lives here. She needed a bit of help and I needed a job so we kind of decided that I should come and stay with her for a while, work in a couple of the cafés, earn some money and then travel.'

'*We* as in Florian?' I gesture to him in the kitchen. He's examining one of the little paintings on the tiling.

'Florian?' she asks, her face screwed up in confusion. 'No, my parents. My family are from Bordeaux. My father's a teacher at the university – he put me in touch with Florian as a bit of company. I help them out at the café when things are busy.'

'So, you and Florian, you're not...'

'Not what?' she asks; clearly the language barrier extends to unspoken assumptions.

'You know... together?'

'Me and Florian?' She laughs at me, a loud, enthusiastic laugh. 'God no, he's old enough to be my dad... well almost.'

'Sorry, I just thought, when you turned up earlier.'

'I was as surprised as you were. He came into the bar yesterday lunchtime. He was in one of his moods.'

'His moods?'

'Oh you know, where he goes all quiet and serious. Something must have pissed him off, you know. Anyway, he stayed till the evening, and then before he went, he just kind of told me I was coming to the lake today. I wasn't going to say no, it's nice to do something different. This place starts to feel as if the walls are closing in at times.' I fixate on her description of Florian and his mood, the mood that started after he walked in on me dancing in my underwear with Archie in the next room.

Inés shrugs. 'So no, just friends, and barely that. You have nothing to worry about.' I notice how she takes me in then, our eyes meeting as if we are sharing some secret. I wonder if Florian has told her about the other night; I don't know why he would but still, I feel exposed.

'Oh, I'm not worried.' I shake my head and clutch my glass a little tighter to my chest.

'He's nice.' I look as she gestures to the kitchen. The two men have found a common purpose: Archie has his back to us, tending to a frying pan on the stove, Florian now has his head down in concentration, chopping up vegetables and depositing them in a salad bowl.

'Who?'

Inés tuts, 'Archie!'

'Oh, sorry! Yes, he's great.'

Archie announces that the food is ready; he calls us to our seats and instructs me to get another bottle out for dinner. I struggle with the cork until Florian rescues it from my grasp with a shake of his head.

Florian goes to sit as far away from me as possible but Archie points at the seat opposite me instead. 'Sit there, thought couples next to each other and all that.' I wince at the word, watch Florian's eyes flutter to mine for the briefest moment before fixing back onto his plate. Archie places a platter of chicken in brandy sauce on the table, followed swiftly by potatoes, the salad and a basket of bread.

We all thank Archie for his efforts who bats them away humbly.

As we start to eat, we descend into a hungry silence, only the sounds of cutlery on plates and wine glasses refilling occupy the table. I do my best to keep my eyes on the plate, to not let them wander to the figure opposite.

'Ava says your exhibition was good the other day,' Archie breaks the silence; I have come to the realisation that he will always find the need to fill a gap in a conversation.

'Yeah, there was a big crowd, makes a change. We normally have to beg people to come, that or invite the schools and then it just turns into a glorified nursery for teenagers who would rather be anywhere else.' Florian skewers a potato onto his fork.

'Are you working on anything else at the moment?' The piece of chicken turns to gristle in my mouth. I think of the sculpture sitting in Florian's studio, think of the counter that we both sat on, think of the way his skin felt under my fingers, how cold and unyielding his lips were. No matter how much I concentrate on chewing down the clod of chicken in my mouth, it won't give up; it catches in my throat. I splutter and cough until I can feel all eyes on me. Archie pounds on my back and I grab the napkin and deposit the contents of my mouth into it. When I look up through watery eyes, Florian shoots me an incredulous look that I know translates to something close to, 'Wow, doing a really good job of playing it cool.'

'Easy, babe,' Archie laughs as he fills up my water glass but I bypass it in favour of the wine instead. I rest my cutlery on the plate and hope he doesn't take offence that my appetite has immediately vanished.

'I'm working on something new but it's a while away from being finished. I have another exhibition in Bergerac tomorrow evening, same old stuff from before with a few additional pieces.'

'Are you going?' Archie asks me when I have returned to a normal colour.

'I didn't know about it,' I answer honestly. Florian shifts in his seat.

'So, Archie.' Florian changes the subject. 'What do you do?'

'I'm a business analyst. Consultancy mainly –finance.' He adds that last bit in as an afterthought.

'Impressive.' Florian's voice is muffled from a bit of bread.

'Not really, just got lucky and people haven't found me out yet.'

'He's lying,' I interject. 'He's great, won awards and everything.' I lean into Archie and he smiles gratefully at me.

'And how did you two meet?' Florian persists. My eyes linger on Archie's, whose gentle smile has now turned into a wry little grin, thinking back to that first awful night that we fell into each other's orbits.

He shakes his head, wipes the corner of his mouth with a napkin. 'Oh, it's a long and very boring story.'

Florian leans forward, resting on his elbows, chin nestled on top of his knuckles. 'Aren't they the perfect type for a dinner party?'

I shoot Florian a warning glance to stop but it's too late; Archie clears his throat. 'We met at a bar?' Archie draws out the word and then looks at me as if trying to gauge how much detail he should give. I appreciate his hesitation. It wasn't my finest evening.

'You don't know or…?' Florian asks pointedly.

'I think he's trying to protect my modesty.' I place a supportive hand on Archie's, put myself back in the firing line. 'It was a friend's thirtieth, his sister's. We were at this bar, he was there, we talked, I went home with him.'

I notice Florian flinch a little before he catches himself. 'Must have been love at first sight.'

'No!' I say quickly, a little too quickly. 'I mean I was *very* drunk.' Archie's hand grows a little limp beneath mine and he pulls it away, replacing it with his drink. 'But he's been amazing, really wonderful.' I try to wrestle him back. 'I'm very lucky that he didn't judge me too harshly for that one night.'

'So, you've been seeing each other for a while—'

'Jesus, Florian, what's with the questions!' Inés interrupts the assault and Florian relinquishes the conversation, leaning back in his chair as if he now knows everything he needs to.

'Sorry, I've never been good with small talk,' he shrugs, playing with the stem of his glass.

'Ava, I'm sorry to hear about your incident the other night.' Inés changes the subject, leaning over the table earnestly. I feel a discomfort start to prickle at my neck.

'Incident, what incident?' Archie pipes up with a mouthful of food. Inés looks immediately uncomfortable, aware that she has just put her foot in it.

'It's nothing bad,' I say quickly. 'It's the reason I don't have a car. I got into an accident but I'm fine.'

'You crashed the car?'

'She hit a deer so it wasn't really *her* fault.' Florian jumps to my defence and I'm grateful for it.

'Oh,' Archie falters, his face dropping slightly before he recovers, 'so you were in the car too?'

'Er, no!' I sweep in. 'He picked me up, sorted the car situation out, made sure I was okay.'

'That's great, thanks mate.' Archie looks visibly relieved.

'It's no problem,' Florian shrugs. 'Wasn't just going to leave her there, was I?' He laughs out the last bit to try to cover the sourness in his voice.

'No of course not, I just meant that it's nice…'

'We look out for each other, don't we, Ava?' It's the first time that Florian has held my gaze all evening.

'Yes.' I nod earnestly. 'Yes, we do.'

After dessert, Archie drains the dregs of the bottle and looks around at the apartment.

'Is that the last of it?' He directs the question at me.

'I think so.'

'Fuck. I didn't realise we would get through so much.' I think of the four bottles lined up on the table earlier and the bottles I'll need to take to the dechetterie tomorrow.

Inés bangs her hands on the table as if she has just had a momentous idea. 'There's wine at your café isn't there, Florian?'

'Yes,' Florian nods. 'Whisky too.'

'Now you're talking,' Archie says.

'Really, shouldn't we just call it a night?' I beg.

Florian shrugs. 'I don't mind getting it, I mean it's only around the corner.'

'You're sure?' Archie asks, not wanting to look like a bad host for sending his guest off into the night.

'Yeah, it's fine. Ava can keep me company.' I look around to see if there's someone else here called Ava, maybe he got Inés's name wrong? But Florian's eyes are fixed on me.

'Me?'

'Thought you might want to see it again, without other people there.'

'Oh… I don't…' I look at Archie who is looking slightly paler than he has done all evening.

'You should go, Ava,' Inés says softly.

'Yeah.' Archie's voice sounds strained. 'Yeah, you should go.'

Florian is already grabbing his coat and making his way out of the apartment.

'I shouldn't…' I step towards Archie. He slackens.

'Go on, it'll do you good to see it again, besides…' he leans into me, 'think of the book.' He presses a kiss into my cheek and jettisons me out of the apartment, leaving me tripping down the stairs after Florian.

Chapter 22

FLORIAN SWINGS THE KEYS in his palm. For a while it's the only sound that disturbs the peace of the Bastide. It's late and this place has fallen into its nightly hibernation. The supermarket's closed, the cafés have all closed, even the tabac is closed, and the only signs of life come from the occasional light emanating from a sporadic window.

'What book?' Florian asks as we turn the first corner.

'Sorry?'

'Archie, he said something about a book?'

'Oh.' It comes out as a squeak. 'I think it's just something from some self-help book he read, about saying yes to things,' I shrug, wondering if it sounds as transparent as it feels, but I refuse to get into this conversation now so instead I add it to the long list of things that I should probably address with my brother-in-law when we are on more neutral, comfortable territory.

'He's a nice guy.'

I nod enthusiastically. 'Yeah, he is.'

'Good cook too.'

'Glad you thought so, he put in a lot of effort, think he wanted to impress you.'

'Dresses well, amazing career…' I feel the conversation souring.

I stop walking, cross my arms in front of my body. 'Your point?'

He stops too, a little ahead of me, holds up his hands. 'No point, I'm just saying he's a very solid guy.'

'Okay.' I carry on until we're next to each other again. We

turn off the main street into the square and I can see the café in the far corner. 'Well, I'm glad you approve.'

'Oh, I don't.' He sort of laughs it out, a mean little snigger. I feel myself squirm under the comment.

'You don't approve of him?' I repeat as if I might have possibly misheard him, but he just shrugs.

'I approve of him, just not with you. Not that it matters of course.' He shrugs it away as if it's nothing, as if his words are just these simple little things that won't send me spiralling down some plughole of doubt and panic and pure fury. The café is a few feet away and we are forced to stand there as he pulls back the shutters, revealing the front door with its curtain drawn down and the closed sign hanging at an angle.

'Well, why? And you're right it doesn't matter, but why? What's wrong with him?'

He doesn't look at me, just starts passing the keys through his fingers until he finds the right one. 'I don't know.'

'Yes, you do!' It comes out as an exasperated little yelp. 'You always know, that's kind of your thing, the man who knows.'

He sighs as if this is all some massive inconvenience to him, to have to explain the most obvious thing in the world. He looks at me, points at my mouth. 'You just don't do the thing you did with Ettie.' Florian turns back to the café, slips the keys into the lock and goes to open it but I stop him with a firm hand on his arm.

'The thing?'

'Yeah, this.' He smiles, catching his bottom lip a little with his teeth and then with a hard tug the door opens. Florian strolls in, flicking the switches on the wall sending the lights fizzing into existence.

'I don't do that!' I tumble in after him, my finger pointing in his direction.

'No, you don't, that's why I said it. But you did.' When the final light illuminates the bar he turns to me, arms crossed, that frustratingly knowing grin tugging at his cheeks. 'With him.'

'Pfftt, you barely saw us.'

'I know but I notice things. That very first day I met you, when Etienne brought you to that dinner with Mum, it was plastered all over your face. I mean I know you never made a secret of being completely besotted with him, but your mouth always gave you away.'

I catch myself in the mirrored surround of the bar, my fingers protectively covering my lips. I have no recollection of ever doing that face, it's not like Ettie ever pointed it out, and I never looked at my own reflection with the same apparent adoration, but Florian's ability to tell the unflinching truth leads me to believing him. 'And I don't do it with Archie?' I sound disappointed.

'No.' Florian shakes his head firmly. 'You don't do it with Archie.'

Fuck. I am disappointed.

'But like I said, it doesn't matter, he doesn't know that and I'm sure you'll be happy and looked after and *safe*.' He starts to revert back to the Florian of minutes ago, the sarcastic one.

'Why do you make it sound like a bad thing?' I take a seat on one of the stools in the bar whilst Florian slips behind the Formica counter and reaches up to the shelf directly above us rooting around for the bottle.

'They're not bad things...' he groans, his arm at full stretch. His chest is in front of me, his shirt pulling up and revealing a dark line of hair and his navel. I look and then when I realise I'm looking, I turn my eyes to my wedding band. Something clinks and Florian makes a celebratory sound and places a bottle on the counter. 'Well, not necessarily.'

'Is that it?' I point to the bottle he's just brought down; it's half drunk and dusty.

'No, that bottle's over there, this is something else.' On his way back to me he grabs two glasses and puts them in front of us.

'We don't have time for this...'

'Just sit here for five minutes and drink.' He pours out a large measure and pushes the glass back to me.

I take a sip and then let my eyes wander away from Florian, start to take in where I have found myself. Nothing has changed. Florian's earlier comments had served as a wonderful distraction allowing me to be here without feeling the weight of the past sitting too heavily on my shoulders. Instead, being back here, bickering with a Grenaud, made it feel almost normal. I look at the door behind the bar, the one that would lead to a narrow wooden staircase and up to Ettie. I try to numb it all out, try to imagine that he is there, but it's getting harder and harder to do that now because three years is a long time, and I have built the person I am now around losing him, around that catastrophic bit of bad luck. The losing him is as much a part of me as the having him ever was.

I catch him watching me, probably evaluating whether I am about to break in some way shape or form. 'Is it hard, being here?'

'No,' I answer honestly.

'I put off coming for about two weeks after I arrived. I mean I was staying at my house promising Jules I'd start my shifts, but I couldn't bring myself to do it.'

'What made you?'

'Money mostly.' He smirks. 'I had none and I needed some. I got drunk, like drunk enough so that I could actually get here without bursting into tears.' At the mention of him crying my hand reaches out and squeezes his; he looks at it for a moment too long, but instead of pulling it away his fingers curl around mine. I don't hate it.

'Anyway, when I got here it wasn't as hard as I imagined. It's as if I finally knew that he really wasn't here any more. It was my last bit of hope, that he would come down slightly hungover, tell me off for freeloading and pour me a drink anyway. When I got here and he didn't materialise, well I knew it was done.'

I marvel at his transparency, how it feels like Florian has been able to see straight through me, gather up all those complicated little feelings and string them together into a sentence that I wanted to say. 'I think I've been imagining the same thing.'

'It was all a little easier after that.' He takes his glass and holds it up, inspecting the way the light pours through it. 'This was Ettie's bottle,' he says whimsically. 'He was given it on his thirtieth birthday. He never opened it, so I did it for him.'

'Is that allowed?'

'Well, no one else was going to open it. I save it for special occasions, things that Ettie would have wanted to toast. When France won the World Cup, when I sold my first commission… you.' He holds the glass closer to me. I hesitate, let the strangeness of it all wash over me. My husband's bottle of whisky, the one meant for him and his achievements, had now fallen into mine and Florian's hands. I let myself think about him, of what he would have made of this, the reunification. I'm sure he would have laughed, enjoyed the strangeness of it all, the closeness we had managed to find in each other. But, there's a discomfort there too that sits so closely to betrayal, an unshakeable feeling that I am doing something wrong just by being here. I used to find it comforting to think of him as some sentient force, finally knowing my innermost thoughts, watching my every move, but since that evening in Florian's workshop, that belief has become less and less reassuring.

'Santé,' I say as the glasses clink together, our eyes locking on to each other as we bring them to our lips to drink. Florian takes a small sip but I choose to swallow down the rest and then when the glass is empty, I slam it down onto the bar and untangle my hand from his. I don't want alcohol to blur the lines again; it makes me question things, like how dangerously easy it is to fall into an intimacy that actually scares me, or think about how much it had hurt when he hadn't kissed me back. I can avoid the shame-spiral when there's other people around, but when it's just us there's something else: a fuzziness, a stupid little voice telling me to do things that logical me would never do.

'We should get back!' I turn away from him quickly.

He looks frustrated but he manages to conceal it quickly. 'Why rush?' he challenges.

I slip from the stool. 'Archie will be waiting.'

'Fuck Archie!' he barks and my head twists to him, my mouth slightly lolling open at his coarseness.

'Florian!'

'After everything I told you, you're still going back to him?'

'Oh, come on, I'm not going to throw him away because I didn't do a particular facial expression in his presence.'

I go to the bar and pull the actual bottle of whisky from the cupboard and then stand expectantly at the door for Florian to follow but he stays rooted in his seat. 'You won't be happy with him, Ava.'

'You don't know that.'

'I do. I mean would you have even invited him out if you hadn't freaked out on me? You. Kissed. Me. Ava.' He accentuates each word and they radiate around the empty café. I look around alarmed as if it isn't as late as it is, and we aren't the only ones here. 'I mean, I didn't even kiss you back, I did the right thing.'

'The right thing?'

It's like this moment of clarity descends on him. He almost manages a smile, a sort of maddened look of acceptance. 'Or is that what this is about?' He slips off the stool.

'What do you mean by that?' I take a step back towards the door, gripping the bottle tightly in my hands.

'Should I have?'

'What, kissed me?'

'Yes, Ava. Should I have kissed you? Because then at least you would have a reason to be angry with me instead of just being pissed for no reason other than your own embarrassment.'

'That's not fair,' I reel at him. It isn't fair. He was the one that stopped it. He was the one that bought reason and logic to a situation that defied both of those things. To bring it all back up now would mean that he hadn't been as okay with the situation as he had claimed to be, or that he was questioning what my intentions had been in the workshop in the first place.

'No, what's not fair is you ignoring me then bringing some random guy from home to distract you, when I sat there and told you it was okay, that you didn't need to be embarrassed, like I got it, Ava, I got that you wanted Ettie, and I was there—'

'I didn't!' The words come out raw and ragged. There it is, the grand realisation I have been working towards, slotting into place all at the wrong time. It's the reason why Archie's here, the reason why I've been avoiding Florian, the reason why everything feels so wrong.

'Didn't what?' He knows. I know he knows but he wants me to spell it out.

'I didn't think you were Ettie. I didn't kiss you because I wanted to kiss him. I wanted to kiss you, okay? That's why this is all so fucked up!' It's only when the words echo back at me that I realise I've been shouting.

I watch the smugness evaporate from his face, his mouth forming and unforming words which never quite make it to the space between us. 'Ava—'

'And I am aware that that makes me the worst person in the entire world, that out of everyone left on this planet that I could have possibly made a move on, it was you. And I am aware that I have a man probably wondering why on earth we're taking so fucking long, who has been dying for me to commit to him for the longest time, and I am so close to fucking it all up.'

He looks guilty now and I realise that he does honestly think that Archie is a nice guy, not just some obstacle to happiness. He reaches for me, but I bat him away. 'He doesn't have to know...'

'I'm not talking about the last time. I'm talking about now, about what we're about to do.'

'What we're about to do?' he repeats, his eyebrows screwing up into a confused frown. It's infuriating how complicated he is making this, how much simpler it would all be if we stopped skirting around the obviousness of it all.

'Oh, don't pretend like you have no idea what I'm talking about. I'm talking about this *thing* that sits in this imaginary space between us, the thing that clearly won't quit, and I'm talking about what's going to happen, what was always going to happen when we left that apartment and came here, when we got in a room on our own together again.'

Finally, I have managed to say something that Florian could not predict, something I can't explain away with grief. Instead, he looks like I have slapped him.

'And you want to...' He is looking at me like I'm a child, like I don't know what I have just said.

I close the final few feet between us and when I'm within touching distance he reaches for my hands, examines them closely and winds me into him, his eyes locking with mine. He is trying to read me, trying to assess for any evidence of hesitation, but I keep my face flat. I have wanted this for longer than I care to admit, I just know it now. I can smell the fire burnt into his flannel shirt, see every freckle on his cheeks, hear how jagged his breathing is as if he has just run a flight of stairs. For a moment we exist in the gap, the little space between the before and the after, a space that will disappear forever when I give him my next answer.

'Yes, I fucking want to.'

It's hard to not be entirely intoxicated by the smile that radiates across his face, the sheer pleasure and relief all mixed into one as his hand reaches for my cheek, his fingers tangling in my hair as he strokes away the redness, marvels at me in a way that makes me feel as remarkable and extraordinary as one of his sculptures.

'Thank God,' he murmurs and we collide.

I know as soon as our lips meet that this is how people should always kiss. The whisky still lingers on our tongues, smoky and deep, and I can feel myself getting drunk on it. His lips break from my mouth and for a moment I think he's going to pull away again until he replaces my lips with my neck. Maybe I should be the one to stop this? Maybe it's my turn to have a conscience? But I can't fathom how I can give this up now.

He lets go of my face, moves his grip to my waist, pulling our bodies closer still. This is different; before it was a kiss, now there's more. He brings his lips back to mine and I groan at how good it feels, how every inch of my body hums, like it is trembling with an energy I never knew I possessed. His breath is becoming shorter, mine too. The elation of finally doing this is replaced by something else: longing, a desire for more.

He spins me round, presses me against the bar. My hands slide his jacket off his shoulders and he shrugs the last of it free from his body, leaving me to work at the buttons on his shirt. I manage three before he grows impatient and tugs it over his head. My hands go straight to his arms, feeling his warm skin under my fingertips. I press my lips into his neck in little staccato pulses down to his collarbone.

He senses the disparity between our nakedness and his hands tug at my t-shirt until it is whisked clean from my body.

'I lied earlier,' he mutters into my ear, his hands tracing their way around my bra strap. 'I was very interested in what your tits looked like.' He chuckles and it sends something spiralling inside of me. I kiss him harder than I had before, faster, my tongue finding his. He groans. My finger traces a line from his chest to his navel and down until I come to the buckle of his belt. I pull the end until it releases, and I rest my thumb on the hem of his jeans. I feel him hardening below me. And I want him. I want this.

And then Archie rings.

Chapter 23

'FINALLY. I WAS ABOUT to send a search party.' Archie's voice brings us both down to reality with a stark, treacherous little crash. Florian brushes his arm past mine, an innocent action but it still makes my cheeks sting.

Archie is standing by the sink, washing up the dinner plates. 'Sorry, didn't realise we'd been gone so long.' I linger by the entrance, watching both men in my apartment feeling terrifyingly responsible for them both.

'Where's Inés?' Florian hulks himself down on the sofa, his eyes darting around as if she might be hiding behind the table.

'She left about twenty minutes ago, said she had work in the morning.'

'Oh.' Florian looks a little shocked. I think we were both banking on letting Inés dominate the remainder of the evening until we could both go.

'Not a problem though, sure we can still have a nice time without her. You get the bottle?'

'Here.' I pull it out of my jacket pocket.

'Well, open it then.' Archie laughs at my awkwardness. 'I'll get the glasses, go sit down.' I do as he says and choose the armchair; it feels perfectly isolating and separate. Florian looks up at me; his hair is messier than it had been when we had left the apartment an hour ago and his fringe is falling over his eyebrows. He looks slightly apologetic and for a moment I wonder if he wants to take it all back, but with one hand he gestures for me to breathe, to calm down and I know that he is simply thinking of a way that we can both get out of this evening with the least amount of damage.

We had walked back in this kind of heavy silence, drunk from touch, bodies aching and heavy from unfulfilment. When we neared the apartment, I had slipped my hand into his and pulled him to a stop.

'I won't say anything,' Florian had answered before I even had the chance to ask. I knew I needed to tell Archie, but tonight wasn't the right time or place to break his heart. So, I had nodded gratefully, smoothed down my hair and then his hair and took a deep breath before climbing up the flights of stairs back to him.

Archie pours out three measures and hands them around the table,

'Cheers.' He proffers up his glass and Florian and I awkwardly extract ourselves from our seats to meet him.

'Santé.' Florian offers his native alternative, but it feels wrong in this language too. Archie downs his measure with a theatrical gasp at the end and then roots into the cabinet behind us, pulling out a pack of cards I hadn't realised were there.

'A game?'

'Of what?'

'Strip poker?' It takes a while for the joke to make itself evident on Archie's face, it's like there's a lag as he looks up at me with a blank face until a small smirk appears. 'Jesus, I'm only joking.'

'Sorry, it's just late, I'm tired.' I make my move, pray that he might get the hint. I look to Florian who positions himself at the corner of the sofa, ready to leap up and grab his coat.

'Bullshit.'

'Sorry?' I look at him, startled.

'The game, a round of bullshit.' Archie gestures to the cards, and I notice how hard my heart is pounding. I look at Florian who is once again miming at me to calm down.

'Oh, I don't remember how to play.'

'Course you do, it's easy.' He starts to shuffle the cards, splitting the deck and running them through his hands, fanning and dividing, fanning and dividing until he snaps them back into one pile.

'One game,' Florian concedes. He has the cool head of someone who has found themselves in situations like this before, an attitude that I – a chronic, anxious overthinker – can only dream of.

Archie starts to deal out the cards.

'You two okay? You look a little… flustered.'

'No, we're fine,' Florian answers flatly.

'Ah.' Archie smirks. 'Do it a lot, do you?'

'Do what?' I ask not liking how his words are slurring, how he looks bedraggled and undone like he has spent the last half an hour waiting impatiently, thinking of all of the things we could be doing.

'Oh come on, you know.' He takes another shot of whisky that I hadn't seen him pour. 'Use your dead husband's café as an excuse to hook up… or is it the first time? I'm assuming you guys have fucked before, yeah?'

My head shoots up to Florian; his coolness has dissipated and his wide, panicked eyes scream at me to say something. 'Archie…' I try to find the words. I think of lying but what good would that do? He knows, he's not stupid, we must reek of it. He throws his cards down, gets to his feet, his hands go to his head, his face lights up with a manic, exasperated laugh.

'Fucking hell, you aren't even going to deny it? I thought you might have at least spun me a good line, Ava, told me something that I could have unravelled or at least believed for a couple of weeks!' He bends down to the table and pours himself another larger measure. Florian's hand hovers near it. I wonder if he's going to say something, tell him that adding alcohol into this mess isn't going to make anyone more coherent, but he thinks better of it.

'I… don't want to lie to you.' I smooth my hair back with my hands and rest them on my temples.

'No, you really are a decent person, you would just rather cheat on me instead.' The word riles me a little; we exist together here, but before this weekend I didn't give a shit if he was seeing someone else, in fact I encouraged it. To call it *cheating* evokes images of sordid sexts and work colleagues. 'It's not cheating… we aren't—'

'Together?' he finishes for me. 'We aren't together, right,' he mutters and then rounds on the sofa, giving it a swift kick. 'Are you actually serious right now, Ava?'

'Look… It wasn't her fault…' Florian gets to his feet, his hands now trying their hardest to tell Archie to calm down, take it down a notch, but he fails miserably.

Archie's attention fixes onto Florian. 'You don't get a say in this, you smug bastard, you got what you wanted so fuck off.' I stand up then, take a step towards Archie.

'Don't speak to him like that!'

'Did our conversation the other day mean nothing to you? I poured my heart out to you and you go and do this?'

'I know, I know, I'm so sorry Archie. I never meant for it to happen…'

'Oh give over, you don't just slip and fall onto someone's cock.'

Florian moves closer, putting himself between Archie and me. 'It's fine.' I try to calm him down. 'I didn't… we didn't have sex.' I shake my head. 'It's not this cold and calculated long drawn-out affair, it's today, just today and things just got out of control, and we didn't have time to really stop and think…'

'I've waited for you, Ava, for so long! Waited for you to be ready to commit, not pushed you, treated you well, picked up the phone whenever you wanted to moan about *him* and when finally you say you're ready, when you let me in, you let him in as well!'

'You haven't done anything wrong, you did everything right.'

'No, I was too fucking naïve. Tried far too hard to be the nice guy. I never thought you could be such a bitch.'

The word hurls itself around the room and comes to rest by my feet. I go to look at Florian, warn him not to do it, but he isn't there; instead he's rushing at Archie, grabbing a handful of his shirt in his fist. They slam into the wall and a picture frame smashes on the floor.

'You don't talk to her like that,' Florian spits, his voice almost terrifyingly quiet. I expect Archie to pale away from the confrontation, but his eyes light up a little.

'I mean fair play, Florian, your brother's Mrs, that was probably the reason Etienne never saw you back then, the poor guy knew what a sleaze you were.' Florian tightens his grip.

'You don't say his name.' He is losing his cool, unravelling. 'Don't say his name.' He stabs him with a finger in the chest. Archie's smirk doesn't fade, I think he wants me to see it, wants me to see this side of Florian, but I have seen a side to Archie too, one that I would never have seen until it would have all been too late.

I put my hand on his shoulder. 'Florian, let go.' I watch his brow furrow as if I'm a million miles away, not standing an inch away from his ear. 'Florian – please.'

He releases and stands back.

'Fuck this.' Archie holds his hands up, gathers his jacket, phone and the remainder of the bottle on the table. He goes to the front door and looks back at me. It's only now that I see his eyes are rimmed with red. 'And fuck you.'

The door slams behind him on his way out.

Florian and I both stare at the door for a moment, the sound echoing around the apartment for longer than it should. 'Are you okay?' he asks.

'You should go too.' I ignore his concern.

'Me?'

'Yes. It's late and I'm tired and…'

'What, so I leave and then you can avoid me for another week and then when we do see each other again, you'll just pretend that nothing's happened?'

'Well, shouldn't we?' I turn on him.

He looks shocked, more shocked than when Archie had found us out. 'What do you mean?'

'Isn't it better if we pretended like it hadn't?'

'Are you fucking serious, Ava?'

'Look, perhaps it's best if we just have some space.'

'Some space?'

'Yes, space, and just some thinking time, you know? Look, Florian, I like you, I do, but we can't seriously think this is going to do anything but backfire on us. I'm leaving in just over a week, Florian. Surely, it's best if we don't try to complicate things any further...'

'Don't use that excuse.'

'Okay, well how about this one: you're his brother, Florian, I'm his wife, in what world would this ever work?'

I watch as a darkness pours over his face, it was the same instinctive cloud that materialised when Archie had said Ettie's name. 'You know what? Fine.' He grabs his phone and keys from the coffee table. 'I'm done. You want time then you can have it, all of it.' He grabs his jacket and exits, leaving me alone in the apartment, wondering at what point in the night I managed to fuck it all up quite so catastrophically.

Chapter 24

I MANAGE TO DOZE off in sporadic, thirty-minute stretches until the sun beats through the curtains and I give up entirely on sleep. My head is a foggy minefield; for every delicious vignette from the café, of flesh and relief and excitement, there are two from the apartment, of Archie and his anger, of Florian's sad, dejected face.

I reach into my bedside drawer for my diary and release it all onto the page until it's all there, in black and white, every detail and realisation taunting me.

My phone vibrates. I half expect to see that it's Florian, getting there before me, but instead my mum's contact card appears. I feel a comforting relief wash over me and I shelve the diary back in the bedside drawer.

'I thought you would still be asleep.' Her voice is full of surprise.

'No, I'm awake.'

'Well, there's a nice surprise. Is it sunny with you? The weather lady said there was a heatwave over Europe at the minute.'

'Yes. It's really nice,' I reply flatly.

'You are getting out of the apartment, aren't you, making the most of it?'

'Yes, Mum.'

'I have visions of you locking yourself in a dusty little attic with just your laptop for company.'

'Not quite.'

There's a longer, heavy pause. 'Are you okay, love?'

I let the silence speak for itself.

'Ava, what's the matter?'

'Nothing, Mum, just saw some friends last night, have a bit of a hangover.' I try to restrain the words that come out at first as a little whimper.

'Florian?' Mum asks. His name physically hurts me, creates this aching chasm that exists in a part of my body that I have no control over.

'Yeah, and some others.'

'On a Sunday?' The judgment starts to pepper through her tone.

'Yeah, I...' My train of thought is interrupted by a quiet knocking at the door. 'Mum, I've got to go, I'll call you back later.' I cut her off before she can protest.

'Hi.' Archie's head materialises around the door. He looks like the old Archie, softer, apologetic.

'Hi.' I swallow back the emotion, try to make my face look as sorry as I possibly can manage at seven in the morning with a burgeoning hangover.

'I need to grab my clothes.' He gestures to the pile on 'his' side of the bed.

'Okay.'

'Thanks.' He enters, starts to root around in the pile of clothes for things that look like his.

'I didn't hear you come in last night.'

'It was just after two. Slept on the sofa.'

'Right.' I nod slowly, pulling the covers up to my neck as if he hasn't seen what's underneath before. 'Where did you go?'

'Nowhere really. I walked around a lot, found a nice little bench to sit on for a bit, came back when I ran out of battery.' He picks up the last remaining pieces, folding them half-heartedly.

'He didn't stay then?' Archie gestures to the empty space in the bed next to me, a space that he had slept so happily in the night before.

'No.' I shake my head. 'No, he left after you.'

'Well, looks like we all had lonely nights.' He goes to leave but something is stopping him, he lingers in the doorway and for a moment I wonder if he's going to tell me it's all okay, that he knows it was just a lapse of better judgement. 'I need to apologise, Ava, I shouldn't have called you a bitch, that was uncalled for. I was drunk and upset but I'm not that kind of guy.'

'*You* don't get to apologise!' I shake my head fervently. 'I *am* a bitch, a messed-up, psychotic bitch.' My nails claw a little at my shoulder leaving sharp, hot lines. The pain is a relief.

He chuckles at the floor and shakes his head. 'No, you're not a bitch – you *are* messed up, I wouldn't go as far as psychotic, but a little messed up.' When he looks up, my heart aches because there he is, the nice, safe, loving man who wanted me, who answered the phone when I called, who came out here at the drop of a hat because I asked him to. It would all be so perfect if I didn't know in my bones that Florian had been right, that it would never quite be enough.

'I know this sounds like a petty excuse, and I would punch someone if they said it to me, but I really don't know why it happened, Archie, I don't remember making the decision to do it. It just suddenly was happening and…' Archie shakes his head, thumps himself down on the corner of the bed, plays with his phone charger.

'Anyone else could see it happening from a mile off.' He looks at me, at my apparent confusion, because then he tuts a little at my obliviousness. 'It's weird because I think I knew even before I came out here; he riled you up too much for it to be nothing. But I wanted to ignore it, believe that it was just the grief talking. I definitely knew when I first met him though, had that twist in my gut that was screaming at me that this wasn't right.'

'Why?'

'I don't know, I mean he was this attractive guy who was standing in your apartment grinning wildly at you dancing in your knickers. And the fact that he looked quite so crestfallen when I walked in, I mean I did enjoy that bit.'

'I didn't know… not really. '

'Oh, I believe you on that front. And I believe that you really did need time, that you needed to take things slow and that you were holding out for a moment where it all felt right between us and I thought we were going to get there. I think if he hadn't turned up, Ava, then I would have worn you down and we would be something.'

'Yes.'

'And what a terrifying thought.' He smirks.

'No, it's not!' I reach out to him, grab his arm. He looks at my hand with a kind of sad familiarity. He pats it softly, removing any hint that once we were in this bed together, legs wrapped around each other, and I was as close to happy as I had been in months.

'I mean for me, to have given everything to a woman who never actually loved me.' I go to object but what can I say that would make it better? I don't love him, I'm not sure I ever would. It isn't his fault, it's not mine either, just a sad, unpleasant little fact.

He gets to his feet with a groan. Clearly his head feels about as heavy and aching as mine does. I think of the three whisky shots he managed almost simultaneously before the verbal assault; at least I had stopped drinking at the café.

'On paper we would have been good together,' he says as he reaches the doorway.

I nod furiously in agreement. 'On paper we would have been the best.'

'Just that "on paper" isn't exactly what romance novels are made of, are they?'

'No.' I manage a little smile. 'No, I guess they're not.'

Chapter 25

'WHAT'S HAPPENED NOW THEN?' The American asked, straightening the napkin onto her lap and nodding an appreciative thanks as the waiter at the hotel restaurant places her martini down in front of her.

'How do you know something's happened?'

'Ava darling, I would love for you to have come here out of the goodness of your heart, to trust that you just wanted to treat an old lady to lunch, but I think I know you a bit better than that by now, and by the look of you…' she takes me in from my unbrushed hair to my un-ironed shirt that I had picked up off the pile on the floor, 'you've had an interesting weekend.'

I chew my cheeks a little, nod slowly, weighing up how much I want to tell her, how much she needs to know.

'Shall we start with your London lover?' She swirls the olive around in her drink not looking up at me.

'Left this morning.'

'Amicably?'

I cringe. 'Not quite.'

'And Florian?'

I bite my lip. 'Even less so, if that's possible.'

She leans back, her hands thrusting theatrically into the air. 'Well, well, well, did bringing the man from home to the man in France backfire in your face? Who could see that one coming?'

'Yes, thank you for that.'

'So.' She goes back to swirling her olive. 'I'm assuming that you figured out that Florian might like you more than you anticipated?' I stiffen a little at the realisation of quite how obvious it had all been. Archie had felt it, Inés too, and this entire time my closest friend had watched me try and fail to navigate my way around it.

'I figured that bit out just as he was taking off my shirt.' The American chokes a little on her martini.

She leans closer to me. 'Not with them both…?' she whispers, her eyes the size of saucers.

'No!' I exclaim, horrified that she could even suggest such a thing.

She looks relieved but plays it off with a shrug. 'Who knows what you young people are up to nowadays; all I ever see when I open up my magazines are articles about open relationships, threesomes, people fancying saucepans.'

'Pans…' My mind wanders. 'Look, it was going fine, Archie was here, we had a nice time, a really nice time – just us two. Then Florian turns up and invites me to the river the next day, except he doesn't realise Archie's here, so ends up inviting both of us.'

The American chuckles. 'How marvellous.'

'Well, Archie's just trying to be nice, make friends, and he suggests that Florian comes to dinner with Inés and all of a sudden last night there's all four of us, around a table.'

'Now that's a dinner party I would like to have attended.'

'Well, I wish you had because maybe you could have persuaded me not to go to the café alone with Florian for a bottle of whisky, where he basically told me that I wasn't in love with Archie and never would be, which apparently is a massive aphrodisiac because five minutes later I had my legs around his waist.'

During the juicier details, The American has managed to lean in a little closer, her necklace swinging into her salad. 'So you… consummated it?'

'Consummated?' I screw my face up at the officialness of the word. 'We're not Tudors, and no, we were interrupted by Archie ringing me asking where on earth we were.' I feel the residual shame of that evening set back in. I have thought of all of the different ways I could have handled things, been more honest with Archie, been more honest with Florian. Quite frankly, honesty would have got me through pretty much unscathed, but it's hard to be honest about something that you don't entirely understand yourself.

'I see…'

'And then we had the delightful task of walking back to the flat where Archie had pretty much become Poirot and called us out over a card game, shouted a bit and then stormed out. His flight took off an hour ago.'

'And Florian?'

The look of devastation that involuntarily appears on my face says more than words ever can.

'The book?' she frowns.

'What?'

'Did he find out about your book?'

'No.' I swallow hard. 'We never got close to that.' My throat becomes taut. 'I… I told him that it would never work and that we should maybe just stay out of each other's way for a bit.'

'Well, what did you do that for?' She almost slams her hands on the table and once again we have become the main entertainment of the small restaurant.

'Because it's mad. It's totally, unbelievably mad to think that anything could happen. He's my husband's brother! I mean surely there's some rule somewhere that says it can't happen, and even if there isn't, I'm damn sure that morally it's wrong.'

'Who says?'

'Every fibre in my body.'

She dabs her lips with her napkin and then leans back in her chair taking me in. 'Can I tell you something?' she says after a minute.

'Of course.'

'Did you know that I once was entwined in my own little love triangle?'

I try not to let my head get too carried away in the imagery. 'You were?'

'Well don't look so surprised, sweetie, I'll have you know

I was a catch in my day.' I sit back, skewer a tomato into my mouth.

'Who were the eligible bachelors then?'

'Wallace – he was a property lawyer in New York, fairly handsome but very straight-laced, the kind of man that the 1960s sort of ignored. And there was Jack – we had been friends since school, he owned land in Maine, it's all vineyards now, made a buck or two I can tell you that now.'

'Which one did you pick?'

'Wait a minute now, there was another name in the mix.'

I raise my eyebrows, play with the stem of my glass. 'You really were a catch.'

She ignores my disbelief, trades it instead for more details. 'There was a French art student who was staying at Jack's parents' house you see, had been there for a few months and well, let's say I was a fan of their work. We had a lot of fun, I learned a bit of French and tried to paint but I was next to useless. We had eight weeks together until I had to make a decision, whether I stayed over in the States, married Wallace or Jack, or whether I ran away to Paris and said goodbye to the life I had spent twenty-four years living.'

'And you chose *the artist*?' I roll my eyes.

'I chose Jack,' she says quietly and a little too quickly.

'What, why?'

'Because I was a smart girl too, Ava. I looked at my life, realised how lucky I was, looked at how much I had to lose, at how my family would never speak to me again, how much harder I would make my life if I went with the choice my heart wanted me to make. I was too smart for my own good. I married Jack.'

'Were you happy?'

'Mostly.' She swirls something in her drink. 'He was a good man, we rubbed along just fine, better than a lot of our friends, probably because we never bothered to complicate our friendship with silly things like passion.'

The conversation has drifted into unfamiliar territory for us. I am used to being the centre of the inquisition; it was a comfortable space for us, her squeezing out my feelings, meeting each one with a quick quip or incredulous eyebrow, but this is deeper, realer, and I realise that she isn't somebody who opens up her own life as quickly as I open up mine.

'Did you keep in touch with the artist?'

'Yes, we wrote to each other every year on our birthdays.'

I manage a soft little smile. 'And did you ever see him again?'

The American chuckles into her salad. 'Jack and I were married for forty years. Did it all properly you know – till death do us part – and then I was seventy sitting in a big house with more money than we ever needed and no one to pass it down to, so I did the first brave thing I had done since I was born: I booked a flight to Paris and made it my mission to find my artist.'

I imagine her navigating Charles de Gualle with a set of those antique trunks that wouldn't be out of place on the Titanic. 'And did you?'

'Yes.' She grins, her whole face lighting up. 'I found them alright, here of all places, living in a tiny little attic apartment on Rue Saint Jacques.'

The name of the road. My road. 'Wait…' I screw up my face, trying to piece together the fragments of a story with the fragments of conversations we had had when we met. 'Your artist's name was…'

'*Her* name was Bluette, yes.' She knows she has floored me, knows that her story has destroyed the little picture I had been drawing in my head and replaced it instead with a million questions.

'She was your "*friend*".' I roll my eyes, frustrated that I hadn't put two and two together before.

'That's what we called each other, it was ironic of course and true all at the same time. It was easier for two girls to co-exist together than it was for the boys, we just looked like companions who liked to eat dinner together a lot.'

'So, you were together, eventually, after all that?'

She nods enthusiastically. 'Yes. This place was a little too quiet for me back then so we only came back when we needed to have a little rest. We travelled together, visited museums and galleries in far-flung cities. We went everywhere: Egypt, Greece, Kenya, hell even Peru, and we did it all together.' And then a sadness passes over her. 'And then Blu got ill, four years ago, so we came back here to rest thinking that maybe she would get better but...' Her eyes are glassy at the memories and I reach for her hand. She lets me and I squeeze it. 'We were old ladies by the time we eventually got to it and it wasn't fair because we had wasted so much of our lives on other people.' She pauses, gathers herself. 'So... you see, Ava, why I have such an issue with you saying that you can't even try to be with Florian because there's some imaginary moral compass that you are judging your actions by, because I used the same compass and it robbed me of a life that I so deserved and wanted.'

'I'm so sorry.' I know how empty and pointless those words are but sometimes there really isn't anything else to say.

'Don't be sorry.' She shakes her head. 'We found each other at the end, when it mattered.'

'When did she... pass?' I find myself making the same face that people have made for me so many times over the years.

'Oh, she hasn't.' The American pales a little, looks down at her bracelet and then when she looks back up at me she has readjusted, drawn back on her smile. 'Alzheimer's. She's in a facility in Toulouse, near her nieces; they were close to her, like daughters really, wanted her near them. I couldn't argue with that, considering I had missed so much. I couldn't face being in that apartment, it didn't make sense without her so I came up with my little arrangement here.'

We are silent for a moment. It's like all the noise and bustle of the restaurant quietens as we try to find our way back to our conversation. 'My point is, Ava, I know how it feels, to be on the precipice of something that scares you. And I think – no, I know – that you have been numbed to the possibility of feeling something other than sadness for far too long, and that you have told yourself, subconsciously or not, that this numbness is your last bastion of grief. But Florian has scuppered your plan because you do feel something with him, you feel everything with him. You said it before the last time you visited me, you said, "I just feel." It wasn't an unfinished sentence, it was everything you wanted to say: he makes you feel. And how utterly terrifying it is to feel again.' The tears start to slip down my face and I let them go.

'You're rather wise, you know.' I sniff back the sob.

'I try my best.'

I shake away the emotion, steeling myself at the memory of how he looked when he left last night. 'You should have seen his face yesterday, he's done, I've ruined whatever it was that we had or could have had.'

She squeezes my hand again and I look at hers, her skin, the thickness of tracing paper, weighed down with a multitude of silver rings. 'I don't claim to know much about men but I do know, in my bones, that if you showed up at his exhibition tonight in a low-cut dress with a sort of sad little smile on your face then he would forget everything he said fairly quickly.'

'And then what, what do we do after that?'

'What's with the labels, the destinations? You don't *do*, you just *be*.'

Chapter 26

THE AMERICAN TAKES ME to her room which on closer inspection is bigger than my entire apartment. She instructs me to sit at the desk with a large vanity mirror and then proceeds to hurl dresses out of her wardrobe trying to find something that 'might work'. I have tried objecting, tried to say that I'm pretty sure I could just wear the same thing I wore at the last exhibition but she had looked mildly horrified, so I knew there was little point in objecting further.

'You do your make-up.' She gestures to the array of products neatly stacked around the vanity with labels like Chanel, Dior, Yves Saint Laurent.

'Erm…' I pick up a lipstick that's probably worth more than my entire make-up bag contents combined. 'Are you sure?'

'Honey, just get to it. We don't have the luxury of time here.'

I watch as she glides around her room, another tasselled sleeve billowing behind her. She moves effortlessly, quickly, with a new sense of purpose. She purses her lips at the hangers, holds dresses against shoes, bags, necklaces and then either adds them to the pile on the bed or discards them back to their hangers.

'Now you've obviously got a bit more meat on your bones.' She gestures to her very slim figure, to where her bosom probably used to be. 'But these should do.'

I stop trying to patch up my eyeliner and turn to the mountain of 'options'.

'There's dozens.'

'Well let's narrow it down. What colour?'

'Black.'

'Revolutionary.'

'Well, I don't exactly want to look like a complete stranger, this is already more effort than I normally put in.'

'Praise the lord.' She holds her hands together and gestures to the heavens. 'Now come over here and try this on.' She holds up a long black silk gown that I fear has an actual train.

'Anything but that.'

'Oh, live a little.'

'What about this?' I hold up a simple black dress with a collar that hadn't made it out of the wardrobe.

'I wore that to Jack's funeral.'

'Perfect.'

'Oh no you don't. What about this?' She thrusts a mini dress in my direction.

'Why do you even have this?'

'It was on sale, you never know when it might have come in handy.'

'No chance.'

'Well, there's always…' Her voice trails off. 'Grab the box from under my bed won't you.' She gestures to the king-sized bed and its ornate linen headboard.

I do as she says and my hands fix on a white cardboard box tied in a dusky pink ribbon with the words 'Dior' printed along its length in cursive lettering.

'Shut up.' My mouth falls open. I may not know much about fashion, or go to the same lengths that she does to present myself to the world, but I know this: I know that in this box there is the promise of something more beautiful than I had ever dreamed of wearing.

'I bought it on my honeymoon.' She smiles as I open the lid and stroke away the crepe paper, thankfully revealing black fabric. I pause, look at her, fearful that she is just being nice, looking to see whether she actually wants to let me and my uneducated, unfashionable self touch it, but she just smiles warmly.

'Well, go on, the taxi's here in twenty minutes.'

I unfold the fabric, heavy and expensive, and hold it out at arm's length, taking in the simplicity, how utterly breath-taking it is and similarly so unlike anything The American has ever worn in my presence.

'It's got sleeves, three-quarter lengths, square neck, all very sensible.' She lists off its features.

'Are you sure…'

'Just try it on.' I do as she says and slip off my jeans and shirt and then stand into the dress, pulling it up over my body. I try to manipulate my hands into the arms and then when I shimmy it over my shoulders, I reach for the zip but find only buttons.

'Here.' She moves to my back, and I feel her trembling hands slowly but surely fix the dress to me, button by button. I expect us to get to a point where it struggles to do up, where my unimpressive chest might still pucker its fabric, it is entirely nonsensical to me that something like this could fit me, but The American pats my shoulder and smooths out the fabric so that it sits flush over my shoulders.

'There, perfect fit, let me take a look.' I step back to allow her to take me in. 'You look beautiful.' I wonder if it's a trick of the light but there are tears in her eyes. 'Here, go take a look.' She gestures to the full-length mirror and when I do, I almost can't believe what I'm seeing. The woman looking back at me is a stranger – refined, elegant, a grown up – and she does look beautiful.

'I have never worn anything so lovely in my entire life.'

'Not even on your wedding day?' she asks, her eyebrows drawn up into a look of concern. I smirk, think of the dress I had bought the night before in Mango, cream because my mum had threatened to disown me if I didn't. She was already put out by the fact that it was going to be a registry affair and that our reception consisted of a meal at Antonio's down the road with twenty friends in attendance. She had asked me no less than six times if I was pregnant that weekend.

'Not exactly, I wore…'

'I don't think I even want to know.' The American stops me before I can disappoint her further but softens once I start twirling around, feeling the weight of the skirt flutter by my calves.

'Now there's a petticoat somewhere…'

'No!' I answer all too quickly. 'This is fine, this is perfect.'

'For once my dear, I completely agree with you. Now sit in that chair.'

'Why?'

'Just do as I say.'

I sit down and she scurries back over to me, her hands going to my hair, pulling out the claw clip and letting the knotty reality of my hair fall. She tuts at it and combs her nails from the roots to the ends.

'Now normally us girls would use rollers but we don't have time for that. No, I think we'll have to do *the trick*.'

'The trick?'

'Bluette called it the French Trick. She said it was a time-sensitive solution to looking "put together".'

'I like it.'

'Now, head back, pass me the brush.' I do as she instructs and watch her, face screwed up in concentration as she starts to pull strands together, smoothing my hair down against my scalp with hair spray, until she starts to twist it in her now rather dexterous hand and pins it to the back of my head.

'I can't remember the last time someone did my hair like this.'

'Not your mother?'

'I was never really the daughter that got her hair done,' I shrug. 'She probably would have liked me to be, but I've come to realise that parents don't often get the child they envisaged having.'

'Now who's sounding like the sage?' She looks at me in the mirror, a mistiness transcending over her. Her hand rests on my shoulders, giving me a reassuring little squeeze. 'Will you do?'

'I think this passes as making an effort, thank you.' I crane my neck and press my lips into her powdery cheek. She closes her eyes and takes it in.

'One more thing.'

She reaches around in a drawer and pulls out a necklace with some blue stones scattered around the neckline. 'I think you should tell him.' She says as she struggles with the clasp of the necklace.

'Tell him what?'

'Why you're really here.'

'I'm trying to get him back not scare him off forever.'

'Don't you think that he should know? Then you can start on neutral ground. Secrets aren't good, Ava, they turn splinters into vast, horrible chasms.'

I shake my head. 'I will tell him, just not tonight.'

'But…'

'Thank you for your help.' I reach for her hand and squeeze it tightly and I watch as her resolution breaks a little, knows that her pleading is falling on deaf ears for tonight.

She straightens her own outfit and then goes to her phone, pressing one button and then waiting patiently by the handset until there is the faint crackle of another voice picking up.

'Your carriage awaits.'

'Maybe I'll just stay here…'

'Oh no you don't.' She reaches into her bedside cabinet, pulling out a bottle of clear liquid. 'Dutch courage.'

'Thanks.' I take the glass she offers and neck it back. 'You should come,' I half offer, half plead.

'Not tonight. Tonight's about you. Now get outta here.' She slaps me on the arse, propelling me towards the door.

Chapter 27

IT'S A FORTY-MINUTE DRIVE to Bergerac, the only city in a fifty-mile radius. It feels refreshingly large, cosmopolitan almost, the old sandstone buildings next to glass offices, buses driving past people cycling home from work. The taxi pulls up directly outside the gallery where a few people are mingling with cigarettes.

A middle-aged woman looks up as I slam the taxi door a little too hard; she takes me in – the dress and my nerves – and reassures me with a small half smile, and it is enough to persuade me that this is a good idea, that I can walk through those doors.

Inside it is starkly modern, the walls are white, the floor is white, the ceiling's white. It feels for a moment like someone's interpretation of heaven, the brightness almost blinding as my eyes adjust. The crowd is different here too, infinitely better dressed than at the last exhibition, the men all in suits, the women in dresses so no one blinks an eye at me, and I feel as if I am wearing camouflage, a woman who is meant to be here, a woman who normally looks like this.

'Madame.' A waiter in all black hands me a flute of champagne. I take him in, think of The American's story of the naked waiters and stifle a smile.

'Merci.' It's nice to hold something in my hand, a distraction.

I take in the room, all of it, start to focus on the little spaces that have been created with some organised seating, pedestals with different multicoloured pieces of art on them. I look for Florian but there are too many people milling about. Instead, I decide to work my way around starting by the door, hoping that I might be struck with some inspiration of what I might actually say when I do see him because, other than the initial words of 'I'm sorry,' I had been drawing a blank. Obviously, I could just recycle what The American had managed to spout out at dinner, but I'm not sure I could convince Florian that I can be that brutally honest.

And then I see him, surrounded by suits. Next to him, the same sculpture as before except this time there are more people around it, admiring it, admiring him. I stand back, try to tune out the background noise and catch the conversation. He has always been more animated in his native tongue; his hands come to his midline, accentuating word after word. He says something, the crowd laughs, he looks pleased with himself and then his eyes wander around his space in the gallery, gauging what's a success, which of his drawings is starting a conversation. His eyes pass over me at first, this absent, polite smile on his face that he must give to all prospective purchasers, but then I watch as he stiffens, stops, rooted in his place. Florian swallows hard and then his eyes drift back to me.

We stand there for a moment, eyes locked, him probably wondering if it is actually me, and me – well I'm trying to figure out if he looks mildly horrified or slightly pleased. The crowd of people around him are still talking, but he looks like he's forgotten all about them; instead his lips pull into a wide grin, the kind that is impossible to fake. Someone in the crowd says his name but he doesn't waver, so instead they turn to see where his gaze has fixed itself, turn to me. I know I'm smiling too; it's as if I'm watching myself exist, aware of everything my body is doing but not quite being able to control it.

'Florian!' the admirer calls again. I gesture to his audience, and it breaks the trance. He blushes, looks at the faces, a couple more astute admirers have knowing grins on their own faces.

'Pardon,' he apologises with a little shake of his head. *'Voudriez-vous m'excuser?'* He slips through his audience.

'Please don't abandon your fans on my account.' My voice cracks a little from disuse and nerves as he meets me.

He dismisses them with a wave of his hand. 'There will be others.'

'You sound so sure.'

He looks at his feet and then brings his face back level with mine, a mischievous little shimmer in his eye. 'My admirers have a habit of sticking around, even if they say they're not interested.'

'Stupid admirers.'

'I've grown quite fond of them myself.'

I let the comment wash over me, try to notice how it feels, how it sticks to me, the strangeness of the relief it brings, and then I think of his face last night when I told him to go.

'Florian, I need to…'

He shakes his head and swallows the last of his drink, resting it on one of the waiters' trays. 'Not here,' he says, grabbing my hand and pulling me through the crowd and some doors onto a small courtyard, with string lights around the olive trees.

There are a few other people milling about, smoking, on phone calls, getting some air but there is an intimacy here that was lacking in the echoing room of the gallery. He leans back against a large plant pot, his eyes meet mine again, his boyish grin returns and it's infectious. I bite my lip, look down, try to play it cool because there's things that need to be said.

'You came,' he says gently.

'I came.'

'You look…'

'Ridiculous?' I interrupt before he can finish.

'No!' he says fiercely. 'No, you look beautiful. I mean seriously beautiful.' I know I'm blushing, I can feel it, the way my cheeks are on fire, the way the heat is thundering down my body. It's a heat so consuming that even the cool evening air is doing nothing to dampen it. I straighten down the bodice of the dress.

'You can thank The American.'

He looks around at the dissipating crowd. 'Just for the dress, or for the fact you're here?'

I shrug. 'Both.'

'I will thank her profusely.'

There's a beat. I could kiss him, try to say everything I need to with one action, but the opportunity to have frank and honest conversations would probably disappear after we do that.

'Florian, look I'm sorry, I'm really sorry.'

'You know when you said you needed some time, I had kind of assumed you meant more than twenty-four hours.'

'Well, I never did specify…'

'Did Archie come back?'

'Yes.'

'How was it?'

'It was like kicking a puppy.'

'I didn't mean to…' He stops, noticing my look of incredulity. 'Okay, well I did mean to, but I didn't want to hurt the guy.'

'I know. I think he knows too. We talked when the dust had settled a bit, but I realised you were right.'

'I hate it when I do that.'

'Yeah, it sucks.'

'So…' He plays with a leather bracelet on his wrist. 'What *do* you want, Ava?'

'I don't know.' It comes out as an exhausted sigh and I watch as his eyebrows furrow, the smile wiped from his face. I don't like it. Now that I know how to make him smile, how to muster up that disarming little grin, I want to do it all the time. I put my hand on his forearm, step towards him so he has to bend his head to keep looking me in the eye. 'I think I want to see what this could be.' He bites his lip and his index finger swoops under my chin, lifting it up so that we are looking at each other, eye to eye.

'I'm sure I can manage that.' His voice is gravelly, low. I know what I want now. I want to go, with him, I want to be with him anywhere other than here.

'Florian!' a voice calls from the doorway. His hands drop, I leap back. Turn my head to see Madame Grenaud smoothing her hair behind her ears. She looks alarmed; it makes all her sharp features more chiselled and angular than normal.

'Shit,' he mutters, scuffs his brogue into the ground and then looks up. 'Mama, I'll be there in a minute.'

She ignores him, steps towards us but still keeps her distance. 'Ava? I didn't think you were coming,' she calls to me over the courtyard.

'A surprise,' I shrug, my stomach lurching at what we look like to her, what poisonous thoughts are now thundering around her head.

'You have buyers, Florian. Stop... talking and get back in there.' She manages to soften her voice at the end, controlling her fury.

'Give us two minutes,' he offers her, looks back at me with a wink.

'*She* can wait, the Trelcats can't.'

The viciousness of the way she said 'she' is difficult to ignore. It was a slap and I can feel Florian stiffening next to me but this isn't the time or the place and nothing is going to be achieved by a screaming match in the gallery garden.

'Go.' I shoot him a pleading look. 'We can talk anytime.' He doesn't look convinced. Instead, he looks like a teenager, someone who was about to hop the wall and play truant at his own show. 'Go,' I repeat, trying to wipe any ounce of flirtation from my voice.

'Fine,' he salutes her sarcastically, but she doesn't leave the doorway until she sees Florian move from his flowerpot and start towards the door. When she turns her back, he holds out his hand behind his body and I take it.

'So... this time I did know she was coming,' he adds, noting the apprehension on my face. 'I just didn't exactly know that you were.'

'How about in future, the first thing we say to each other is whether she's in the vicinity?'

'Romantic.'

'Do you think she saw anything?'

'Saw what, Ava? We haven't done anything.' He lets go of my hand as we get to the door where Madame Grenaud is waiting to sweep him up under her arm, he turns his head around to me before being swamped by his well-wishers and with a wink he

mutters, 'yet'. My head fills with every delicious detail that I had
worked hard on trying to ignore, allowing myself the pleasure
of private reruns of how it felt to be touched like that, to want
to do nothing so badly as to rip his clothes off that I was blind
to my surroundings, dumb to whether we had been five seconds
or five minutes.

I lean against a wall, away from where Florian is being shown
like a pageant girl to some expensive-looking men in expensive-
looking suits. I like looking at him from a slight distance; it's like
I can see him more clearly, the whole picture, not just a fragment
of an emotion. I think of Ettie, of how he could never quite give
up on his little brother, that he always knew that this version of
Florian would be worth sticking around to see. He just couldn't
quite make it to the finish line himself. When another person
pats him on the back I decide to head towards the bathroom.

'Avoiding the crowds?' I look in the mirror above the sink to see
Madame Grenaud watching me from the door of a cubicle. I try
to not shrink away from her gaze. Ettie had joked that you had
to treat interactions with his mother the same way you would
with a black bear: stand tall and don't run.
 'Something like that.'
 'Me too,' she shrugs.
 'Why? Your son's the man of the hour, isn't that what you
want?'
 'Ha.' She comes to the sink next to me, we continue to catch
glances at each other through the mirror as if looking directly
at each other might turn us both to stone. 'People keep talking
to me as if I know who he is.' She rummages into her bag for
a lipstick and begins applying it delicately to her lips, pursing
and unpursing, letting the vagueness of her comment stick. She
always had a quality about her that I imagined some celebrity
would have: the ability to say anything, do anything and people
would listen. She could make reading the weather forecast
sound momentous.

'I don't think anyone knows who he really is.' I pull a couple of handtowels from the wall, dry my hands quickly and then manage a half smile before grabbing my bag. 'Have a nice evening, Maxine.'

'I think that's a lie, Ava,' she says as I reach for the doorhandle, within touching distance of freedom, so close to getting out of this altercation unscathed. 'I think you know him better than most people.' I stop, try to ignore the daggers in her voice. 'And by the looks of things earlier, it's all getting a little incestuous, wouldn't you agree?' I don't turn around. I let her comment soak into me, the implication, the venom, the satisfaction that here I am, the girl she always knew I was, one who clearly never loved her favourite son as much as I should have.

I open the door and disappear back into the noise.

The gallery's attendees are thinning out. I look at my watch: it's nearing ten and these things rarely lasted until the early hours, especially on a Monday. Florian's fans have aged significantly, and he is now being cornered by four elderly ladies who lay their hands on his arms and tell him how wonderful he is. I slip in next to him, stringing my arm through his. He looks mildly alarmed that I have broken the wall between us, the private and public spheres of physical touch.

He leans over to me whilst one lady is deep into telling her crowd a story. 'You okay?' he murmurs.

'Your mother,' I manage with a grimace. Something passes over his face – anger? An understanding? It's hard to translate but his hand snakes its way around my waist and rests itself on my hip. I feel the weight of it, the way it pulls me into him, the way it feels like the most intimate thing we have done and yet we're still fully dressed.

One by one the crowd disperses until it's only waiting staff and a few stragglers. Florian gestures to the door and I follow him. As he holds open the door I look back for any signs of Madame Grenaud.

'She'll have gone home.'

'Thank God.' It's cold out, there's a wind that ricochets off the wide bend of the river – the end of the premature heatwave. Florian throws something heavy and warm at me from where he stands a few metres ahead, arms crossed, jacketless.

He drops back, offers me the crook of his elbow as we walk up the sideroad. 'What did she say to you anyway?'

I think about telling him, but I don't see what good it'd do; it would only mean that I stoke an already established fire. 'It doesn't matter.'

Florian stops as if the thought is only just dawning on him. 'How are you getting home, Ava?'

'Not sure,' I shrug, play the idiot. 'I hadn't planned that far ahead.'

'That's very adventurous for you.'

'Well, I figured that if this whole plan blew up in my face then I would probably have enough time to call another taxi.'

'And if your plan worked? How were you planning on getting home then?' He smiles, watching me try to grapple with some excuse.

'Like I said, hadn't thought that far ahead.'

We stop next to my beloved old car. 'Fine, I'll drop you home.' He sighs dramatically, patting the bonnet of the car with his hand. 'Or better yet...' He reaches into his pocket and pulls out the keys, swinging them from his finger.

'I've had a drink.'

'Thank God. I've had two.' He throws the keys at me and immediately heaves himself into the passenger seat. I reluctantly make my way to the driver's door, pull it twice until it eventually gives way and I smooth out the dress before slipping into the seat.

The familiarity hits me again, how it feels like my own personal time-capsule, the smell of the cigarettes still ingrained into the leather. 'How does it feel?' he asks.

I grin at him. 'Like yesterday.'

Florian reaches over the gearstick and pats my thigh playfully.

'Just so you know, if you hit another deer then it's your problem.'

'Fuck off.' I put the keys in the ignition and the car spits into life.

'So where exactly am I driving us?' I keep my head looking straight out of the windshield, my eyes darting over to his lap where he starts to tug again at the leather bracelet around his wrist.

'To yours and then I'll drive back to mine.' He clips his words at an attempt to sound definitive, entirely sure of himself.

'And will you be coming in?' I look over then, allow myself the luxury of watching the idea pass over his face before he steels himself.

He chuckles. 'Not tonight.'

'Am I allowed to ask why?'

'Because I don't want to give you a reason to freak out on me again.'

'Freak out on you?'

'I just think that this, whatever this is, is complicated enough at the moment and there's feelings involved, big confusing feelings, and I don't want to rush into something that you're going to turn around tomorrow and regret.'

I prickle at his assessment. 'What if you were the one who'd regret it?'

He looks at me, one eyebrow raised so high it disappears into his fringe. 'I know that simply wouldn't happen.' I focus on the road to try to hide the triumph on my face. 'Look, Ava, I want us to go out.'

'Go out? Where?'

'I don't know, dinner maybe? That feels like a normal thing to do.'

'We did dinner… didn't exactly go to plan.'

'I mean a dinner where both of us are on a date with each other, wouldn't that be nice? A good, uncomplicated dinner where no one ends up crying?'

'Okay,' I nod. 'Dinner sounds nice. I should probably let you know that I don't put out on the first date though.'

'Your track history tells me otherwise.'

I pretend to be offended. 'I wasn't going to sleep with you the other night!'

'Oh, you weren't? Sorry, must have misinterpreted your hand when it slipped down my—'

'Yes, very much misinterpreted!' I shut him down quickly. I don't need a play-by-play. I had already committed my version to memory.

'Well, I'm glad we cleared that up.'

'Me too.' I let a comfortable silence envelop us. He's humming a song I don't know, tapping his fingers on his thigh. He is content; it feels good to know that I have had some part in it.

I indicate off the main road towards Monpazier. 'So, you want to do Wednesday?' I ask. His humming stops abruptly. He looks at me a little too long and I wonder if I have managed to land in some parallel universe where the earlier conversation had been entirely imagined by myself.

'Wednesday?' he repeats.

'Yeah…' I turn to look at him, the way his face is slightly paler than it had been before. 'I mean isn't it moules frites night at L'Octave?'

'You don't remember?'

I screw up my own face, rack my brain for whether we had already made plans, whether he had told me about some other exhibition he was hosting perhaps. 'Remember what?'

'On Wednesday it will be four years since Ettie died.' He says it slowly, his voice void of any inflections, emotions.

'No… it's…'

'May the ninth,' he fills in. I start to do the calculation. May had snuck up on me; the fact that we were only two days away from it being four entire years since I lost him was impossible.

'Oh my God.' I feel sick, a kind of wave of panic spreading through me. Florian gawps at me as if I'm having a stroke.

'Are you okay?' he asks and I'm unsure if he means physically or mentally. I am not doing great on either front.

'I forgot.' I screw my face up a little, the sourness of those words sitting heavily on my tongue.

'You've had a lot going on…'

'I forgot, Florian!' I say again; this time the words are cutting, fierce. I grab my wrist on the steering wheel, pinch a bit of skin with my nails until I can feel the sharpness, wince a little from the pain.

'Stop that,' he scolds. 'Ava, it's okay,' he lies, a poor attempt at making it seem alright, to forget the landmark date now automatically etched into my calendar, which should be this big red beacon in my year that makes the grief almost unbearable. Instead, I've been playing dress up and fantasising about getting with his brother.

He tries to reach out, rescue my hand that is starting to redden, but I snatch it away and I drive the last mile up to Rue Saint Jaques in an uncomfortable silence.

As soon as we park up, I throw myself out of the car and slam the door, the hem of the dress getting caught and ripping a little as I pull it away.

'Fuck!' I yell and slump myself down on the steps of my front door. Florian hangs back, leans against the car, arms crossed. I cry. I properly cry. All the anger and fury dissipates and despite the dress, the intentions, the bravery of tonight, I'm just a girl, sobbing on her own doorstep.

'Hey.' He takes a few slow steps towards me until he knows I'm not going to lash him again and slips his body down beside me. He wraps his long arm around me and strokes my arm gently. 'He would be happy.'

'That I forgot the day he died?' I ask incredulously.

'Yes. Of course. It's a horrible day, Ava. He would be happy that you aren't living your life around a dead man.'

'He's my husband… was my husband.'

'What, and he never forgot an important date, your birthday, a Valentine's Day perhaps, your anniversary?'

'I – ' I stammer, remember the dinner reservation that I made on that first year, him entirely unaware why we were there, me breaking apart a little at his lack of awareness of what I considered a pretty vital day in our lives. 'Did he tell you?'

'He didn't need to,' Florian chuckles softly. 'I know Ettie; he's not exactly the kind of man that would have tried too hard to purchase a calendar.'

'But you remembered Wednesday?'

'Only because it's my least favourite day of the year.' He presses his lips into my head and I relax a little, feel the strange sensation of genuine care wash over me. 'Mum makes us go to the graveyard, lay down some shitty flowers and then we have this awkward little dinner, just the two of us, and we both get entirely too drunk until it gets late enough that we have an excuse to go home.'

'That sounds disgusting.' I manage a stifled snigger.

'Oh it is exactly that.'

'Don't tell her that I forgot.' I sound like a child, my voice warped by the aching void of sadness that has set up camp in my throat.

'Ava, I would never.' He sounds sad that I would ever think that he would. 'Here's an idea.' He clears his throat. 'Maybe this year you can join us?'

'Seriously?'

'Why not? It would be nice to have the company. You can absolve yourself of your guilt about forgetting and I get to have someone there who I genuinely want to talk to.'

'And your mother?'

'Well maybe we can both revel a bit in the fact that it will really piss her off.'

'Ha,' I splutter and then the sadness descends again. 'I've never been back there.'

'Why would you? It's a shitty place.'

'Okay.' I sniff and then wipe the snot that has accumulated around my nose with the back of my hand. Hardly the glamourous impression I was hoping to give.

'I'll pick you up at three on Wednesday.'

'Are you sure I can't tempt you inside for a drink? Am I not the definition of sexy right now?' I gesture to my face, how I know the eyeliner and mascara will be forming little rivers down my face.

'Quite sure.' He pats me on the shoulder, groans as he gets to his feet. I watch as he stretches out his long body until he stands there, hands slipping into the comfort of his pockets.

'I'm really happy you came, Ava,' he says earnestly. 'But if you hadn't, I was going to head here tomorrow anyway. There's no way on earth I was going to let you get away that easily.'

I am flooded with a delicious relief.

'I'll see you Wednesday.'

Chapter 28

I DON'T KNOW WHAT to wear to a graveyard. I didn't know what to wear to his funeral either. Mum suggested I wore his favourite colour, but I didn't really know what that was. And then I cried some more because I would never get the chance to ask him. I've never really liked colour at a funeral anyway, it feels wrong. I wanted all the colour to drain out of the world, do a Queen Victoria and wear a little black veil for the rest of my life.

I imagine Ettie sitting on the edge of my bed, rolling his eyes as I stare at the void of my wardrobe, how the clothes are mostly thrown into drawers and sagging off hangers. He would tell me that it didn't matter, just shove on something and get out of the door. I reach for jeans and a bright-green jumper that we had bought together when I hadn't realised that a couple's trip to Prague in March might be a little brisk.

'Perfect,' he would say, emphasising the 'f'. 'You look like a couple hundred euros.' And I would hit him and pretend to be offended.

I do my hair, my make-up even, put on my jacket and then sit on the sofa checking whether my phone clock has actually stopped working because once again, despite trying my hardest to be late, I am on time; no, in fact today I am early.

The apartment is strangely calm. I had filled it with as much noise as I possibly could, but typically it's only now when I have five days left of my tenancy that I realise quite how peaceful it is, how it feels safe and warm and clean, how it feels like mine. I don't have a place that's mine when I get off the plane. I have a bedroom with a fresh beige carpet with beige walls and a beige bed. It will be spotless, vacuumed, dusted, there won't be cobwebs and dust and birds on the walls and it will feel like I am a million miles from home even though I am there.

I reach for my diary from underneath the coffee table; it's still left open from my session after Florian had dropped me back after the gallery. Amongst the guilt of forgetting why Wednesday was significant were particularly vivid reruns of details I never want to forget: his smile when he saw me, the protective arm around me in the gallery, his jacket on my shoulders. I turn to a fresh page, write the date, press my pen to the first blank line and feel a distinctive and recognisable tremor of inspiration. I close the diary, reach for my shopping bag and throw it in along with some fruit and wine for the meal tonight, Florian had made the decision that he would cook; said that perhaps more space might defuse the tension than sitting at a restaurant for other people to listen.

When Florian rings me to say he's outside I'm grateful to see the front seat is empty.

He gets out of the car, holds open the passenger door with an outstretched arm. I hover before getting in, take him in. He has gone for the same approach to his outfit as I have, like if we treat this as *normal* then maybe it might feel it eventually.

We stand there assessing each other for a moment, an awkwardness descending that feels so alien now. I place a hand on his shoulder as he presses his lips to my cheeks and then we pause, bodies still locked together and then I lean in, stealing the simplest of kisses. His cheeks flush.

'I'm never sure what the protocol is,' he mutters, eyes still half closed.

'I'm not sure there is one for this specific situation. I think we get to make up the rules.'

His hand slips to my waist. He chuckles and then he kisses me back. 'I like it.'

*

'Is she not coming?' I ask, gesturing to the empty backseat as Florian thunders down the cobbles, the entire car vibrating beneath us. I know I sound entirely too hopeful.

'She's meeting us there.'

'And does she know that *I'm* meeting her there?' Florian swallows and then nods a little apprehensively, the ghost of a conversation he clearly hadn't wanted to have still lingering in the air.

'She does.'

'And I'm guessing she wasn't best pleased?'

He manages a sideward glance in my direction. 'No comment.'

I feel the saliva dry in my mouth, an all-consuming nausea descending on me. 'Maybe it's a bad idea, we can go anytime just you and me...'

'I'm not doing this on my own.'

Ettie was buried in a town thirty kilometres away. It wasn't his home. It made no sense. The only connection to the fortress balancing precariously on a hilltop was the fact that the Grenauds had a family vault there, where three generations of his family had rested their own skeletal remains. Whilst I tried to protest, I had been too numbed by Valium and shock, so I quickly gave in.

Ettie and I never wrote a will; I'm sure we would have got around to it eventually, maybe if we ever decided to have kids, but it was never exactly high on his agenda. I came to realise that part of his attraction to me was my age: he could get away with ten more years of pretending that he wasn't ageing; ten more years of drinking too much; morning, lunchtime and afternoon sex. He wanted lie-ins and cigarettes for breakfast. And I wanted him.

Florian parks the car at the bottom of the hill and we have to walk up a steep cobbled pathway until the dome of the Basilica comes into view.

It is impossibly beautiful. It does make the thought of him being here a little easier, that he gets to lie at the foot of this

vast and entirely ridiculous tribute to a God that I'm not sure
Etienne ever believed in.

'You know the Virgin Mary showed up here.' Florian kindly
stops, letting me catch my breath as we ascend higher. 'Over
there by the caves. A starving girl saw her, and she gave the girl
bread. That's why this is here.' He gestures upwards to the white
stone temple that looks like it should belong in Rome, not up a
hill in the middle of nowhere.

'Funny how these saints always show up in pretty places, isn't
it? They never just pop out of the woodwork in Hounslow or
Staines.'

Florian's face is blank; it is one of the only times I am aware
that we are from entirely different places, that our mother
tongues are not the same. 'It doesn't matter.'

Madame Grenaud is perched on a marble bench overlooking
the gates to the graveyard. She is wearing black; of course she
is wearing black. Her dark glasses and hat speak slightly of a
theatrical performance and even Florian looks slightly taken
aback.

'Mama, you look… smart.'

'Thank you.' She kisses him like a stranger, afraid that he
might wrinkle her black two-piece perhaps.

'Ava.' She barely glances in my direction. Florian clears
his throat. 'I am glad you could join us today,' she adds as an
afterthought, and I wonder whether he had threatened her into
at least being civil.

'Thank you for letting me come, Maxine.' I smile and she
bobs her head at my own civility.

'Well, shall we?'

She gets to the gate but pauses, gestures for Florian to open it
and then grabs onto the crook of his arm before he can register
what's happening.

There is sad grey shingle on the ground, the occasional
cluster of green weeds struggle out from under the stones and
swing defiantly in the breeze. It is a little strange, contradictory

almost, that life is still managing to slip through the cracks.

Immediately we are banked on both sides by large marble tombs in muted greys, blacks and browns. I hang back from my two companions, my feet performing some sort of macabre wedding march, my eyes taking in the unfamiliar names, the dates, the small faded pictures in marble frames that indicate whose bones I am walking past.

Ettie is in the far corner, under the shade of a budding oak tree. It is a peaceful place with far-reaching views over the valley, a valley that probably looks as it did when his great-grandfather was the first body to be interred.

The gravel stops crunching under our feet as we reach the family vault. It is a gargantuan box of granite that rests a metre off the ground, covered with the names and faces of distant relatives that in some bizarre way I am, and always will be, related to. I take in the faded sepia cameos of the dead. I recognise a few faces from photo albums, most notably the picture of Mr Grenaud, a man who I never met. His picture is an old one; he probably was the same age Ettie would be today, smiling, in a brown suit with the same wild hair Ettie had inherited.

We all stand there in an uncomfortable silence. I watch as Madame Grenaud steps towards the monument, places her hands on the stone and starts muttering in French. Florian folds his arms to his chest, and I notice how his lips mouth an 'amen' when she finishes. I don't embarrass myself with joining him; there is a strong possibility I might combust.

Madame Grenaud then steps back, gestures for Florian to do something. He reaches into a bag I hadn't realised he was carrying and pulls out a little wooden box and hands it to his mother. She takes it gently, opening up the clasp to reveal a small oval picture frame carved out of a crisp sand-coloured granite. She looks at it fondly, her hands smoothing the edges. She says something to Florian in French, the words make him soften. She places the picture on the grave, on Ettie's grave. It looks so out of place, too fresh and clean amongst the other weather-beaten tributes that have seen decades of rain and snow and bleaching sun.

Madame Grenaud makes space for Florian to approach. They both lay their hands on the stone again except this time they don't mutter a prayer: they just stand there, as if they are touching something more than the cold, hard nothingness beneath their fingers. I feel like a voyeur, so far removed from the sentiment and purpose I might as well be a stranger.

Florian breaks first; he crosses himself in a way that is as automatic as washing his hands and then he falls out to my side.

'You made it,' I murmur, pointing to the frame.

'Yes. Mum's request.'

'It's beautiful.'

He closes the distance to my ear. 'You should see what she made me carve in the back.' He makes his voice low so that she can't hear.

'What?' I match his tone.

'Read it when you get a chance.'

'Florian.' Madame Grenaud turns towards us. 'Are you ready?'

He clearly registers my look of relief that this is finished, but grimaces a little.

He gestures to the gilded dome of the Basilica that towers over us. 'We go there… to pray.'

'Oh…' I stumble a little on my feet. 'Right, okay.'

'Not her.' Madame Grenaud whips around, her eyes narrowing in my direction.

We both stiffen as if reeling from an attack. 'Why not?' Florian challenges her.

Madame Grenaud shrugs. 'She's not Catholic.'

'Neither are half the tourists in there now.'

'Ava can wait here.' Madame Grenaud gestures to a bench by the grave. 'We won't be long.'

'Are you serious? She…' Florian's voice rises, his body growing taller, stiffer. A few faces from the ramparts above turn to us.

'It's fine,' I say quickly, my hand reaching for his arm, steadying him. 'You go. I won't know what to do in there anyway,' I shrug, shooting him a pleading glance.

He wavers for a moment before relenting. There will be no winners today.

'We'll be quick,' he promises and then makes his way back out of the graveyard towards the doors to the Basilica.

I scuff my feet into the shingle, moving pieces backwards and forwards until there is nothing but chalky ground beneath my trainer. A pigeon flies in, lands a few metres from my feet and pecks at something that my unintentional landscaping has brought to the surface.

I watch it for a moment, the only living company in this place, until it too gets bored of me and scuttles away in a clumsy flapping of wings.

I take a step towards the grave, my hands wavering on top of the stone until I give in, press my palms down onto the smooth top and feel something in my body unravel.

I look at the carved tribute of a face that now feels like it's fading from my memory.

'Hey.' My voice is shaky, holding on for dear life. There's a silence. Of course there's a fucking silence.

'So, it's been a while.' I keep going. 'Sorry about that, you know what I'm like when it comes to running away from my problems. Not that you're a problem, apart from – well the dying bit. I don't know if you can hear me… I don't think that you can which is another reason why I feel so fucking stupid, talking to a bit of sodding rock.

'I… I… really miss you, Etienne. I think I just need to say that, to admit it. That every day I wake up and for a fragment of a millisecond I think you're there. Everything would be easier, my life would be easier, your family's life would be easier, if you had just stuck around a bit longer.

'I don't know how much you know, if you are some sentient being just flapping around the place then – well then I guess you kind of don't need some announcement about just how dramatic

I have managed to make things. I don't know how you'd feel about the whole thing. I know you were a bit of a hedonist in your life, but I'm not sure your liberal attitude to love extended as far as your brother.

'I think if you knew this version of him there would have been more dinners, more fun, more family. And I know it hurts him that you never saw him like this. I guess in some way he's making it up to me instead.

'I love you, Ettie. I still love you. I thought it might fade or change or lessen but it doesn't, there's just more space in me now. And I think that space is for him. With Florian. If that's cool with you of course, and if it isn't then like send me a sign or something and I'll back off or better yet, maybe resurrect yourself and tell me in person?

'I...' The rawness starts to catch in my throat, everything becoming tighter. 'I'm always going to love you, Ettie, I just think that you need to know that... God!' I wipe the tears from my eyes, the roaring ache relaxing as I take a deep sobbing breath. 'I'm going to go now.' I step back, take my hands off the slab, break the connection.

There is a clarity, a relief that radiates through me, a release of something that had been gripping me so tightly and for so long I had forgotten that it was there at all.

I cry some more and then remember Florian's instruction. I reach for Ettie, turn over the frame in my hands to see the back and then let out a manic cackle that I have to put great effort into suppressing. My French might not be perfect but I can translate this.

La famille avant tout: *Family over everything*.

There is still no sign of my two companions when I exit the graveyard, so instead I amble around the ramparts, the grotto where prayers have been inserted into cracks into the rocks. A statue of the Virgin Mary stands sentinel, her hands in prayer, and a couple of tourists linger at her feet.

I find a bench that looks over the valley, sit down, reach into my bag and grab my notebook. For the first time since I opened this thing and started my random narratives I think about what I'm saying. I structure my sentences carefully, pause to select my words. It's slow at first, like running after a six-month hiatus, but after the first paragraph it starts to come back to me until I am sprinting through the page, a clarity descending that is both so alien and so fucking euphoric I think I might even be smiling as I write it.

I write three pages in ten minutes until I add the final full stop. And for the first time in months, I know that what's written down is good. That I have my ending.

'Hey.' Florian thumps his body onto the bench next to me. He lets out a long sigh and his limbs slacken.

'How was it?' I dare to ask, although I feel like I am already anticipating his answer.

'She made me do confession,' he hisses.

'Confession? The whole wooden box and priest and sin thing?'

'Yes.'

I pivot my body towards him. 'And what sins were you confessing to?'

He stretches his arms over the back of the bench, his thumb catching my shoulder, the mischievous grin returning to his lips. 'Well there was some gluttony... lust, coveting thy brother's wife, you know – all the good ones.' I let out an unattractive snort.

'And what's your punishment?'

'Oh, just the five hail Marys and enduring dinner with my mother.'

'Sounds like a fair deal.'

He looks at me with one raised eyebrow and I know in that moment he would rather take a physical beating over what the next few hours had in store. 'What's this?' He looks at my lap, finds the notebook and before I can register his interest, he reaches for it.

'Don't!' I snatch it away before he can take it, and he screws his eyes up at what he clearly thinks is an overreaction.

'Alright, calm down.' He holds his hands up, the wonderful lightness we had managed to inject into a rather shit day evaporating.

'It's just a diary,' I shrug.

'You took your diary out with you, here?'

I don't have an excuse, I don't have the time or the energy to explain either. I will one day, I'm sure of it, just not yet. 'Yes, and your point?'

'Okay, my apologies, it's a perfectly normal thing to do.'

'You're excused.' I throw it into my bag. 'Now, can we possibly go so that this evening can be over and banished to my distant memory?'

'Yes, Ava. Yes, we can go.'

Chapter 29

Madame Grenaud is perched precariously on the edge of the sofa, the evening news a welcome guest at this dinner party.

I don't join her; I think Florian realises that it would be too cruel to insist that I do, so I pour the two of us some wine and hide in the kitchen, acting as an entirely useless sous-chef.

'What are we having?' I peer over to the stove where something dark and rich is simmering down.

'Boef Bourguignon,' he shrugs as if he might as well be chucking some chicken in the microwave and hoping for the best. 'Here.' He holds up a spoon for me. 'Taste it, you can let me know if it needs anything else.'

'I think we both know I'll be next to useless at providing culinary advice.'

'Still.' He swings the spoon in the air, pouting a little until I give in, leave my glass on the side and let him scoop some sauce onto the spoon. I try to take it off of him but he scolds me until I stand there like a guppy with my mouth wide and he deposits the liquid onto my tongue directly and then stands there, waiting for my reaction.

'It's good. Really good.'

'I'm glad. Now go set the table.' He winks.

I do as he says, retrieving some placemats and mismatched crockery. 'God, I'm going to miss the food here,' I say to the room, beginning to organise the table into three distinct little areas. Check that there is enough distance between everyone in case things get difficult.

We work in a busy silence, Florian stirring something rather vigorously whilst I focus on folding napkins into little shapes.

'I think we should talk about that,' Florian says quietly.

'About what, my textile origami?' I gesture to a wonky swan with a flourish.

'About you going.' He doesn't look at me, focusing intently on hooking out something from his pot with a spoon.

'Oh.' I stop decorating, look out of the doorway to where Madame Grenaud is perching, eyes still fixed on the TV. I rescue my wine from the sideboard and lean back against the sink, eyes fixed on the back of Florian's head, willing him to turn around so I can at least gauge where to pitch my defence. 'Well, we can talk but my flight's on Sun—'

'I don't think you should go.'

I'm not shocked that this is where the conversation has headed. I think I've been waiting for him to say something since I had bought it up the night I kicked him out. He is pretending like it isn't happening; I think in some way he actually thinks it won't.

'You don't?' I keep my voice soft and measured.

'No.'

'Can I ask why?'

'I think you're happy here.' He brings his shoulders up to his ears.

'You never saw me in London, maybe I'm happy there too?'

'Are you?'

'No, but that's beside the point.' I scoff at how stupid it all sounds. Of course I wasn't happy there, but I had survived it by convincing myself that it was the grief talking, that I could be anywhere in the world and it would feel just as terrible. The reality of how wrong I had been was starting to set in. Besides, the one distraction I had tried to make in London was now back in his glossy apartment, probably trying to forget about the ordeal I had put him through. Over here, grief still woke me up in the morning and followed me around until I went to bed, but in the day when I was having drinks with The American or cooking a meal in the apartment or spending any period of time with Florian, then that feeling dulled, it became manageable.

He turns around then. I am unsure if he did ever find the thing he was so desperate on fishing out of his dinner.

'Don't go,' he says simply, sadly. I know now that he has grasped the magnitude of the situation, the reason I had been so unwilling to see where things might go in the first place.

'I have to!'

He looks slightly disgusted at my inability to stretch my little imagination to a place where I could want to stay. 'You don't "have" to do anything.'

'I have commitments, my parents, I mean I don't have anywhere to live here when my lease is up.'

'We can sort something out. The American loves you, I'm sure she'd let you have the apartment for longer.'

'It's not that simple!' My voice frays at the edges and it's enough to loosen Florian's dogmatic resolve. He comes over to me, taking my hands in his. He chases my eyes around with his until I can't avoid looking him square in the face.

'Ava, I cannot accept that I only have four days of *this* until you go… it's simply not enough time.' He brushes some stray hairs out of my face, his thumb resting on my lips. 'Delay your flight, stay at the hotel… stay here?'

I shake my head at his last comment. He doesn't mean it. He's grasping at straws. He pulls away.

'I'll come back.'

He scoffs, crosses his arms like a petulant child. 'I don't believe you.'

'Hey, come here.' I hold onto his shoulders and then lock my hands together behind his neck, keeping him close to me. 'I promise I'll come back.'

He relents, relaxes a little. 'When?'

'Soon. I need to do some things, tie up some ends…'

'What are you doing back there that's so important?'

'I… I can't say, not yet.' I don't like lying to him. Especially when it feels like Florian's 'thing' is radical honesty. But I also don't like the thought of my life without this book. It is the only thing that I have truly done for myself and before there was Florian, before there was even Archie, there was a bashed-up diary with blank pages ready for me, all of me.

And I will tell him soon, when everything's finalised, when there's a final approved manuscript, I will hand it to him, let him see for himself what it really is. Not my attempt at profiting from Ettie's death, but something that has meant that I could keep living in a world without him in it. He can't hate me for it then.

'So many secrets,' he murmurs into my ear. I slacken. Unravel. His breath is warm at the crease of my neck. I can feel his steady breaths, thinking about what to do next. I want him to kiss me. I want him to press his lips into my neck in long drawn-out pulses. I am bereft when instead of doing that he pulls away and looks at me with a wink. He knows exactly what he's doing.

'Dinner tomorrow,' I tell him.

'I think that might be a good idea,' he smirks and then a timer goes off and we jolt back into the reality of why we are here, of who is sitting in that room next door, most likely pretending to be watching something on the TV.

I am been prepared for dinner to turn into many things. I'm not prepared for it to be a relatively uninteresting and normal affair.

The food is delicious, and we eat it in a polite and comfortable silence, offering around the various accompaniments to each other, filling up our plates, thanking Florian. I am mainly a bystander in the conversation, and I am grateful for it. We choose Florian as our neutral middle ground, his art and upcoming commissions proving a fertile ground for a few minutes of distraction until we are finished, and I offer to take the plates.

'Just leave them on the side,' Florian gestures, heaving in the large ceramic casserole dish.

'Sure?' I waver and he nods emphatically.

'I think this is the most uneventful dinner we've ever had. Don't want to ruin it now.' There is a look of sheer relief coupled with a dash of confusion. I think I might have the exact same expression on my face too.

We re-join Madame Grenaud who has started to unpack some hunks of cheese onto a wooden board.

'You didn't have to do that, Mama,' he softly scolds but grabs some plates from the side.

'Well, you cooked, it's nice to contribute.'

'Ooh!' I squeak, remembering my own offerings in my bag. 'Wine!' I run to the sofa where I had thrown my bag when I came in but instead find it in the corner by the fireplace. Florian must have cleared it away. I find the wine quickly but something is off; there's more room in the bag than there was before, it's lighter too. I start to play a game of spot the difference until there is a knowing and all-consuming worry that transcends over me.

'You alright, Ava?' Florian calls out, aware that I'm taking too long.

'I've lost it!'

'Lost what?'

'My diary, I had it, it must have fallen out of my bag by that bench. I need it.' I rush to the door, grab my coat.

'It's just a diary, Ava, we'll look for it in the morning...' I think of all the people that might have visited that place after us, the others that will get there tomorrow for the sunrise, hundreds of people all able to get there before we can, people that might find it and read it, take it or bin it. I think of the work, the hours and nights spent spilling my guts into its pages. The last chapter, how I won't be able to write it again because I can't even remember what it says. My whole life. My whole future is in those pages.

'It's not just a diary, Florian!' I shout. He looks like I've hit him square across the jaw.

'No, it's not...' Madame Grenaud breaks up the conversation. She is still sitting in her chair, a small smile on her face, her hands tracing over the patterns on my diary that she has placed on the table. 'But it is incredibly enlightening.'

I can feel the life draining from me, and a heavy, uncomfortable dread makes itself at home in my chest. This can't be how he finds out. 'Give it back.' I run to her, try to snatch it back, but she whips it out of my hands.

'Not yet,' she tuts.

'Mama? That's Ava's...' I catch Florian's confusion, the way he is standing back, looking at the book that he had dismissed hours earlier.

'Oh, I know. I know a lot more than you think I do. I mean, it's not exactly a secret, you plastering yourself all over the internet like that.' My blood stops circulating. My stomach lurches. I feel a wave of adrenaline-induced nausea come over me.

'What is she talking about?' Florian is looking at me now, this sort of helplessness on his features. He doesn't know the details, but he knows that something bad is about to happen, the same way that animals know hours before an earthquake hits.

'Florian...' I shake my head. 'I was going to tell you—'

'Here, see for yourself.' She reaches into her lap and pulls out her phone. She fiddles for a moment until the screen illuminates her smug face. The phone is placed face up on the table and she slides it towards Florian. I see the header, the font, the colours; I know what it is and I know that I'm fucked.

'What is this?'

'A blog... quite a successful one at that too. I found it when I was at the hairdresser a few months ago; it featured in a magazine with a picture of a girl who I thought looked familiar.'

'You've known all this time?' I ask her, my fury turning into this heavy and inescapable sadness. This has been my fate since she realised I was here. Any ounce of happiness I had managed to seek out for myself would always be stamped on and squeezed out by her plan.

'Oh yes.'

'Why didn't you say something sooner?'

'I thought you would get your fill, sell your story, whatever you needed and then you would be gone, just like you were the first time around, and then you would leave my family in peace.

But then I saw how you were with him, the way you wrapped yourself around another shiny thing, and well, I won't let that happen to another one of my sons.'

I look at Florian whose face is illuminated by the screen that he is slowly taking in, I see him scrolling, taking in the words, the headers, the pictures.

'You make it sound like I've been planning it to work out this way. It wasn't some scheme, it just happened. And it isn't just me!'

'You've written a blog about him?' Florian interrupts, his voice spacey and distant.

'Yes, but it isn't about him, not really. It's about me, about how losing him affected me.'

'Okay. That's fine?' It comes out as a question. 'I don't see what the issue is here, I mean I don't know why you didn't tell me about it but it's no big deal, Mama.'

'You have always been a little too naïve for my liking, my darling. Go on, Ava, you tell him what else has been going on, why you're really here.'

I look from her to him, the venom in her eyes and the expectant disappointment in his. But there's no use avoiding it; in a few minutes every secret I ever kept from him will be common knowledge.

'There's a book.'

'A book?'

'Yes, that's what my loose end is. The blog got bought by a publisher a year ago and I've been working on it ever since. She told me I needed to come here because I needed to find some ending to it. She thought that me coming out here would give me some closure and then I was meant to go home and get the thing published and that would be it.'

'That's why you came?' His face falls into a stony stare. 'Not because you missed this place?'

'I didn't want to come.' The truth slips out now even when it isn't needed, like I can't stop it. 'I had no intention of ever coming back here. I only came because she told me that if I didn't then there wouldn't be a book.'

'But why not tell me?'

'I was going to, but you made this big speech about how making art about Ettie would be sort of profiting from his death and… I wanted to wait, wait until it was finished and I could show you properly and… then you would see… see that, that isn't what this is.'

I watch as the memory of the conversation we had in his studio plays through his mind. 'I—'

'And I didn't think it mattered anyway!' I don't let him finish, I won't let anyone say anything until it's all out there. 'Because you didn't matter, not at first… until you *did*.' My voice cracks, all of the bravado and confidence evaporating. 'Until I started to realise that I cared about you, that I do care about you, Florian, but it all got too big.'

Florian softens a little, for a moment it is all salvageable. He'll ask her to leave, we can talk this through. It's a harmless lie. No one gets hurt, no one dies, we can put it down to a complication. I have a second chance.

'How dare he. How fucking dare he.' Madame Grenaud's voice cuts across the table. We are both put off guard by the words coming out of her mouth, until I see the open page of the diary and realise that they aren't her words at all, they're mine. '"How does he get to be alive, him with all his fuck ups and bad decisions, how does he get to live and Ettie doesn't? He's selfish, just some selfish drug addict who's entirely occupied with protecting his own back. Ettie would hate that he's back here, in our place, living out the life that Ettie should have had."'

'Florian…' I look at him, the pain of those words carving into his skin and through any chance of redemption.

'I didn't know that's how you felt.'

'I don't! I wrote that after the first time I ran into you… it's a diary, it's just a stream of consciousness.'

Madame Grenaud clears her throat, an almost gleeful look of anticipation on her lips. '"I want to wipe the taste of him off my lips, to undo it all. I hate the person I am with him."'

'Stop it! You're twisting it!' I scream at her, snatching the diary out of her hands and standing there gasping, looking from the woman next to me to the man a few feet away whose softness and adoration have now entirely vanished.

'You need to go,' he says flatly.

'Please, Florian, don't,' I sob, all dignity lost.

He steels himself; I watch the hardness wash over him. 'Get the fuck out of my house.'

Chapter 30

'AVA?' A VOICE BREAKS through the stagnant air of the apartment. Apart from the radio and occasional Instagram reel, I have not heard another voice since I started my self-imposed confinement, two days ago.

'Ava,' the voice calls again. For a moment I imagine it's Florian. I had spent all of Wednesday night and most of yesterday thinking, hoping, praying that he would just launch himself into my apartment and shout at me some more just to tell me that it didn't matter. That we were worth more than this. I gave up on that dream when midnight hit and my eleventh call and twelfth text remained unanswered. Deciding instead to smoke the last of my cigarettes and drink the rest of the whisky from the other night as a kind of pathetic tribute to what we could have been.

'Ava?' the voice calls again and then the bedroom door opens, The American peers around the corner cautiously as if she isn't quite sure what she might find. 'Oh, thank God, you're not dead.' She sighs, surveys the state of the room and then the state of me. Her face immediately switches from relief to sheer pity.

'How did you get in?' I groan, the sleep still sitting heavily on my bones.

'I have the keys, remember.' She waves something silver and shiny in front of my face.

'Doesn't that break some sort of rental law?'

'Probably.' She collapses onto the end of my bed and I move my feet to the side to accommodate her. 'But I think it is also called a welfare check and that tends to be looked on more kindly in a court of law.'

I pull myself up to a sitting position and push some hair behind my ears. 'I'm fine.'

'Clearly.'

'Okay, I've been better but I'm not dead. I just need to exist here for another forty-eight hours and then I can be on the next flight home.'

'Without saying goodbye?' Elderly people really know how to stick the knife in, I think their puppy-dog faces could beat any four-year-old's.

'I...' The truth of the matter is that I hadn't really given anyone else a second thought. Perhaps, naively, I just assumed that everything would sort itself out. 'Florian and I got into a fight.' I offer up my reason for the abandonment as my excuse.

'I guessed.'

'You were entirely right, I should have told him about the book.'

'I know.'

'And I would just like to sit here and wallow for a bit longer if that's okay.'

She sighs, gets to her feet and then pats some imaginary dust off of her skirt as if the messiness was contagious. 'A week ago, you'd told him that you weren't sure you wanted to be with him and now you're acting like some lovesick seventeen-year-old.'

'Urgh,' is all I can manage.

'Right, get up.'

'What?'

'Come on, up you get.' With surprising dexterity, she pulls the covers off me and the bed.

'Give them back.' I pathetically reach for them, but she bats me away.

'You are going to get into that shower whilst I make you something that doesn't have an alcohol content and then we can talk.'

I lie there staring at the ceiling for a few seconds until I relent. I snatch up my dressing grown from the floordrobe and head towards the shower.

*

'Better?' The American glances in my general direction as I emerge from the bathroom. She is standing in my kitchen, washing up some mugs that I'm guessing needed some elbow grease to clean.

'A bit,' I shrug, not wanting to admit quite how much better I do feel after soaking myself for about twenty minutes in water that was close to boiling.

'Right, sit down.' She gestures to the dining room chair where she has laid up a place for me. 'I assumed you might not be feeding yourself so I took the liberty of picking up some provisions.' She struggles over with a tray that she places in front of me, full of bread, croissants and a pot of coffee.

'Thank you, that's very kind.'

'Don't worry about it. I quite enjoy looking after people in need.'

'I'm not *in need*,' I scoff and it is met by an incredulous eyebrow. 'I just needed to lie low for a bit, that's all. I'll survive, but I do appreciate the food.' I hold up the corner of the croissant.

'I should let you know that I did run into Florian.'

'You did?'

'So, your state isn't much of a surprise.'

'What did he tell you?'

'Not much. He didn't need to.' I look up from my croissant, appealing for a little more information. 'He looked awful, better than you, but still awful. I asked where you were and he told me you were probably here, packing up your stuff and looking forward to going back.'

'So, when you say he looked awful…' I start, 'I mean, was that a physical assessment or more of a mental—'

'He was a bit dead behind the eyes. Looked away when I said your name. There was a particular malice when he said you were probably packing for your return. I don't know any details yet. He said that you would probably fill me in anyway, but I should let you know,' she adds, pointing her finger in my direction, 'I tend to play the role of Switzerland in these situations.'

'His mother's a scheming witch, nothing new there. Told Florian about my blog. She stole my notebook, read him some passages that weren't exactly flattering. He told me to leave.'

'Oh...'

'Yes "*oh*". So that's what I did. I left. You know, an hour before he was asking me to stay, asking me to bloody live with him and now... well now there's this.'

'So, he didn't take the book news well?'

'No.' I take another bite of the croissant. 'It's fair to say that went down like a lead balloon, which is pretty ironic really.'

'Why?'

'I'm going to pull it. I've got a meeting in London next Thursday with Sam to tell her.'

The American's coffee cup crashes against her plate when she sets it down a little too quickly. 'What! Why?'

'How can I publish something that has already caused so much drama? His family don't want Ettie immortalised in that way, for me to profit from losing him. I mean, aren't they right?'

'But all your work?'

I shake my head. 'I simply don't care any more. I just wish I never came here, never got to know *him* again, I was making progress and now I'm back at square one all over again.'

'Ava.' She reaches for me but I snatch my hand away. I can't deal with niceness, with platitudes or care at the moment. It just makes me want to cry. 'I think that is the opposite of the truth.'

'I guess I just thought that the next time I got on my flight back home I would feel like I had achieved something, had some greater purpose, that losing Ettie would mean something, but I don't feel like that and losing him just means that he's gone.'

The American dabs her mouth with a tissue, ignoring my self-pity. 'I've been thinking.' She reaches into her bag and pulls out a small piece of white paper, embossed in gold lettering with multicoloured balloons tracing the borders. She pushes it across the table towards me.

'Your birthday party?' I ask sceptically.

'Yes.'

'But it's this weekend, my flight's on Sunday.'

'I'm very aware of the clash. That's why I also went to the liberty of purchasing this.' She pushes over a boarding pass with next Tuesday's date on it.

'What did you do that for?'

'Well I thought it might give you one less excuse to use. I want you there,' she says simply.

'I don't think I can stay here another day... I...'

'This will do you good, Ava. Treat it like a holiday before you go back, an opportunity to really relax. It's not here. It's a house a few miles away, I've rented it for the weekend every year since I got here. It's wonderful, all paid for and there's a room with your name on it.'

The holiday away from here sounds tempting, a way to delay the inevitable I guess, but it wouldn't erase what has happened; if anything, being surrounded by a bunch of happy people, inevitably couples, could be sheer torture.

'Ava...' She can see me weighing it up, the slight splintering of my resolve. 'I am eighty-two years old, eighty-three on Sunday. Come to the damned birthday party. I don't have that many more to go.'

'Are you really guilt tripping me?'

'Well. Can't blame me,' she pouts.

I take her in, how there really isn't anything lower than rock bottom, so where would the harm really be?

'Alright,' I sigh.

'You'll come?' Her face illuminates.

'For you. For everything. Yes.'

Chapter 31

'THIS IS THE PLACE?' I ask, slack-jawed as the taxi indicates off of the road and down a track lined with budding cypress trees towards an imposing grey stone chateau flanked with two round turrets.

The American peers out as if I'm seeing something she isn't. 'Yes, is that okay?'

I turn to her. 'You said it was a *house.*'

'It is a house.'

'It has a moat.' I point to the bridge we are about to pass over.

She shrugs. 'Still a house,' but I can see her trying to hide her smile.

There is a grunting from behind and Crispy's head appears between the two headrests. 'Doris has always done her birthday in style; every year she says she's going big because she thinks it's her last.'

I crane my neck to look at him. 'How many of these have you been to?'

'Well, let's just say Doris has been dying since 2012.'

The American scowls at him, bats a fan in the direction of his face but he manages to duck back into the rear seat without injury.

'Ooh, looks like the others got here first.' She claps her hands together and we look out of the window to see a few cars already pulled up on the forecourt. I had forgotten about the prospect of others. Whilst I consider myself a semi-sociable person, who can at least pretend to be confident and nice for a few hours, I wasn't looking forward to switching dynamics, to having to start from the beginning with people who I would probably never even meet again. I am bruised too, slightly emotionally bedraggled and the rawness of it all still catches me off guard. I had been able to cope in the apartment, until I had braved the outside and headed to a shop to purchase The American a present and bumped into Inés. She had apologised about the other night and I had been confused about what she meant. I had almost forgotten that the last time I had seen her she had disappeared. A lifetime had happened in a week; something had blossomed, existed and swiftly died in seven short days.

The taxi pulls up, crunching over the gravel as it comes to a halt. I slip out of the other door whilst the driver spends a few minutes helping The American and Crispy from the car. It is good to surround yourself with octogenarians when you're feeling a bit shit about yourself; it does make you reflect on how good it is to be relatively agile and to have complete control of all your limbs.

'Sabine!' The American opens her long arms, made longer still by yet another butterfly sleeve, in the direction of a plump, petite woman dressed in a black suit in the doorway.

'Madame, bon anniversaire,' the woman called Sabine greets The American. The two women meet in a mele of cheek kisses and excitement.

'Sabine's the housekeeper,' Crispy elaborates into my ear.

I turn on my heels to look at him properly, to see if there is any hint of a joke on his face. 'We have a housekeeper?'

'Oh yes!' he nods. 'Just wait till you meet the chef.'

We are interrupted by The American ushering us towards the front door, flanked, like the rest of the full-length windows, with burgundy shutters.

Inside, it feels like we have stepped into a museum. The floors are grey flagstones and the walls are panelled in a dark wood. Scattered around the space are what can only be described as relics: a few busts, portraits in gold frames, candle sconces on the walls and in the corner a sentinel suit of armour.

'Bloody hell.' I brush my fingers over a piece of wooden furniture in the corner.

'The estate has been here since the twelfth century.' Sabine steps in to give me the tour as The American and Crispy are already heading towards some double doors at surprising speed. 'The chateau that we are in now was built later in the eighteenth century. It has been in one family's ownership since then.'

'It's beautiful.'

'I think so.' Sabine smiles. 'There are worse places to work I am sure.' There is the sound of a door opening and a sudden onslaught of noise: cackling, cheering, groaning. 'The others are in the courtyard having a welcome drink.'

'I should probably join them.' I know that my face gives my lack of enthusiasm away. Sabine gifts me a reassuring nod and gestures towards the door for me to lead on.

The American's friends are as varied as I had imagined with one thing in common: they are clearly fans of at least one outlandish item of clothing. There is a woman with comically large glasses and a silk turban called Debbie who was a nude model in the seventies, her husband Frederic – probably my age – who is wearing an almost entirely white suit, a writer named Winona who looks like she could give Jackie Collins a run for her money, a Rupert in red chinos, an Alphonse who has a pipe lolling out of his mouth, an Evangeline who looks even older than The American and is using a rhinestone cane, and a final woman, who Crispy informs me is called Jeanette, who looks distantly famous, with a suspiciously un-lined face and bright-red hair.

I wonder where I fit into this motley crew. They greet me as an old friend regardless. They say they have heard lots about me, and I wonder how The American has pitched her little lodger, a bright young thing with a book deal, or a slightly down-and-out widow who needs to be clapped on the back and told she's doing well.

We are served champagne in delicate little coupes and have canapes of prunes and cheese and caviar waved under our noses for our approval.

I politely pick at the food, mainline a few glasses until The American shoots me a look that lets me know I am being watched and decline the next one Sabine offers. I know it's a party but even I can't pretend that I'd be getting drunk just for the festivities.

It feels as if everyone has been here for months and I am the late arrival. They know the order of the day, where the bathrooms are, they slip in and out of rooms, and I am left entirely out of step, like I'm at one of those shows that requires audience participation, except I'm drunk and wasn't aware I'd even bought a ticket.

'You look like you're dying on your feet,' The American mutters into my ear.

'I feel it.'

'Why don't you go and lie down before dinner, have a bath, freshen up?' she suggests. 'Might make you feel better.'

'And you can keep me sober for longer?' I ask. She shrugs.

'You just have to make it to nine, half of us will be in bed by then and the other half will be drunker than even you can manage.'

'There's one issue.'

'Yes?'

'I don't know where my room is.'

'Oh! Sabine!' The American suddenly calls out and seconds later, the familiar bobbed figure of Sabine emerges, the same unfazed smile she had greeted us with earlier fixed onto her face.

I am whisked into the quiet calmness of the house, having to trot to keep up with Sabine as she slips up the stairs. 'Now most of the bedrooms are on the ground floor, due to the...' Sabine pauses, thinks about how best to phrase it, 'access.' She pauses, looks at me to see if I understand that she is politely letting me know that most of the party aren't a fan of stairs. I can only imagine the situation becoming practically perilous when alcohol is added into the mix. 'So, it's only you and one other guest on this floor.'

'Okay.' I suddenly notice the vastness of the corridor, the creaking darkness of the passageways. 'I don't suppose there are any ghosts lingering about, are there?'

'Oh no.' She shakes her head quickly. 'Only rumours.'

'Rumours?' My neck snaps to her.

She pouts her lips. 'Well, yes, but I've lived here for twenty-two years and never seen anything of concern so don't be alarmed.'

'Brilliant.' I manage a straight-lipped smile as she reaches for a key, stopping at a door painted a dusky blue with a brass knocker. She lets me enter first. The room is thankfully much lighter than the corridor, with tall deep-set windows upholstered into window seats with banking views over the grounds. The bed, a ridiculous four-poster, sits opposite the windows and I am desperate for the morning, to sit there with a coffee and take in the early sun. Everything is in shades of blue and white, from the periwinkle on the walls to the magnolia patterns on the curtains, and culminates in a willow-pattern eiderdown on the bed.

'Madame picks all the rooms for the guests,' Sabine says, watching me take it all in. 'She says you were in need of something...' She looks for the word, racking her brain for the English word, 'peaceful,' she shrugs.

'She was right.' I run my hand over a chalky white armoire with a bunch of hydrangeas in a white porcelain vase. 'It is very peaceful.'

'You have a bathroom.' She opens the door onto a large marble space with old brass fixtures and a claw-foot bath by the windows. I notice a box of toiletries already prepped on the side. 'You also have access to a balcony. It's shared with your neighbour, I hope that's okay.'

'Yes,' I nod. 'That's fine.'

'Wonderful. Well then, I'll leave you to it, there's the itinerary for the weekend on the dressing table.'

'An itinerary?'

Sabine just grins at me. 'She is quite strict about it too, so don't keep her waiting.'

'Thank you.'

'You're welcome.' Sabine closes the door leaving me on my own. I take in some more of the room, try to listen for voices but all I can hear is the occasional snippet of birdsong, the frogs beginning to wake up for the evening.

I find the itinerary in pride of place on the bedside table along with a little bag. Sabine was right: by every event there is a dress code, a time and a location. I baulk a little at the dress code; prior warning would have meant I could have at least packed to order. I look for my battered old carry on but it isn't anywhere to be seen. I open up my wardrobe to find to my horror that everything has already been packed away, even my incredibly old and slightly holey knickers have been pressed and put into a drawer. The biggest concern however is that there are definitely more clothes than I had packed. The American had clearly taken her own initiative.

I collapse onto the bed with the little paper bag and pour out the contents onto the quilt. There's a couple of face masks, an array of expensive-looking skincare, a couple of pre-mixed cocktails in mason jars and a box of chocolates I recognise from the chocolatier in the village. I think The American may have far more money than even I realised, and by God, is she on a mission to spend it before she goes.

My phone pings. For a moment that idiotic hope lingers until I see that it's my mum asking how I am. I take a picture of the room and send it to her. She sends a vomit emoji back followed swiftly by a love heart and then sends a rather long-winded apology about clumsy thumbs and not wearing her glasses.

Chapter 32

DINNER IS A BARBECUE on the terrace, a strangely casual affair considering that we all look like we're going to the opera. Not only had The American gone to the effort of selecting my outfits, she had labelled them with the specific nights they were to be worn leaving me little room for manoeuvre. Tonight is a red satin dress with a plunging neckline that makes me look like I am attending the Oscars in the 1990s. I have rebelled somewhat by leaving my hair damp and putting on as little make-up as possible without looking as if I am actually a corpse. She rolls her eyes when I appear, exactly at seven, and tells me I am being immature. I tell her perhaps we should both act our age.

We mill about on the terrace in little packs, still slightly unsure of the others in our party. It is clear who has met before; they laugh loudly at the other's jokes, place hands on each other's shoulders and waists for a little too long.

I am allowed to skirt the edges, occasionally being included in a conversation. I learn that Debbie has been married three times before she met her Frederic who is actually a year younger than me. They met at the ballet which Crispy later informs me is a load of bollocks unless 'ballet' was a new name for a dating site for younger men who want to be bankrolled through their thirties in exchange for a few nights of passion a year.

Rupert with the red chinos seems to be the only semi-normal person here. He was a theatre agent in a past life and now spends his retirement selling art.

*

The American flows through the crowd effortlessly. She looks younger, like she has spent her life in a constant state of rehearsal for these things. I think about the story she told me, the life she must have lived, how in many ways this was the one thing a marriage to a man she never really loved allowed her. I think of how sad it is then, that the one person she probably wants to be here more than anyone, isn't. I feel that familiar sadness seek me out again, but it's sharper than it has been, with frayed raw edges because I'm not thinking about Etienne.

'Do you approve?' The American asks when it's my turn. She places her arm around my waist pulling me into her. She smells of lavender and gin, a delicious combination.

'It's beautiful and you've been very generous, some would say too generous.' I gesture to the dress.

'No such thing. You look beautiful. It's important for young women to feel beautiful or they end up becoming all sad and boring and settle for sad and boring men.'

'I get your point.'

'And you're feeling okay?'

'Yes. I'm feeling better. I'm happy I'm here.' I kiss her cheeks again and she holds me so close to her I think for a second that she won't let me go.

In a clearly well-rehearsed routine, some young men in suits push the tables away from the floor, leaving space for the band who have begun to play something more upbeat. The guests begin to congregate on the dancefloor whilst I stay back, a happy observer. That is until there is a tap on my shoulder and Crispy, wearing a silver suit and the same red cravat, stands there holding his hand out expectantly.

'Is there any point in me saying no right now?'

'Not one bit.' He winks and pulls me into the middle where he immediately starts to pirouette me until I squeal for him to stop and threaten to vomit.

'That's better,' Crispy shouts over the music.

'What is?' I ask, my face screwing up in confusion.
'You're smiling.'

Crispy has the guy at the bar at his beck and call, delivering large gin and tonics directly into our hands.

'Do you smoke?' Crispy slurs after our third goldfish ball of Tanqueray.

'Occasionally,' I nod, expecting Crispy to present a little packet of cigarettes but instead he nudges me in the direction of some stairs. I take our drinks and follow him down to a hidden patio where some expensive-looking loungers are scattered around the swimming pool.

He collapses into one with a groaning thump and rifles in his jacket pocket for a little silver cigarette case.

'That looks expensive.'

'Was my grandfather's, you can see the dent a bullet made over in Ypres.' He opens it up to reveal eight rather suspicious-looking cigarettes. 'I rather like the fact I'm using it for nothing but debauchery now.' He takes one out and the smell hits me.

'When you asked if I smoked, I thought you meant cigarettes.'

'Oh no.' He curls up his lip in disgust. 'This is purely medicinal.' He shrugs as if it is some consolation, lights the spliff and then immediately passes it to me.

I think about saying no. I haven't done this since university and even then, I distinctly remember throwing up almost immediately.

'Fuck it.' I grab the spliff and take a short, half-hearted drag before spluttering most of it out immediately.

Crispy takes it back off me with a slightly incredulous look and lies back in his deckchair staring up at the sky.

'Fucking lovely, isn't it?' he says. I look up too, take in the splattering of stars, the heavy moon, the glow and laughter emanating from the house.

'Yeah. It's pretty nice.'

'She's happy you're here.' He takes a long breath. 'You know the past few months, it's like I've got the old girl back again.'

I turn to him, his eyes still lost in the sky. 'How do you mean?'

'She's not been the same since...' He pauses, looks at me to see if I know, if I look blankly at him he won't finish his sentence because he doesn't want to give The American's biggest secret away. I admire that protectiveness, can see the depth of the friendship that The American builds with those she lets in.

'Since Bluette?'

His shoulders relax. 'You know?'

'I have the synopsis, you know, the major plot points,' I add.

'I met them the first day I moved here. They were at the same bar and they sniffed me out. We were inseparable from then on. They made it all easier in those blurry months when you're just trying to find your feet.'

'What were they like? As a couple?'

I watch as his face glows a little at the memory. 'As happy as clams.' He nods. 'Yes, you know, it sounds a bit saccharine, but it made me truly believe that there was such a thing as soulmates because when you saw them together, how easy it was for them to be in each other's company after all that time, everything sort of made sense.'

The sentimentality hovers over us. I allow myself to imagine them, drinking in cafés for breakfast, reading extracts of books to each other, Bluette painting whilst The American put together another mad outfit, just the mundane moments of complete happiness that made the sadness of losing it all worth it.

'And Bluette?' I add. 'What was she like?'

'Doris's total opposite,' he smirks. 'But lovely all the same. Blu was kind, soft, almost shy, she liked to sit back and watch people, but there was a gentleness to her – no judgement, just... peace.' He gulps back a lump in his throat which seems to bring him out of the memories, back to the here and now. 'God, we shouldn't be crying this early into the weekend, it's not even the big day yet.'

I squeeze his spare hand in agreement.

'Well, anyway.' Crispy takes another drag. 'You're a good friend to her, Ava, she appreciates good friends.'

I feel myself blush, the heat spreads down my chest. But this is my chance. Crispy is my chance to finally figure this out. 'Crispy...' I start. He looks up. 'This is going to sound really stupid but I don't think I can be considered a very good friend because... Well, I don't actually know her name.'

Crispy grins, his whole face ruching up, and then he starts laughing. It's silent at first until the air catches on his breath and he starts to honk.

'You still haven't figured it out yet? Good God, Ava, I thought you were meant to be smart; I mean there are enough clues in that sodding apartment.'

'There are?'

'I hope you figure it out by tomorrow otherwise I'll owe her a hundred!'

'She knows? You've placed bets on it?'

'Oh my dear, Doris thinks it's the funniest thing that's happened to her in a long time!'

I feel the heat in my face subside. 'And she doesn't hate me?'

'Hate you? Darling, she adores you. You just remember that. She just wants you to be happy.'

I let the reality sink in, how one of my biggest embarrassments has actually been something that The American has been revelling in, all this time.

I sigh, pull a hand through my hair and prop myself up on the lounger looking at him properly with a grin. 'You're going to tell me now that your name isn't actually Crispy, aren't you?'

'Well, aren't you clever,' he smirks. 'Unfortunately, I wasn't as lucky in the nickname department. I was a dancer in my youth – ballet,' he adds and brings his arms up above his head in a static pirouette. 'Pretty damn good if I do say so myself and my birthname wasn't exactly inspiring.'

'Go on...'

'Oh...' He looks around to see if anyone's listening and when he realises the coast is clear he sighs. 'Bernard.' He side-eyes me. I try to wrestle the emerging grin from my face.

'How lovely,' I choke back.

'You're an awful actress, darling,' he pouts. 'Well, anyway, when I started auditioning I wanted a stage name, something refined, classy, unusual, so I became Crispin Fée.'

'Wow… that was a choice.'

'Crispin was one of the old prefects at my school, had his name carved into one of those plaques that I had to walk past every day and it kind of rubbed off on me I guess. Anyway, when I met Doris and Bluette all those years ago, they took one look at me and thought I could do with being brought down a peg so I swiftly became Crispy.'

'I mean it's not the worst…'

He offers me another drag but I shake my head, deciding that the third gin was enough of a tranquiliser for one night. He takes another deep breath and the smell of the weed sticks to the air.

'Doris told me about your late husband,' Crispy says to the sky, as if he's addressing some far-off galaxy. Like he has his own personal constellation of lost souls that he talks to nightly like this. He takes another drag. 'And if it's any consolation I think you're doing marvellously.'

I scoff, 'I am?'

He turns to me, taking me in with a reassuring little squint. 'Losing people, grief, well it acts as a mangle. I know death, it been a sad sort of companion in my life and I've watched as the grief consumes people, becomes them until it's hard to see them as anything else. You, my girl, there's still some life in you yet.'

I look at him hard, look at the sadness that I realise has been there the whole time, a sadness he has tried to mask with red cravats and silver suits. 'You think?'

He reaches over the arm rest of the chair, takes my hand in his and rubs it vigorously. 'I do.'

He gives me the headline pieces of gossip about each of The American's guests until we hear some commotion from the dance floor, some cheering, more voices, a different hum.

I sit up, start the process of standing up. Crispy pulls at my dress.

'Oh, don't go!' he pleads.

'We're missing the party.' I pull free of his grasp and Crispy quickly scrabbles to his feet.

'But we're having fun!' he pouts as I start to leave, precariously edging my way around the pool towards the exit. 'Five more minutes.' He trails after me, clawing at me to stay.

'What's happening?' I ask, my eyes narrowing at him. The protestation is too much to just want me to stay here innocently.

'Nothing's happening! Just stay here for a few more—' His sentence is stopped prematurely, replaced instead by a small strangled little shout and finished with a loud, thunderous splash. I look around to see Crispy underwater, his hands the only thing visible above the water line, desperately flapping about, his body making no attempt to surface.

Without thinking I jump in after him, reaching for the silver suit and when I have it in my hands, I desperately try to pull him to the edge until my knees catch on the bottom and I realise just how shallow it is. Barely a metre deep.

'Just stand!' I plead with the half-drowned figure who eventually returns to the surface, spluttering and choking. He slowly draws himself to his full height, the sad spliff hanging limply in his mouth.

When he finally gathers his breath he takes a look at me, hair sopping, dress weighed down by the water and lets out an almighty bellow of a laugh. He cackles at himself, at both of us, for a full minute until it becomes contagious and I am laughing too.

'You arsehole.' I splash him. 'I thought you were going to drown.'

'I shouldn't walk and smoke,' he booms and splashes me back.

When we turn around it is clear that the shrieking and splashing has drawn a crowd of concerned and confused faces and the guests are standing by the shallow end, watching us.

'She saved me!' Crispy wraps his arms around my neck and pretends to swoon. I push him off of me and watch as he clambers to the side, still hooting merrily.

'What on earth?' The crowd parts to reveal The American shuffling as fast as she can to see what all the commotion is about. I almost don't notice the person at her side, how his concern turns to steely fury when his eyes meet mine and take me in.

'Shit,' Crispy hisses into the water.

'Florian…' I struggle for the words. His lip twitches in recognition of his name on my lips, the rest of his body rigid apart from a fist which he is clenching repetitively.

I manage to regain control of my face, it draws up into a hopeful smile – confirmation of how much I have wanted him to be here, of how much I wanted to see him again.

I wait for him to move, to smile, to wink, to grin in that way he has perfected, but a coolness hangs over him and then I watch as he turns his back and begins to storm back the way he entered.

'Florian – wait!' The American calls, staggering after him. I can feel all the other eyes of the guests on me, at the sopping wet girl in the pool.

'You knew he was coming?' I look to Crispy, all of the fun, the tipsiness fading from me. He doesn't meet my eye. In that moment I know this has been just one big elaborate ruse.

I make my way to the steps with as much grace as a very wet three-legged giraffe and stumble out of the pool. The dress feels like someone has sewn weights into the hems and I trip only to be caught by Rupert who holds me at arm's length like I might combust. I reach for a towel on the wall and manage a half-hearted attempt at mopping up some of the water but it's a pointless exercise, so I limp towards the direction that Florian and The American had left in.

'You lied to me!' Florian shouts from house, the words echoing through the doors to the terrace. I see the open doors, spy their heads a few metres in front of us and brave the floor, leaving a trail of pool water in my wake.

'I didn't lie. You assumed she wasn't here,' The American protests, her voice laboured from the exertion.

'You didn't say she would be!'

They turn to me when I come into view, both looking as exasperated as the other but it's hard to shake the look of sheer hatred in Florian's eyes.

The American breaks first. 'I wanted you to be here. I wanted you to both be here.'

'Did you know?' He looks at me with a ferocity that stings. The first thing he has said to me since that night.

'Know what?'

'That I'd be here. Was this some plan to...'

'What – to get you back?' I scoff, furious at his self-assurance. 'No, Florian, I wasn't made aware that I would be playing the starring role in my own shitty rom-com tonight.'

The American hangs between us, arms out on either side as if we might draw swords. 'Neither of you knew. Things just got out of hand. I didn't know things were as bad as they were when I ran into you and I thought you needed cheering up, Florian. I... knew that Rupert would be here and I genuinely thought it would be a good opportunity to connect.'

'And her?'

'I saw Ava after I saw you... You hadn't said whether you would come and she's my friend, Florian. I wanted her here.'

'Well, have her here, I'm going.'

'Stop it!' A soggy Crispy careers into the room. 'All of you stop it, you're acting like children. There is no reason on God's green earth that we can't all be here at the same time enjoying this wonderful weekend. This place is big enough for the both of you to avoid each other all day if you want to, we don't care. Doris is eighty-three years old for goodness' sake and she wants you two to both be here. So, grow up and get over yourselves.'

We stand there staring at each other in a kind of stalemate until Florian breaks. He kisses his teeth, throws his hands in the air. 'I need a drink.'

We watch him go without moving ourselves. I feel their eyes turn to me, waiting for me to explode.

'Ava…' The American starts but I wave my hand to get her to stop.

'I'm sure your intentions are completely honourable but right now I need a drink and to be on my own.'

I take a bottle of wine from the side and disappear up the stairs leaving the party and the dancing and the fun behind me.

Chapter 33

BREAKFAST IS A SIMPLER and more subdued affair. Despite the strict start time of nine, only four of us, including The American, have managed to make it. I didn't exactly care whether I was going to be punctual or not, in fact I am pretty sure I would have a free pass this morning to sulk, but the truth was that I had woken up at three in the morning to my neighbour crashing around and been unable to go back to sleep. Therefore, to at least have somewhere to go and something to do was a more savoury option than stewing in my room on my own for the rest of the morning.

The American is uncharacteristically quiet, averting her eyes from mine whenever she can. Crispy has not materialised and neither has Florian, although I don't begrudge him that.

I pick at pastries whilst the other guests filter in, in dribs and drabs, clutching their heads and turning a little green at the sight of the sausages on the side.

'Remind us of what's on the agenda today?' Rupert asks The American. He is one of the only people who looks like he normally functions at this time of the morning.

'Well, there's some free time in the morning and then the opportunity for some art after lunch followed by lawn games and then dinner at seven,' she replies.

I can't help but roll my eyes at the quaintness of it all, how it feels both like a retreat and a place for extreme exposure therapy at once.

'What time are we contractually obliged to meet?' I ask, my voice carrying over the table. I sound pissed off. I am pissed off.

'Uh, does one o'clock work?' The American has switched her fascist party-planning techniques to something much more libertarian. I know it's entirely for my benefit, to try to demonstrate that I have some control of the situation.

'See you then.' I don't look at her as I gather my things, down the last of my coffee and clamber up the stairs to see Florian emerging from the room next to mine.

My noisy three o'clock neighbour. The only other guest here apparently capable of doing stairs.

'Are you fucking serious!' I shout to the ceiling, enjoying how it carries along the ornate woodwork and down the stairs, hopefully to the ears of The American who will know that I have indeed discovered her attempts at organising a meet-cute.

I also take a lot of pride in the fact that my exclamation causes a slightly hungover Florian to squirm from the noise.

I let myself into my room before I can say anything else. I need to rehearse it anyway.

I think of all the things I can do with my morning and decide to rescue my swimsuit from the wardrobe and wrestle it on. I take my book for good measure, hoping that it might serve to quieten the thrumming internal monologue that is proving to be a rather exhausting companion.

In the daylight, the pool with its sheltered little courtyard feels much less dramatic. The deckchairs that Crispy and I had lay on before his betrayal had been pushed back together, fresh towels at their feet. The only sign from last night are my shoes, which have been neatly placed on a small side table.

However, in comparison to the rest of this place it is empty, and unlike my bedroom, there is air and a breeze and something to do.

I dip my toes in first; there is the faint promise of heat but as I let the water wash over me it still takes my breath away. I swim a few laps, at first trying to keep my head above the water until I can feel the wetness tracing its way up the back of my neck and decide to dunk my head under the water. I stay under for a few moments, let the cold drown out the voice in my head, the constant hum of emotions that I hadn't realised I had been carrying. I stay there until my lungs start to feel as if they might burst open and when I emerge, gasping, Florian is sitting on the edge in a pair of salmon-pink swimming trunks, dipping his calves into the water.

'Thought you might not be coming back up for a moment there,' he coughs.

'Considered it.' I take a few deep breaths until the world around me begins to turn crisp and cold again. 'I assumed you were going to breakfast.'

'Couldn't face it,' he shrugs. 'I thought this might clear my head; didn't anticipate you'd be doing the same thing.'

'Well, my foggy head was caused by my neighbour waking me up at three o'clock with some drunken crashing about.'

Florian manages a dry chuckle, a warmth returning to him. He looks up to the house, to our shared little terrace. 'You have to congratulate them on their ingenuity.'

'Do we?' I scoff.

'If it wasn't so misjudged.'

'I suppose.'

He bites the bullet and lowers himself into the water, his whole torso tensing, and I can make out the faint line of an ab. 'Your flight was today.' He shivers, bringing his shoulders under the water line and then bobbing around a few metres from me.

'I changed it.'

'So that's what it took to keep you here – a party.' He says the last bit with a flourish, his hands splashing around manically.

'Don't say it like that. I didn't exactly have anything to go back for after all that.'

His head snaps up to me, a clarity descending. 'What?'

'It doesn't matter.' I shake my head.

He looks unconvinced but also still bruised enough that he doesn't want to give me the pleasure of knowing I have spiked his concern. 'Okay.'

'Am I allowed to ask why she wanted you to meet Rupert?'

I counter, feeling like I have earned at least one question this morning.

'He's an art collector, has connections in various galleries. He likes my work, wants to work with me.'

'Great.' I try a supportive little smile.

'And I've apologised for causing a scene last night. I was just caught off guard. I said we would be civil.'

I nod and start to propel myself to the steps. 'I can do civil.'

'Don't go on my account.' Florian looks slightly apologetically at me. 'I didn't mean to interrupt your alone time.'

'It's fine. I'm done anyway,' I shrug and launch myself out of the water, reaching immediately for a towel. Yes, he may have seen half of my naked body in the café but that feels like a million years ago now.

I settle my damp body on a lounger on the lawn that overlooks a handful of guests playing a lazy game of Pétanque. I take the book out of my little bag and try to find the specific dog-eared page but after reading the first few lines, I have no idea what's happening and instead start from the beginning, hoping that at least then I have something longer to distract me.

My plan is short-lived as I hear heavy, raspy breaths and the sound of feet shuffling towards me.

'Are you talking to me yet?' The American heaves herself down into the chair next to me, a large sunhat and glasses concealing most of her face.

'Depends on what you have to say.'

'I'm sorry?'

'That's a good start.' I bring my knees up to my chest, wrapping my arms around them and linking my fingers together, watching as Alphonse stands behind the line and deftly launches the silver ball in the air where it swiftly lands a few inches from the jack. There are some cheers, Rupert shakes his hand vigorously before pulling him into a sort of half-hug.

'Did you and Florian talk any more?' The American persists. I meet her eyes, genuinely curious and well-meaning.

'What, in our adjacent rooms?' I peek at her over my sunglasses. She looks a little bashfully at the floor, realising she has been well and truly caught out.

'You're the only ones here with your original hips, the room situation was sort of out of my hands.'

'Well, I caught him in the pool. We said we would be civil to each other.'

'Civil,' she tries the word on her tongue, 'how…'

'Sad?' I smirk. 'Yeah, well at the minute I guess I'm lucky to at least have civil.'

'Did he say anything about the other night?'

'No. It wasn't a conversation I think either of us realised was going to end well.'

'Still,' she shrugs, 'it's a conversation you need to have.'

'Well why don't you orchestrate a game of sardines and lock us up in a cupboard together, sure we'd have the conversation soon enough.'

'Tempting.' She looks as if she is genuinely weighing up whether it would be worth it.

'Look, I appreciate how invested you are in my love life, honestly no one has tried harder, but at the end of the day some things just can't be worked through. This is one of them, and it's sad and it hurts but I can't say I didn't give it a good go and whilst I don't believe that everything in this life happens for a reason, I do believe that if despite your best efforts things still aren't working out, then you probably should admit defeat.'

The American's eyes move to the group below who have now set up another game. She lets out a deep and sad sigh.

'I like him, Ava. I just think it's very sad.'

Chapter 34

I HAVE ONLY EVER seen a 'white party' on an episode of *The Real Housewives* and had assumed that, as we most definitely did not run in the same social circles, I would never have to attend one in my life. Obviously, I had never factored in meeting a flamboyant American geriatric who thought lime green was a neutral and who lived for a bit of theatrics. So, when I slip on the white maxi dress left in my closet, that is all too white and all too sheer simultaneously, I can't help but feel as if I've fallen into some alternative reality.

It is a small mercy that the dress is what some would describe as 'beachy' and not 'bridal' as I have a sneaking suspicion that The American might think that decking me out in a white dress with a train would be an excellent opportunity to demonstrate to Florian how right we are for each other.

I unscrew one of the pre-mixed cocktails from the gift bag and down it in four gulps, not stopping to feel the sting just knowing that in a few moments whatever's waiting for me downstairs will feel much more manageable.

The bell rings for the second time from downstairs and I grab my bag and take one last glancing look in the mirror before leaving. When I get to the top of the stairs, I hear something slam behind me; I turn to see Florian who freezes on the landing. He looks frustratingly good: linen trousers, brown brogues and a white linen shirt left open at the collar.

I feel my cheeks redden, debate whether to say something to him, but I know that anything that falls out of my mouth will be idiotic and unfathomable. Instead, I manage a sort of sad half smile, the kind you shoot strangers in parks when you walk past them and you're trying to be nice. He receives it and matches mine with an equally awkward gesture until I turn around and make my way to where the music is coming from.

I am grateful to see Crispy's face at the bottom of the stairs. He pretends to faint at the sight of me.

'Well look at you.' He presses his red cheeks into mine and makes me stand back for appraisal.

'I feel ridiculous.'

'You look Grecian,' he says suggesting an alternative and I take it. 'Bloody hell!' he suddenly guffaws and I look at where his gaze has fallen, onto Florian who has been snapped up by Debbie with the three husbands. 'Doesn't he look dashing?'

'Does he?' I lie through my teeth and catch Crispy's disbelieving look. 'Okay, yes he looks good.'

'Tits up, darling, remember why we're here.' He pats me on the shoulder and then strings his arm through mine leading us both to the terrace.

We are greeted by a long table made up with white linen sitting in pride of place under a net of festoon bulbs. Along the length of the table are silver candelabra with white peonies scattered in tiny stem glasses.

'It's stunning,' I say almost annoyed at how pretty everything looks, how in any other circumstances I would be so happy to be here, to experience this. I know that when I get on that plane on Tuesday, I probably won't ever be somewhere like this again.

'God, she's always so dramatic,' Crispy rolls his eyes. 'I'm almost expecting Liberace to fall out of the closet.'

I'm unsure if everyone had the same wardrobe treatment but every guest has stuck to the dress code in their own way, choosing to express their individuality with yet more strange additions to their outfits in the form of flower crowns, palm-sized jewellery and designer headscarves.

The only person who hasn't yet made their presence known

is the lady of the hour, so we all mill about, drinking coupes of champagne, waiting for the grand entrance.

Florian and I play the part of the opposing poles of magnets: when I go to the bar to order a drink, he is at the other end of the room talking; when he moves closer to the table, I find an excuse to talk to somebody on the terrace.

At half past seven, a string quartet begins to play in hushed tones, and the chateau feels as if it comes to life, as if this is the only true way to experience it. The chatter and laughter begin to subside. When we turn towards the staircase I see *the dress* before I see the person wearing it. She makes her way down the stairs, Sabine's arm in hers, in a cloud of chiffon and lace, so much material that it almost dwarfs her. She is beautiful, her silver hair loose and longer than I had realised it was, the same peonies that are scattered over the table embroidered onto the train as she sweeps down the last step into the lounge.

There's applause then, some wolf whistles, and I watch how she glows at being looked at, at being admired, and suddenly she makes sense to me in a way she never has before. All the clothes, the jewellery, the scarves, this dress – all a massive fuck you to a world that has told her that she should grow old gracefully, should retire into a world where she would be ignored. She has never wanted to be ignored. She wants everyone to pay attention to the fact that here she is, very much alive and kicking.

The American beams at her enthralled audience and moves to the head of the table, to a seat that might as well be called a throne. Everyone follows, makes notes of the little place cards on the silver chargers. I linger at the bottom of the table, my name unfindable until Crispy nudges me.

'The Queen has requested your presence tonight.' He bobs into a curtsy and gestures to the seat next to hers.

I suspect a trap, look for Florian, but he is seated away from me, about as far away from me as the table allows.

She watches me as I take a seat cautiously.

'No games tonight.' She shoots me an apologetic little smile.

'Just an old bat wanting the pleasure of your company for one last evening.'

I feel the tears welling in my eyes; of all the emotions I expected to feel tonight, sadness wasn't one of them.

'Are you sure?' I ask.

'Very sure.' She nods and I plant myself gently in the seat next to her.

'You look very beautiful.'

'I never thought I suited white.' I gesture to the dress awkwardly.

'Darling, everyone suits white, but you suit it especially well.'

Dinner is a four-course affair, with waiters in white tuxedos butterflying service and presenting elaborately decorated dishes of veloutés, scallops and duck. At the end of the meal a cheese board is placed at the centre of the table for people to groan at but still pick through greedily as if it would be rude not to. I try not to count the bottles of champagne and wine that are taken away empty almost as soon as they arrive.

I don't feel drunk though, I feel happy. The conversation flows easily at this end of the table and whenever I do shoot a glance down it, I notice that it is a similar story across the board. The hum of contentment.

There is a clinking of a glass and our eyes shoot to Crispy who is standing up, enjoying the attention of the eyes that find him.

'Well,' he starts, 'it is tradition at these kinds of things to say some kind words about our birthday girl, but I've been to many soirees with her at the helm, so fear my stocks are running a tad dry on original content. So I have taken the liberty of choosing someone else to do the honours.' The table falls into an uncomfortable silence. We look from face to face, waiting for someone to stand but when that doesn't happen, Crispy clears his throat. 'Ava,' he holds up his glass, 'would you do the honours?' I feel the colour drain from my face, a clammy discomfort spreading over my shoulders and down my chest.

'Oh… surely not me?' I look to The American whose hand is placed on mine.

'You are our wordsmith,' she encourages. I stand up, reach for my glass but miss it, instead sending it spilling its contents over the table. My neighbours jump back, away from the liquid and I throw a napkin on them hoping to cover the worst.

'Shit, so sorry!' I gabble out an apology. My eyes flit from one expectant face to another until I see Florian's. His eyes are gentle, soft and entirely void of judgement. *Go on*, he mouths and, in that moment, I find my breath.

'I would have prepared something…' I start. 'If I had known… but I'm pretty sure that anything I would have prepared wouldn't have really been able to summarise you.' I look to The American who grins at me. 'I had thought that my trip back to France would be something that I needed to endure, that there were no more surprises that this place could throw at me, but that couldn't be further from the truth.' I can't help but let a wry little smile fall from my mouth. 'I never expected that my landlord would have shown up in a black, tasselled kimono to give me her own guided tour of the home I have come to love as if I have been there all my life. I'm not sure if all landlords in France are expected to show the amount of dedication to their tenant's experience as you have, but I have to say that even though I may not have always seemed it, I am nothing but grateful for your company.

'And continuing the theme of things I never expected, I definitely never thought that my closest confidant would be you.' I hold my glass in her direction. 'That you would allow this mess of a woman to sit there and bore you with my almost daily dramas, and yet you gave nothing back but good humour, sage advice and a hell of a wardrobe.' I gesture to my dress and Crispy hollers some wordless response. 'But you have been more than a friend to me, you have been the person I needed, a person who I am honoured to know. You are incredible. Truly, the most incredible woman I have ever met. I have never believed too much in signs and destiny and fate, but I think that someone up there knew exactly what I needed, who I needed, and they sent me to you and what a privilege it's been to know you for even the shortest of times.' My voice wavers and I fight to control it. 'I think I love you,' I snigger. 'I think that you might be one of the best people I have ever met,' I add as she grabs onto my hand, watery tears in her eyes. 'And I think I'm going to miss you the most when I leave. Happy birthday for tomorrow, you old thing.' I hold my glass up to a chorus of happy birthdays and cheering until I am allowed to take my seat again where I immediately find my eyes back on Florian who nods approvingly in my direction.

'I would like to say something.' The American slowly gets to her feet, the wine going some way to make her look her age. All eyes and ears turn back to her. 'Thank you, Ava, your speech was far better than anything I've got out of Crispy now for a decade.' She winks. 'I would like to say that when you live as long as I have, you realise that this table should be far bigger, that I could fill it fourfold with the amount of people that I have loved and who loved me but it is the curse of age and having far too much fun. But when I look at you, I see them too – see my parents, Jack, all the friends from every corner of the world I built my life around, I see Bluette and all the birthdays we should have had together celebrating, but tonight, I feel fulfilled, feel incredibly lucky that I get to still do this, to sit at a table with people who mean the world to me, old and new. Thank you for letting a lady have a bit of fun.'

We dance and drink for the next three hours until my feet start to scream at me and I've drunk so much I've almost started sobering up. Florian and The American are arm in arm dancing gently around the terrace. I let my eyes blur, the same way I had when we had been in his studio, blur them enough so that in the right light I can see his and Ettie's brotherly similarity, knowing that Ettie would have loved this more than anything. He would have won The American over in an instant and would have whisked her off to waltz under the stars too, probably much more dramatically than Florian is managing, perhaps with deathly spins and a backbend. He would have danced with me too, the kind of dance in which his hands would be everywhere and I feel the longing spread through me.

And the thought of him, that kind of lingering awareness of what could have been, The American's little comment about having a host of ghosts at every party, makes me miss him more in that moment than I have since I got here. I don't want him here to cheer me up, or keep me company, or because it would make my life easier. I want him here because he would love it and I want to see him love it myself.

There are feelings that, once you have them, you can't shake off with another drink and a nice conversation. So, I put the glass on the side and make my way back into the house, to end my night without crying on a dancefloor.

I take off my shoes when I get into my room and catch a half-hearted glimpse of myself in the mirror, hair wild, make-up smudged and clinging on for dear life, dress dangerously close to exposing my right breast. I straighten myself up and let myself onto the balcony.

Out here, in the darkness, I make out the orange glow of the little towns scattered over the horizon like fairy lights. I trace some headlights from one side of the hill to the other until they disappear. The sky is impossibly clear, and I look for the familiar constellations, notice how the Milky Way sits high in the canopy; a cloudy glaucoma in the night.

The music is still playing, there are the occasional pockets of drunken laughter, guffawing, stumbling, and somewhere a glass breaks. I rest my arms on the railing, hunch my shoulders over and take it all in, the sounds, the smell, the feeling, knowing that I never really will get it back again; this month will evaporate into a bank of memories for me to return to time and time again, becoming more dog-eared and faded with every day that passes.

The balcony door creaks open and I turn to see Florian emerging from his room.

'The American sent me,' he says quickly. 'Said you looked upset.'

I take him in too, try to bookmark how he looks in this exact moment. How his shirt is slightly creased, his skin tanned and freckled, the boyish fringe that had been gelled into submission at the beginning of the night, now fraying at the edges and on his cheek is someone else's lipstick, pink and faded as if he had tried to rub it off. He doesn't look like Ettie now. Not even in the slightest. I guess when you start to know someone, truly know them, it's like you start to see them in a different way, as if you know them by a specific aura. It makes their face, their features, as unique as a fingerprint. Ettie could be standing next to him now and I think I would struggle to find any similarities.

'I'm fine, just feeling a little emotional,' I say flatly, any actual emotion wrung out of my voice.

He doesn't look convinced, but I'm sure the temptation of the pack of cigarettes in his hand is overriding his wish to try to stay as far away from me as possible.

'Here.' He offers the pack to me first and I take one gratefully. 'Thanks.'

'Just being civil.' He manages a strained smile, and I am grateful for it; it feels like a small part of him is back, that the stranger that has implanted himself into the weekend is fading. He flicks open his lighter and takes a step towards me. I bend over, let the flame engulf the paper and fizz into life.

I turn back to my view, taking a lazy drag until my head spins.

Florian matches me, his shoulders a few inches from my own. 'I'm sorry I've ruined your weekend.'

'You haven't,' I shrug but he scoffs a little to let me know that I'm entirely transparent.

'I wasn't exactly in the right mindset for this anyway.' I gesture to the dress, to the champagne.

'Why did you come?' he asks.

'She made me. I was quite happy locked up in the apartment until it was time to go home. Guilted me that this could be her last birthday and then presented me with a new flight a few days later.'

'And the literary world can wait a few days, can it?' He looks at me expectantly, knowing the goading should solicit some response, perhaps a shouting match; maybe that's what we need but I can't give it to him, not yet. Instead, I clamp my hand onto the railing a little harder. 'What?' Florian persists. 'I thought you were desperate to get back, sure you have some people eagerly waiting for the next instalment?'

'There isn't going to be a next instalment. There isn't going to be a book. I've got a meeting on Thursday, I'm going to tell them that I can't do it.'

He looks at me as if he can't quite figure me out, like he's not really seeing me properly. 'What?'

'Isn't that what you want?'

'No!' he exclaims quickly.

I straighten my body from the railings, look at him square in the face. He shies away, turns his gaze instead to the band on his wrist. 'Why not? I know you think I'm selling out. You can't even look at me, Florian, you know that, you can't look at me without glazing over in this kind of disgusted disappointment. So no, there won't be a book.'

He looks as if I've shoved him. 'I don't look at you like that…'

'And if this sodding book never existed then we wouldn't be in this situation, would we? So, I just want it all to go away.'

He lets out a short, sharp puff of air. 'You're being a child.'

'A child?'

'Yes, you're acting like a kid, Ava. It's happened, you can't go back and change anything, pulling out of the book isn't going to mean that you didn't lie to me, that you didn't write those things…'

'No, but…'

'And this is what you've worked on, yeah? What you've been doing to deal with Ettie?'

'Yes, and I never wrote it to hurt anyone. To be honest, for the longest time I didn't think anyone would even care, it wasn't like you were there much. And I know now that I was wrong. I just don't want anyone to get hurt, Florian.'

He hardens at the mention of being hurt. He shakes his head and the angry stranger who thundered through the chateau to try to get away from me last night reappears. 'Too late for that, Ava, far too fucking late.'

'I'm sorry,' I try but I know I've already lost him, lost the conversation, lost the argument, lost whatever it was that we had.

'Publish the fucking book. Publish everything. Tell the world about how much you detest me, how I'm just Ettie's "druggy brother". I honestly don't care any more.' He stamps on the cigarette, grinding it into the stone and storms back to his room, slamming the door behind him making all the glass in the windowpanes shake.

I am trembling too; everything feels as if it's so precariously balanced that one step in the wrong direction will topple me entirely. I stub the cigarette out on the railing. I can't leave it like this, with him thinking I detest him, that he has just been some distraction for me, an obstacle to write about.

I run into my own room, reach into my bag and grab the tattered diary, the nondescript little object that has caused my world to collapse in on itself. I take a deep, deep breath and then launch myself out onto the balcony again and into Florian's room.

He is sitting in an armchair by the window, his hands gripping onto the arms so tightly I notice how white his skin is, how prominent and green his veins are. He jumps as he registers what's happening, that I am here in his space, not willing to give up just yet. He bolts upright as if I have caught him doing something he shouldn't. We stay like that for a moment, staring at each other, wondering whether to fight our corners or give in entirely. His eyes trace down my body to the little green object in my hand and he rolls his eyes.

'You going to write about this too, are you?' he sneers. 'Might as well get the full narrative arc.'

'You need to know one thing, Florian. This is my diary. I didn't lie. This is the place where I scrawl down everything and anything I am feeling without it being filtered down or thought out. It's me, just me and my confused little thoughts sitting there on a page. It isn't the blog. It isn't the book, it's just ramblings.'

'But it's you, Ava, why can't you see that's the issue? You are the one that thought of me like that. You are always going to think of me like that.'

'That's a lie.' I shake my head fervently. 'Your mother... she picked the worst bits.'

'Don't bring her into this.' He looks pained. I wonder if he has spoken to her some more, maybe even been counselled by her, if she's added some more poison into the pot.

'If you could just read the rest of it...'

He scoffs. 'I'm not going to give you another chance to point out my flaws, Ava.'

'Florian, please...'

'Just go, take that fucking thing with you.'

I look at the door, the way he looks so despondent, so completely and utterly done with me. My finger brushes the fabric of my diary, I open the cover, look at Ettie's little signature in the corner. I take a breath and run the pages through my fingers until I find it.

'I wanted to kiss him.' My voice is shaky, trembling. *'And it terrifies me. I haven't been that impulsive before, not for a long time. He said it was because of Ettie but it wasn't, in that moment, in that brief second, I wanted nothing in the world except him.'*

I look up to see whether he still looks like he might break something. He is staring at the ground, fists still curled up, his expression unreadable.

'I can't stop thinking about him. I keep replaying what happened in the café on this unavoidable, pornographic little loop. He knows me. I don't think I've been so easily read before. Archie tried but I think he

only saw the person I was pretending to be. It's like Florian, he sees through it all, he can see the sordid, dark little feelings I have tried to smooth over. I think I see past him now too. I think he likes that, that he knows I don't just see him now, I see who he was, who he has fought to become. How I am still utterly fascinated with him. And like all nice things I win for myself, I have fucked it up entirely by telling him to go.'

'Ava, stop it, please…' My head is dragged from the pages and towards Florian who has now moved his gaze from the floor and onto me. He looks desperate, shadows eating up the shallow planes of his face.

I flick through the pages again, over more ramblings, through all of the hours and days I have spent thinking about Florian Grenaud, trying to tell myself that this was a normal response to his reappearance in my life. The pages slip through my fingers until I find the one at the end, the one that has been dog-eared and reread multiple times over the last few days. It has been tragically cathartic to know the exact moment that everything in the entire world stopped being so fucking complicated.

'I didn't think I was ever going to love someone again. Not the way that I loved Ettie. But I do.' I feel the emotions catching at the back of my throat, I try to steer myself through the next bit, try to gain the smallest semblance of control. *'It's terrifying, complicated and entirely ill-advised but it is unavoidable. I sit here, on a shitty bench overlooking my husband's grave, desperate for Florian to finish pretending to pray and come back, to sit next to me, to talk to me and I know – I am desperately and against all of my better judgement, in love with Florian Grenaud.'*

The words sit in the air longer than the others, so heavy and thick that I can almost see them, swimming around the space between us.

He runs an exhausted hand through his hair and when our eyes meet again, I realise that there are tears that he is struggling to keep contained. I, on the other hand, am having no such luck in trying to keep my feelings under control. When I let out a sigh, it escapes in pieces, shattered from trying to hold on to it all.

'I understand if you hate me.' I fold the book back up, grip it tightly against my chest, grateful for something to do with my hands. 'I just couldn't let you hate me without knowing it all.'

He nods, swallows something hard in his throat.

And I know that in that moment there is nothing more that I can do. I know when to admit defeat. I know when to walk away.

I leave Florian to his room, closing the door to the terrace behind me and returning to the security of mine. Something smashes on his side of the wall but I don't react; instead I exist in this haze of anaesthesia, numbed by the knowledge that this is over.

Chapter 35

I AM WOKEN UP abruptly by the sound of hammering on the patio doors. I look at my phone. It's two in the morning. Sleep hadn't been a conscious choice. I had slumped myself into bed, fully clothed, drunk the last of the room cocktails and cried for a bit until clearly my body couldn't handle it any longer.

I look up to see a dark figure shadowed by the gauze curtains. It takes me a while to adjust to the light, to recognise his figure, the slim, effortless athleticism of his body, his hair, wild from an evening spent nervously fussing his hand through it in an attempt to keep himself busy.

I pull myself from the bed and make my way to the door. I slip the bolt free from the lock and it swings open.

'Say it now,' Florian thunders, a murderous look in his eyes.

'What are you talking about?' My eyes are still stinging from sleep, head raging from the cocktails I consumed just to be able to stop thinking about him.

'Just say it out loud, not reading it from some fucking book. Say it.' His intensity is terrifying, his chin trembles slightly as he speaks and his fingers rap on his thigh like rain.

'That I love you?'

'Yes.'

'I… love you?'

'You don't sound sure.'

'I love you.' I say it again, this time without the question, this time with all of the confidence and assurance I have. His eyes meet mine. I watch as they narrow, scan from one iris to the other as if he might be able to read me, be able to tell if I'm lying.

I step towards him again and when he doesn't immediately jump back, I take my hand and press it onto his shirt, his heart pounding under my palm.

My fingers brush up the side of his neck and come to rest on his cheek. I pull his head down to face me until his forehead is resting on mine.

'I love y—' I don't have a chance to finish.

Florian grabs me, his mouth is on my mouth, one hand is on the back of my neck, pulling me to him, the other on my hip stopping me from leaving. Not that I would want to.

He kisses me hard, I kiss him back harder until we are tripping back into my room. My hands work quicker than my head. I strip him of his shirt, and he sheds it like some useless second skin.

'You look so fucking beautiful,' he gasps in my ear as he plays with the straps of my dress. 'All night I just couldn't stop thinking about how much I wanted to take this dress off of you.'

'Why rush?' I challenge. Part of me wants to talk, wants to see whether this is forgiveness or some last-time, one-time thing. I don't think I'm strong enough to endure that.

'I'm not risking losing you again before we do this.' It is the sexiest thing that I have ever heard come from a man's mouth. I reach for his belt, run the leather through my hands until he's free of that too, but just as my fingers start on the buttons of his trousers, he pushes me back onto the bed with a thud. I look up at him, standing there over me until he sinks to his knees. The sight of him, prostrate at my feet, sends something inside of me throbbing. He bites his lip and slips his hands up my knees pushing my legs wider apart.

'Fuck,' he mumbles, pressing his lips against my knees in short little pulses.

'What?' I gasp, scared that at any minute he might pull away, leave me here waiting for something that might never happen. I would take death by firing squad over not getting to experience him here between my thighs.

'You're not wearing underwear,' he groans, his lips moving up and up until I can feel his breath, the warmth there at the very centre of me. I think he might just need to touch me and I might lose it. 'I fucking love that you aren't wearing underwear.' And then he's there, and I let out an immediate, guttural groan. He works slowly, methodically, as if we have done this hundreds of times, as if he knows where to plant every kiss, where exactly to put his tongue in order to send me somewhere that I think only he could ever take me. I reach down for his hair, run my hand through it and grab a clump between my fingers. He swears under his breath again and moves harder, longer. I am forced to lie back and he hooks my thighs over his shoulders, his hands on my hips, pulling me into him until something starts building, something I haven't felt in a very long time. I start to groan, protesting every time he pulls away, clenching my eyes shut, one hand still in his hair, the other tugging at the fabric on my dress until a heat starts to spread through me in waves.

'Yes.' I manage to splutter out an affirmation. 'Fuck yes,' I repeat but instead of this encouraging him, he slows down; his kisses move back down my thighs. I prop myself up on my elbows and look at him aghast. He is acting like nothing has happened, like we normally do this. 'I'm not done,' I protest.

'Oh, I know,' he smirks, starting to unbutton his trousers, stepping out of them and kicking them to a chair in the corner until the only clothing on his body is a pair of boxers, satisfyingly tight in the crotch.

'You know, it's good practice when you have a girl trembling at your tongue to let her finish.'

'That's not how this is going to go.' He shakes his head and then peels off his final item of clothing. I feel slightly cheated. I had hoped to be the one to do that. He comes to the end of the bed, takes my wrist in his hands, pushing my back into the mattress again. 'The first time, we finish together.' He kisses me hard on the lips. The heat starts to spread.

'And the second time?' I grin.

'I'll let you choose.' He starts to press his lips into my neck and down the straps of the dress, pulling them below my breasts and exposing my nipples. He takes one in his mouth, and I arch my back to him, just in time for him to catch my thigh in his hand, pressing it to the bed and pushing himself down onto me.

I feel him. The hardness. The expectation. It makes me shudder.

He breathes hard, slowly, bringing his head back up to mine. He smiles at me, and I am grateful for the familiarity. I trust him. I want him.

'How do you want it?' he asks, pressing his hips into mine again so I can feel what's coming, what is about to happen.

'I don't care. Just with you.'

My answer satisfies him and with a breath he plunges himself into me. I gasp, arch my back to accommodate him. He stays there for a moment, both of us catching our breath until he starts to move.

I have always enjoyed sex. I enjoy the initial awkwardness, how, the first time, we bare all to a relative stranger. How good sex is a levelling force, how bad sex will fuel the topic of girls' night for months. This sex though is something different entirely.

I marvel at Florian, how brushing my hand against his cheek feels just as intimate as him inside me. He leans over me, his arms bracing beside my head. Sometimes, when he gets close, I watch as he closes his eyes, bites down hard on his lip and then his eyes shoot open, find mine and it's like he is tuning into me, translating every single twitch and groan and 'fuck' into a language that his body acts upon until everything begins to tighten. It starts with a dull ache so deep that it is almost unpleasant until something else takes over and it begins to spread down, down to a depth I didn't know my body could reach. I start to grip the sheets in my hands. My calls for him grow wilder. I know he feels it too because he becomes more frenetic, harder, giving me everything he has left. I watch him cracking, take in the beads of sweat on his forehead, the darkening of his eyes, the way he grabs on to my breast so hard in the final throes I think I might bruise, but I don't care.

He waits for me, waits for my body to stop convulsing, waits until my calls for him have quietened, waits until my body goes limp beneath him like all of the life has been squeezed out of me. I watch as he lets go. How every muscle in his face tightens, his angular jaw pointing up to the ceiling. His eyes clenched shut. The way he lets out a ragged, guttural moan that is so fucking satisfying I wish I could do it all again immediately just to hear that specific sound again.

He slips from me, rolling to the side, his arm immediately winding itself around my shoulder. I adjust myself, rest my head on his chest, listen to his heart regulating back into its normal rhythm.

'Was that okay?' he asks although I know he knows the answer. I'm pretty sure that no one has enjoyed themselves during sex more than I have in that moment.

'Yes,' I nod and then let out a croaky laugh. 'Yes, that will do.'

He kisses my cheek and it becomes apparent quite how hot and sweaty we are. He grins at me boyishly. 'To think, I was almost going to give that up.'

I shake my head, still fighting to get my breath back. 'That would have been a very unfortunate situation for both of us.'

I trace an invisible pattern on his skin, my fingernail winding its way from his torso all the way down his arms and up his neck. He lets me, looking at me as if I'm something that doesn't quite belong to the earth, something he has never seen properly before.

'I wasn't just saying it for you to sleep with me,' I say. 'Or for you to not hate me as much.'

'How do you mean?'

'I do love you.'

There is a silence, a momentary lapse of conversation that makes my heart plummet. I know you're meant to say these things without the expectation of hearing them back, but the fact that he hasn't said it once when I must have uttered it three times in the last hour has put me slightly on edge.

'Come here.' He gets out of the bed and offers me his hand. He pulls me to my feet where a delicious ache in my limbs greets me. It's colder away from the mattress and I reach for the quilt, wrapping it around my body as Florian leads me to the bureau. He stands behind me, his hands wrapping across my waist, and points to the mirror.

'Look,' he insists. I stare at the reflection of us and the confusion sets in.

'What exactly am I looking at?'

'Look,' he says again as he presses his lips into my neck. 'Look, there, see it?' He takes his thumb and traces my lip, the way my teeth have caught it in the corner, the way my cheeks are blushed and warm: exactly the way Florian had described that I used to look at Ettie.

'I do *the thing* with you.' It comes out as a statement. An obvious little declaration because of course I do; it figures that Florian would be able to uncover the deepest of my secrets before even I can admit to them.

'When we talk, when we flirt, when we kiss, just then, sometimes even when I just catch you looking at me.'

For some maddening reason, I find myself blushing. Of course I love him, I've just made that abundantly clear but the fact I had made it all so obvious makes me feel like a teenager again, nursing a petty crush. 'And how long have you noticed this?'

'It started when we built that cairn.' He looks almost bashful, admitting now that he had been reading me all along.

I turn to him, mouth hanging open. 'That's cheating.'

'It's not *cheating*.' He acts like the word leaves a sour taste in his mouth. 'Just helped me stick around when everything else was telling me to run.'

'Well, it's not fair! Why do you get to know every little thing about me when you remain such a mystery?' I pretend to be offended, pout a little for effect, and he just shakes his head and then holds me a little tighter than before.

'I'm not a mystery to anybody but you.' He strokes some hair behind my ear, his eyes moving across my face, mouth slightly open. 'I think it's clear to anyone who's ever met us that I'm madly in love with you, Ava, and that I think I'm going to be for an awfully long time.'

Chapter 36

THE NEXT MORNING MY first thought is of The American; well perhaps not my first, but the idea of her smug reaction to our coupling looms large in the bedroom.

'How do you want to play this?' I turn to Florian, the morning light casting gorgeous little lace shadows on his face. When he had kept his promise and I was left shuddering on the bed for a second time, I half expected him to go back to his room, to let us gather ourselves and try to figure out what on earth had happened. But in its own way, it had felt like whatever had happened hadn't quite finished yet, that the lying there, his hand stroking my back, my fingers tangling in his chest hair, was just as much a part of the sex as the actual sex was.

'I think we should probably put some clothes on…' He gestures to my naked body, how I don't even attempt to pull the sheets up to protect my modesty. I'm pretty sure there isn't an inch of my body he hasn't seen, modesty feels pretty redundant now.

'I'm being serious.' I pick up a pillow and bring it down onto his chest. He feigns that it's much harder than it is. 'What do we do? What do we say?'

'You think you're going to go down for a birthday brunch and the first thing they're going to ask you is whether we slept together?'

'I wouldn't put it past her.'

'For once in your life, can you just go down there without any prior planning and expectations? Let's just throw some clothes on and go celebrate some eighty-three-year-old's birthday party.'

'Okay,' I smirk. 'Yeah, I think I can manage that.' He heaves himself out of bed and strolls to the bathroom, my bathroom, and I hear the water start to thunder out from the taps and then there's his gentle, husky humming. I lie there, eyes on the ceiling, listening to him, feeling every single inch of soreness on my body and I am so fucking happy.

It turns out I shouldn't have worried about making an announcement. By the time Florian and I emerge downstairs, the crowd are already scattered around the long dining table, balloons and presents arranged carefully around the birthday girl who today is dressed in a purple tea-dress with a red beret, gloves, shoes and bag. I think it is my favourite outfit of hers yet. They must hear us coming as someone starts a drum roll and when we round the corner into the dining room, we enter to rapturous cheers and a mixed chorus of 'Finally!' and 'It's about time!' amongst other things.

I catch Florian blush, thread my hand into his, bringing it up into the air and then plunge into a bow, pulling him with me. There is more applause and more squeals of delight until we take the two seats that have been left for us and the noise subsides.

'Well, thank you for joining us,' The American greets politely, the table following her lead. 'I have to say I've had some interesting birthday presents over the years but seeing you two together is up there with the most unique.'

'I bet you're wondering how we all know,' Crispy pipes up from the opposite end of the table. 'Well turns out that despite being on an entirely separate floor, passion truly does know no bounds... or wall thickness.'

I choke on some of my orange juice. 'I'm sorry...' I gabble, looking around the table at the faces of people struggling to meet my eye.

'Hey, sweetie,' Debbie the multi-marrier calls out. 'If the sex really was *that* good, then I suggest you never let him go.'

I want to die. Florian however looks frustratingly unflappable.

*

The line of questioning is interrupted by the elaborate affair that is the presents. One by one her guests scrabble to their feet, wish her a happy birthday and bestow a gift in front of her like they are the Magi and she is a very colourful and American Jesus. She opens up bottles of wine, more jewellery, books, some stationery until it's my turn. I reach for the bag by my feet and make my way towards her with my rather pathetic offering of another colourful scarf.

'There's more?' she asks, pretending to be overwhelmed. I lean over her, kiss her hard on the cheek.

'Happy Birthday, you mad old thing.'

'Thank you.' She kisses me back and then looks into the bag for something that isn't there.

'There was a card,' I fill in, catching Crispy's eye. He's looking expectantly in my direction hoping that he might now be one hundred euros richer. 'Well, this is going to sound fucking ridiculous but… I don't know your name,' I shrug. 'One whole month I've known you. You know my darkest secrets, my biggest ambitions and I don't even know your name.'

'Crispy!' The American clicks her fingers and a groaning Crispy starts to root around in his wallet for the notes required to pay off his debt.

'And I know that makes me the worst friend but so much time passed and after a while it just felt rude to ask…'

'Ava, stop.' The American places her finger on my lips. 'It has been the highlight of my year.'

'You need to get out more.'

'I thought I gave too much away at one point, I was pretty sure the moment I told you about my Bluette you would have cracked it.'

'Why?'

'Because you've lived in that place for a month with my name staring you square in the face, multiple times a day, written into the walls.' She says it like it's obvious, like her name is actually written in big black letters on the fridge but it isn't – I know; I've checked.

'The only things on the walls are the...' my voice trails off. 'Birds.' It comes out a whisper. 'Bird... sparrow... robin...?' She smirks at my attempts. 'Birdie?' I try it on my lips and even before she confirms whether I have it correct I know it's her name. Of course it's her name.

Then there is another cheer from the table, an eruption almost, with yet more clapping and whooping and laughing. I look at Florian who shrugs at me as if it is the most obvious thing in the world.

'Well done.' He raises his coffee cup.

'What, you knew?'

'I've known almost since day one. Birdie Daniels, her reputation preceded her. She just asked me not to tell.'

'That's not fair!' I thunder, but his grin breaks me as it always has, as I'm sure it always will.

The American just reaches for my hands that are secured on her shoulders. She squeezes them affectionately.

After the brunch, the guests start to scatter back up to their rooms to gather their possessions and pack away another weekend of their lives. Florian yawns next to me.

'Didn't get much sleep last night?' Crispy asks, eyebrows rocketing up into his diminishing hairline, his lips screwed up into a knowing little smirk.

'Something like that.' Florian doesn't avoid the eye contact. Instead, his own little smirk lets everyone still lingering know that he is incredibly proud of that fact. It makes my insides glow. 'I'm going to go for a swim.' He pecks me on the cheek before practically gliding from the patio.

Soon it is just The American and me, our comfortable little twosome that I had grown rather fond of.

She lays her hand out on the table, reaching for mine.

They find each other, tie themselves in a little knot.

'Well done, old girl,' she says, a sincerity so unusual for her that it triggers some bizarre emotional response that I have to fight to steer under control.

'Thank you.'

'Thank *you*. I'm not sure I've had as much fun as I've had with you for a very long time.'

'The feeling's mutual.'

'I have a feeling I might be being replaced.' She winks, gesturing to the figure walking towards the pool.

I can't help but grin. 'You could never be replaced. I feel like I'm going to be running to you with my problems for as long as you'll listen.'

'Do you promise?'

'I promise. Like my first problem is that a good friend of mine bought me a plane ticket that I very much don't want to use. Do you think she'll hate me if I waste her money?'

'And your meeting?'

'Well, turns out Florian was actually quite a fan of the last chapter. He thinks the project might have some legs.'

'Does he now?'

'So, I've cancelled the meeting, told Sam that she'll have the final chapters by the end of the week and I'm going to call Mum in a bit and tell her everything.'

'That's the best news I've heard all year.'

'And the plane ticket?' I nudge.

'Well, Ava, I think you may find that if you turned up at the airport with that ticket in the first place you may have realised that it wasn't exactly entirely legitimate.'

Chapter 37

Two years later

THE BOOKSHOP IS BUSY. Too busy to comfortably host the crowd that have turned up. I made the rookie error of inviting everyone, thinking that if just a quarter actually did turn up then I might be able to make it look less sad. I hadn't anticipated that almost every guest would attend, from the publishing team to my old English teacher, everyone is here smiling expectantly at me, waiting for an audience as if I'm somebody more than I am. And they're all chatting, laughing, holding copies of *the* book. My book. The book that is, as Sam so lovingly put it, 'finally fucking done.'

I'd grown used to its heavy presence in my life, how long it had taken to edit the bloody thing, how every time I sent it off to Sam, it felt like there were more question marks and suggestions than before. But it had been this constant anchor, something that kept me occupied and busy when a French winter had threatened to engulf me, and Florian had been off travelling to various exhibitions and meetings. Seeing it in other people's hands had been both everything I wanted it to be and also something I was struggling to come to terms with. I couldn't protect it, couldn't control how people would receive it. I had done my best to guide the narrative, to portray myself as best as I could, but ultimately there will be people who won't like it, they wouldn't like me by proxy and therefore I find myself outside of my own book launch, on a cold dark London street with a cigarette in one hand and a drink in the other.

I am expected to do a reading, to sit at a table and sign copies, to slap on a face that says, 'I am confident that this book will do well,' when in reality, I am petrified. It is the last thing that Ettie and I will ever do together, a product of our relationship, the only dependant we can ever produce, and it's only now when I look through the windows at the people who have turned up to toast and listen and celebrate that I realise what it is, what it truly means.

'Hey.' I look up to see Florian peeking around the door. He looks impossibly handsome, re-wearing the linen trousers and white shirt he had worn so fucking well at Birdie's birthday that I had blushed when I saw him. He shouldn't be here; three sculptures and a parade of sketches are currently sitting in a gallery in Marseille being stared at and talked about by the Riviera's richest admirers, but he is. I knew that he would be. It's the kind of certainty that I have grown incredibly fond of, that he would be wherever I needed him, even if I didn't exactly know when and where that was.

'Hi,' I grimace. 'Please don't tell me someone needs me.'

'I won't.' He holds his hands up. 'I just wanted to see if you were okay.'

'How do you do this all the time?' I ask incredulously. 'Stand there while people stare at the things you've made and judge them?'

'You'll get used to it, at the next launch.'

'Ha ha,' I guffaw, stub the cigarette out in the ash tray and replace it with his hand. I told him to promise me that I would never do this again. 'How long do I have you for again?'

'Rupert gave me the night.' He winds me into him, pulling me into his warm and safe chest. I breathe him in, the smell I hadn't realised I missed quite so much until he had turned up at my house this afternoon with some flowers and a bottle of wine – the shit one he had rescued me from all those months and years ago.

Rupert became Florian's agent exactly one month after Birdie's birthday and things had changed fast. Florian sold two sculptures for double what he had anticipated and suddenly there were so many commissions that Florian had started having to say no to some. He had taken on two apprentices who worked like little elves in the workshop and became a constant presence in my life, even when Florian was away on one of his many trips, meeting clients, sourcing stone (a surprisingly time-consuming experience) and showing his work. It was exciting to watch him, to see him in his 'public mode' when he was at a gallery, the Florian that oozed confidence and charm, and he deserved it all, every article, every accolade, every glowing review.

Etienne Grenaud would have been so bloody proud. He would have gone to every show, told every customer in the café about Florian's latest project, helped him out at the weekends, smiling smugly the entire time because he always knew how great his little brother could be.

Madame Grenaud had made one appearance at a show in Bordeaux, uninvited. Florian was adamant that he was going to ignore her but I pulled him over for a strained hello. It seemed like the right thing to do. The rage I had once felt for her had subsided a little, replaced with a pity that only the smug and ridiculously happy seem to possess. Florian however, had doubled down on the resentment. He had told me in the car on the way home from that particular exhibition that her 'help' had almost cost him the best few months of his life and he didn't think he could ever see past that. So, she remained at arm's length, her house an obstacle we drove past, her figure at the weekly markets ignored.

'Think your parents will mind the house guest this evening?' We both turn to the window, where my parents are talking to last year's winner of the Booker, probably completely unaware.

'I think they'll love it.' It's the truth. When I had eventually told Mum the reason why I wouldn't be coming back to London she obviously had her concerns. She and Dad came out to visit later that month; I am entirely certain they were checking whether I needed to be sectioned, but when they met Florian I think everything sort of slotted into place. Mum said that she hadn't seen me happy in so long, she had forgotten quite how lovely it was.

'Just one more week,' he sighs. 'One more week and then it will all be done and we'll be on that plane.'

'Oh yes,' I nod. 'I can't wait.' The holiday had been a gift from The American, flights to San Sebastian for a long weekend. She said it was a very late Christmas present but I knew her game, knew that she thought an opportunity somewhere far away, with Spanish wine, beaches and culture might inspire Florian to do something with the little box he had been keeping in his bedside drawer that he thinks is well hidden. I had come around to hoping that she might be right.

'Have you spoken to her?' he asks into my hair.

'She's holding up.' I grimace, thinking of her in Toulouse, holding Bluette's hand, the woman she had spent her entire life loving slipping away from this world to somewhere else. She had told me that she was taking some comfort in it, that she was grateful to be able to say goodbye, and I understood that. My goodbye exists in the form of a three-hundred-page memoir currently in the hands of everyone in the store.

'We'll have her for dinner after we get back.' He plays with my fingers, staring at them a little too closely, noticing something different about them. How empty they are perhaps.

'I did it this morning.' I reach into my dress and pull out a gold chain with a little circle of gold at its base. 'Mum gave me the chain. I thought that today was as good a day as any; the book is proof that we happened, it's enough.'

He nods, still looking at my fingers, inspecting where the dent from eleven years of wear was still circling my ring finger. 'I love you,' he says quietly and his hand scoops my chin up so we are looking at each other. 'I'm so fucking proud of you.'

'I know.' I kiss his cheek. 'I'm proud of you too.'

'I'm going to say I haven't seen you.' He breaks away, a glint in his eye. 'I'll distract your fans.'

'That would be much appreciated.'

'I'll check in, in a bit.' He gives my hands a final squeeze and returns to the crowd.

It's like a revolving door: when the shop consumes Florian, it spits out Sam who looks slightly frantic.

'Ava,' her voice thunders around the corner. 'There you bloody are.'

'Sorry I just… I needed some space.'

She doesn't look angry, instead she just waves my apology away. 'You'd be surprised how many authors go missing at their first rodeo. I found my last one necking a tequila in a pub up the road.'

'You know, tequila does sound quite appealing.'

'I'm on it. First though, I've got someone I want you to meet.'

'You do?' I panic that she is about to present someone far too important, someone rich and clever who I will undoubtedly embarrass myself in front of.

'Ava, meet Lauren.' She pushes a girl towards me, a pretty girl who looks so familiar for a moment I wonder if we're related.

'Hi.' The girl shuffles her feet a little, struggles to meet my eye.

'I'll leave you to it.' Sam gives her shoulder a squeeze and then slips back into the shop.

'Are you with the publisher?' I ask. It's a question I have asked multiple people tonight, people who I don't immediately recognise. She shakes her head quickly.

'No, no. I got an invite a few weeks ago on Instagram from Sam. My name's Lauren. I've been following your blog for a really long time.'

Everything starts to slot into place, the mechanism of memory and a faintly remembered conversation with Sam when I doubted I was ever going to be able to finish the damned thing.

'You're MylifeasLaurie-94?' I recite the username I had seen so many times over the past five years.

'That's me,' she chuckles. 'God, if I knew people were actually going to see it then I might have picked something a bit better.'

I barrel into her, hugging her so tightly that she stumbles back and it takes her a few moments to realise what's happening.

'I can't believe you're here. That you're real!' I say and then she squeezes me back.

'I never knew you noticed me.' She laughs.

I pull away, hold her by the shoulders and look her sternly in the eye.

'You were the first person that ever read anything I'd written. You read everything. Even when I thought it was shit, even when I was about to give up with it all, you liked it, commented, you were there. This wouldn't be happening without you.' I know there's tears in my eyes, that they are falling down my cheeks, smudging my make-up but I don't care.

She brings the copy of the book up to her midline, looks at it for a long moment and strokes her fingers over the cover delicately.

'You were the first person that ever wrote exactly how I felt.' She shrugs and I notice how the words are catching in her throat. 'My boyfriend died when he was twenty-four. He was in a car crash – drunk driver. We'd been together since we were fifteen.' In that moment my heart physically hurts. 'No one knew what to say to me; they tried but I knew they all just thought I was young enough to find someone else. They would say things like "at least you weren't married, at least you didn't have kids together", like that actually helped me reason with my grief. He was my soulmate, and I knew that we were meant to do all of those things together. It was random but your post just kind of appeared the evening of his funeral and it was like you had gone into my head and transcribed everything I had been feeling but couldn't say and it helped a little. It made me feel like I wasn't the only person going through it.'

'I'm so sorry.' I shake my head. 'It's just not fair.'

'I just wanted to say that I'm so happy for you. So proud that you've made something of this. Ettie sounds like a wonderful man, I think him and Tom would have got on. And this sounds really corny, but reading about how you've been able to meet someone else, that you can love again. Well… it gave me the confidence to put myself out there. I don't want to be known as the girl whose boyfriend died for the rest of my life; I want to be someone's person again. I want a new chapter.'

I look past the books to Florian, the figure I think I could spot in every crowded room. He's talking to my parents. My mum's laughing, really laughing. Dad's grinning at a joke that I don't need to be part of. And I am happy, so blissfully and stupidly happy in a way that I had never imagined I would be again.

We exist because Ettie and I no longer do, I know that. I have wrestled with that complicated little dichotomy in which both the loves of my life can never co-exist. I know that Florian feels it too, is occasionally startled by the guilt that creeps in when we least expect it, like when we're wrapped in bedsheets on a lazy Sunday morning or when we see a child with its parents at the park and catch each other's eyes fleetingly.

I am learning to cope with it, the guilt that my happiness comes with. It just feels like I have two lives, that the woman here now who loves Florian, who would always choose him, is a very different person to the twenty-one-year-old who fell in love with a waiter in a French café. And that's the way it should be: the change, the movement, the improvement, the second chances.

I turn back to Lauren, and with all the honesty and conviction I can muster, I smile.

'We all deserve a next chapter.'

Acknowledgements

It's a strange thing reflecting on this abstract little page of thanks. I am almost paralysed to write it, terrified of forgetting anyone that has contributed in some way shape or form to this book being here but what a pleasure it is to put in writing my appreciation to everyone who has made this possible.

Firstly, to my incredible agent Emily MacDonald. It's been a journey, and I am so grateful to have had you by my side. Your ideas, support, wonderful guidance and great tact have helped form *After Ever After* into the book it is today. Thanks also to the team at 42 MP who have made this experience such a joy, special shout-out to Chloe Morris who has been so generous with her time and expertise.

My editor, Rebecca Weigler, thank you for believing in this book and your dedication in getting it out into the world. Thanks also to the wider team at Bedford Square, for your tireless work in getting *After Ever After* ready for publication.

Publishing a book is not just a professional endeavour, in fact the last year has felt easier in comparison to the years before when this book and books before were mere ideas, but before there was a professional publishing team, there were the people listed below who offered their endless support.

Mum and Dad, thank you for giving me the most wonderful life. Thank you for the constant support and for sharing in the excitement. Thank you also for those perfect French holidays – turns out they were pretty fundamental to this book being published! To Matt for never objecting to a writing-retreat and stepping in for extra bedtime shifts when the going got tough. To Karen and John for offering your attic to write in and the babysitting! Beth, Will, Kirsty and Conrad, thank you for sharing in the successes and for all the support. To the whole of the Luckett clan, for everything – I feel so lucky to have you all at the end of the phone.

I would also like to thank Barbara and John Samuels who are not here to share this part of my life with me now, but have been such a fundamental part of who I am. My nana's love of reading, stories and books heavily influenced my life throughout my childhood and teenage years. I know she would have loved sharing this chapter with me.

To my dear friends, I am so lucky to have you to do life with. Special thanks go to Marissa for the voice notes that rival any professional cheerleader, Gwenno for being one of the first readers, Claire for pre-ordering quite so many copies and for Emma – I'm so glad we had that snow day!

To my old colleagues at Ashford, especially Rachel, Hilary, Ed and Jo R for being there through the highs and lows of it all with nothing but unwavering support.

To my new colleagues at Kings (especially everyone in Team English) who have welcomed me and my funny little side-project with enthusiasm and understanding.

Thanks to the team at Curtis Brown Creative for getting me to take writing seriously and for supporting me on the other side. This also includes the incredible people I met on those courses, especially Jennie Godfrey and Laina West for those early days of beta reads.

Katie, I want to make sure you have your own paragraph. How lucky am I to have got you as part of the package deal when I married your brother! You kept me going when I wanted to throw in the towel, you gave the speediest responses to all my panicked queries and requests for a read-through. It has been so much fun sharing this all with you.

And finally, for all the students that I have had the pleasure to teach over the years at Royal Harbour, Ashford and Kings. It has been an honour to be a part of your lives for however short a time. I hope you never give up on your passions – you never know what might happen!

About the Author

Image credit © Matthew Murphy

Hannah Luckett is a writer and English teacher based in Canterbury, Kent. She graduated from the University of Kent with a degree in English and Creative Writing in 2017 and has been an English Teacher for 7 years, splitting her time between teaching her students how to write whilst writing for herself. A self-confessed unromantic-romantic, she primarily writes about modern womanhood in all its forms, and is obsessed with the intricacies and nuances of relationships.

@hannahluckettwrites

Bedford Square Publishers

Bedford Square Publishers is an independent publisher of fiction and non-fiction, founded in 2022 in the historic streets of Bedford Square London and the sea mist shrouded green of Bedford Square Brighton.

Our goal is to discover irresistible stories and voices that illuminate our world.

We are passionate about connecting our authors to readers across the globe and our independence allows us to do this in original and nimble ways.

The team at Bedford Square Publishers has years of experience and we aim to use that knowledge and creative insight, alongside evolving technology, to reach the right readers for our books. From the ones who read a lot, to the ones who don't consider themselves readers, we aim to find those who will love our books and talk about them as much as we do.

We are hunting for vital new voices from all backgrounds – with books that take the reader to new places and transform perceptions of the world we live in.

Follow us on social media for the latest Bedford Square Publishers news.

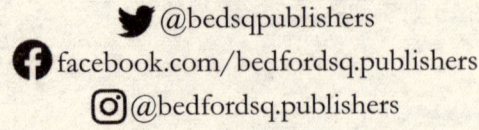

@bedsqpublishers
facebook.com/bedfordsq.publishers
@bedfordsq.publishers

bedfordsquarepublishers.co.uk